Snowbound Blessings

LAUREL RIDGE SERIES, BOOK #5

TARA BAISDEN

STERLING RIDGE PRESS LLC

Copyright

Cover designed by Sterling Ridge Press LLC

Published by: Sterling Ridge Press, LLC www.sterlingridgepress.com

ISBN: 978-1-966093-07-7 Printed in the United States of America

First Edition: December 2024

For permissions, contact: tara@tarabaisden.com or visit www.tarabaisden.com

About The Author

Tara Baisden is a Contemporary Inspirational Romance author who proudly calls the beautiful state of West Virginia her home. Nestled on a sprawling mountainous property, she is surrounded by the peace and serenity of nature. Her days are happily spent in the quiet of country life, writing heartwarming stories of love, faith, and second chances. Tara also enjoys quilting, working in her garden, tending to her beloved pets, and soaking in the beauty of her surroundings.

With deep roots in West Virginia, family is everything to Tara. One of her favorite pastimes is gathering on the front porch with loved ones, sharing stories, laughter, and enjoying the simple, meaningful moments that life offers. When she's not crafting her novels, Tara can often be found exploring the rich history of her home state, visiting local historical sites, and, of course, stopping by every bookstore she passes! Her passion for reading and discovery always fuels her next adventure.

Tara is the author of the Laurel Ridges Series of novels, which includes: Season of Hope, Finding Grace, His Perfect Plan, Love Redeemed, Snowbound Blessings, and Sheltered Hearts all of which have been beloved by fans of inspirational romance. Her novels reflect her love for faith, family, and the timeless beauty of West Virginia.

Known for her sweet and clean romances, she creates characters that feel like family and settings that make readers want to visit again and again.

You can find out more about Tara and her latest releases at www.tarabaisden.com or follow her on social media for updates and behind-the-scenes glimpses of her writing process. Stay connected—you won't want to miss the heartfelt stories of love and family she has in store!

Also by Tara Baisden

<u>Laurel Ridge Series</u>

#1. Season of Hope

#2. Finding Grace

#3. His Perfect Plan

#4. Love Redeemed

#5 Snowbound Blessings

#6 Sheltered Hearts

About Laurel Ridge

Welcome to the fictional town of Laurel Ridge, West Virginia!

Nestled deep in the heart of the Appalachian Mountains, Laurel Ridge is a place where time slows down, allowing visitors and residents alike to enjoy life's simple pleasures. With its quaint, brick-paved streets, historic storefronts, and the ever-present backdrop of rolling hills and dense forests, Laurel Ridge is a hidden gem that attracts tourists looking for both serenity and adventure.

A Rich History

The town was founded in the early 1800s by pioneering settlers who were drawn to the fertile land and abundant natural resources of the region. Laurel Ridge began as a small logging community, relying on the towering forests that covered the surrounding mountains. The New River, one of the oldest rivers in the world, provided an essential transportation route for lumber, as well as a lifeline for the early settlers.

As the years passed, the town evolved from a logging outpost into a thriving hub for craftspeople and artisans. By the late 19th century, it had developed a reputation for its hand-crafted furniture, textiles, and pottery, all made by skilled locals. The town's proximity to the New River also made it a destination for adventurous souls seeking to kayak, fish, or hike along the riverbanks.

A Place of Renewal

Though the logging industry faded by the early 20th century, Laurel Ridge adapted to the changing times. Its natural beauty and deep connection to West Virginia's mountain heritage drew travelers from near and far, transforming it into a beloved tourist destination. Local shops, run by generations of the same families, line the town square, offering handmade goods, locally sourced foods, and, most of all, warm hospitality.

The town's signature event, the Harvest Festival, began in the 1930s, celebrating the craftsmanship, music, and traditions passed down through the generations. Each year, visitors flock to enjoy live Ap-

palachian music, taste locally grown produce, and witness demonstra-
tions of old-world techniques like blacksmithing and weaving.

A Town of Faith and Community

At the heart of the town stands Laurel Ridge Community Church, a
small, white clapboard building with a steeple that reaches toward the
sky. Built in 1876, the church has been a pillar of faith and strength
for the community for over a century. Its bell, crafted by the town's
original blacksmith, has been ringing on Sunday mornings ever since,
calling townsfolk to worship and reminding everyone of the enduring
values of faith, hope, and love.

The church's history is intertwined with the town's, serving as a refuge
in difficult times and a gathering place in moments of joy. Over the
years, the church has grown to include an outreach center that sup-
ports local families and tourists in need, providing everything from
free meals to spiritual counseling. The church's welcoming atmosphere reflects the town's deep sense of unity and service.

A Growing Tourist Haven

Today, Laurel Ridge has grown to a population of around five thou-
sand people, yet it has managed to retain its small-town charm. Its
thriving tourist industry draws visitors year-round. Tourists can stroll
through mom-and-pop shops, and dine at the beloved Martha's Diner, famous for its homemade pies and retro charm. The town square,
with its white gazebo surrounded by flowering bushes, is often the site

of outdoor concerts and farmers' markets, creating a sense of nostalgia and small-town pride.

For nature lovers, the New River offers breathtaking views and the thrill of adventure, whether it's fishing in its crystal blue waters or hiking along the rugged trails that weave through the wilderness. Tourists and locals alike cherish the scenic beauty, often finding peace in the simple pleasures of watching the river flow or taking in the panoramic vistas of the Appalachian Mountains.

Laurel Ridge, with its rich history, strong community spirit, and natural beauty, is more than just a tourist destination—it's a place where past and present blend seamlessly, offering everyone who visits a chance to experience the best of West Virginia's mountain heritage. You'll find that Laurel Ridge is a town that captures the heart.

Welcome to Laurel Ridge. I hope you fall in love with this charming small town and its residents.

Dedication

To the ones who remind us that even in the fiercest storms, love, faith, and hope can create a shelter stronger than any walls.

To the caregivers who pour their hearts into others, the resilient souls who choose courage in the face of pain, and the dreamers who believe in second chances—even when it feels like winter will never end.

And to my readers, who carry these stories in your hearts: may you always find warmth in unexpected places and blessings where you least expect them.

This story is for you.

Contents

Chapter 1

The January wind howled through frost-laden branches, weaving its icy breath across the rugged mountains. Gray-blue skies loomed heavy with the promise of a fierce storm, their chill seeping down the ridges and into Debbie Ferguson's very bones. Snow-packed roads turned what should have been a quick drive into a nerve-wracking ordeal. White-knuckled, she gripped the steering wheel, her tires crunching cautiously along the slick, narrow road that wound its treacherous path up the mountain toward home.

The windshield wipers beat a steady rhythm, struggling hopelessly against the thickening snow, which swirled like a dense, chaotic curtain across her view. Inside the car, Debbie's breath fogged the glass as she leaned forward, straining to see through the blinding white. Her body was a knot of tension, every muscle aching from the effort of keeping the vehicle steady.

The storm system barreling across West Virginia was worsening by the minute. Heavy snow, ice, and inevitable power outages were no longer a mere possibility—they were a foregone conclusion. Flashes of lightning lit up the swirling storm clouds, followed by sharp cracks of thunder that reverberated through the mountains. The surreal phenomenon of thundersnow added an eerie, otherworldly edge to the night, as if nature herself was showing off her raw, unrelenting power.

In a perfect world, Debbie would already be safe at home, curled up by the fire with a steaming cup of coffee, maybe reading or playing a board game with her seventeen-year-old twins. But duty had called, and her devotion to her patients had won out. As a traveling nurse for the county, Debbie's job took her to the homes of housebound or recovering residents, providing care and companionship to those who needed it most. Her days were often long, stretching well past typical hours, but today she'd been fortunate. Her rounds in Laurel Ridge had been manageable, just enough to ensure her patients were safe and prepared before the storm arrived.

The sharp curve ahead loomed through the swirling snow, prompting Debbie to slow to a crawl. She tapped the brakes lightly, guiding the car upward and around the bend with practiced care. The narrow road was treacherous, but she knew its twists and turns like the back of her hand.

"Lord, help me get through this," she murmured, her voice steady but laced with urgency.

A brief image of her children waiting for her at home softened the tension in her chest. At seventeen, Nathan and Danielle were her rock—her partners through life's trials, her joy in the hardest moments. She thanked God daily for the blessing of raising two such remarkable kids. Nathan's steady, practical nature was the perfect counterbalance to Danielle's vibrant, boundless optimism. Together, they reminded her why she kept pushing forward, weathering both the literal and figurative storms life threw her way.

"Just one more mile, Debbie," she whispered, gripping the wheel tighter. "You've got this."

When the familiar outline of her log cabin finally emerged through the swirling snow, Debbie exhaled a shaky breath of relief. Nestled against the backdrop of rugged mountains, the two-story structure stood as a steadfast sentinel against the storm. It wasn't just a house—it was home. Her parents had gifted it to her after her divorce two years ago, a lifeline when her world had felt like it was crumbling. Though they had retired to Georgia several years back, her parents had kept the cabin out of sentiment, a place filled with memories and a haven for family visits. For Debbie and her twins, it had become a fresh start—a place to rebuild and find peace.

The cabin's weathered log walls glistened faintly with a dusting of frost, the chinking between the timbers snug against the biting cold. A wide front porch, its wooden railings now capped with snow, stretched across the front of the house. Debbie loved that porch in the summer, draped with hanging flower baskets, but tonight it looked like a postcard of winter's fury. Out back, another porch offered a view of the rolling forest, which seemed to stretch endlessly into the ridges.

Behind the house, a large pole barn stood sturdy against the wind, its steel roof gleaming faintly in the muted light. It housed the equipment needed to maintain the sprawling thirty-acre property. Nearby, two woodsheds sat side by side, stocked to the brim with neatly stacked firewood. The smaller of the two had been built by her father decades ago; the larger one was her addition, a testament to her determination to provide for her family through the often harsh mountain winters.

The cleared acre surrounding the cabin offered a stark contrast to the dense forest beyond, its bare expanse softened now by a thickening layer of snow. The towering pines and bare-limbed hardwoods surrounding the property stood like a protective wall, their silhouettes sharp against the storm-darkened sky. It was remote here, but that was part of the appeal. This was her sanctuary—a place where faith, hard work, and love for her children had created a life of quiet resilience.

As Debbie turned carefully into the driveway, her car fishtailed slightly on the incline before settling back into place. Her headlights illuminated the cabin's snow-blanketed roof, and she caught a glimpse of light spilling from the living room windows—a beacon of warmth in the storm. Smoke curled lazily from the chimney, a reassuring sign that one of the twins had started a fire in the hearth. Relief washed over her at the thought of the crackling flames waiting inside, warding off the bitter cold.

Guiding the car into its usual spot in the circular driveway, the tires crunched against the fresh layer of snow; the sound muffled by the relentless rumble of the storm. Debbie turned off the engine, and for a moment, the world was still, save for the swirling snow and the roar of the wind. The cabin stood before her like something out of a painting, its soft glow framed by the dark woods and the swirling white of the blizzard.

She paused, gripping the steering wheel, letting her heart slow. The absence of movement, apart from the tumbling snow, made the scene feel almost surreal—static, yet alive with nature's raw power.

Finally, she stepped out into the cold, the wind immediately biting at her cheeks. Snowflakes danced in chaotic spirals as she trudged toward the porch, her boots sinking into the deepening drifts with each step. The bitter air stole her breath, but she pressed forward, drawn by the warm light spilling from the windows.

"Home," she whispered, her voice nearly lost in the storm. The word was a prayer and a promise—a reminder of the safety and solace waiting just beyond the door.

"Mom!" Nathan called out, rushing onto the porch. He stopped near the steps, his tall, lanky frame shivering against the biting wind. Snow swirled around him, clinging to his dark hair, and his blue eyes—so achingly like his father's—were wide with worry. He tried to sound calm, but the crack in his voice gave him away. "We were starting to think you wouldn't make it back."

Behind him, Danielle hovered in the doorway, her arms wrapped tightly around herself against the swirling cold. The usual spark in her demeanor was dimmed, replaced by an expression of concern. Even standing still, she radiated the kind of nervous energy Debbie had come to recognize as her daughter's way of coping. The protective instincts that often bubbled beneath Danielle's lighthearted surface were clearly in full swing.

Debbie waved a hand to reassure them, though the tension in her body lingered. "I'm all right," she said, her voice steady but heavy with exhaustion. "Let's get inside before we all freeze."

Nathan reached for her medical bag and helped her up the last few steps, his movements quick and deliberate. Debbie didn't miss the way his eyes scanned her, checking for signs of trouble even as he ushered her inside.

The wind howled behind them, tugging at the door as they closed it firmly against the storm. Inside, the house felt like a cocoon, the warmth from the fireplace immediately enveloping them. The crackle of logs burning in the hearth and the faint scent of apple and cinnamon candle wax filled the air, grounding Debbie in the safety of home.

Without a word, Debbie pulled both her kids into a tight embrace, her arms circling them with a fierceness that caught Nathan off guard. He stiffened for a moment before relaxing into her hold, and Danielle leaned into her mother's shoulder, her warmth reassuring. Debbie held on a little longer than usual, letting the tension she'd carried home finally dissolve.

"I made it back," she murmured, her voice soft but heavy with gratitude. "And I'm so thankful. This storm is no joke."

Pulling back slightly, she studied their faces, her concern shifting into practicality. "Did you double-check everything? Generator? Supplies?"

Nathan nodded immediately. "Twice. The generator's good to go. We have plenty of gas, the firewood's stacked on the back porch and some inside, and I tied down all the outdoor furniture."

Danielle chimed in with a small, confident smile. "We filled the bathtub upstairs with water, and three five-gallon buckets of water are in the downstairs bathroom, just in case the power goes out. We're ready."

Debbie felt a swell of pride and relief at their thoroughness. "Good. You two did great," she said, her voice warm with approval. She gave them both another squeeze before stepping back, her eyes lingering on their faces. The storm outside might be fierce, but inside this house, she knew they had what mattered most: resilience, teamwork, and love.

"Okay," Debbie said, taking a deep breath and shaking off the last of the chill. "Let's hunker down and ride this out." The words carried a sense of purpose and calm, grounding them all as the wind continued to howl just beyond their sturdy walls.

Another distant rumble of thundersnow rolled through the mountains, the low growl reverberating through the house and rattling their very bones. The sound seemed to settle deep in the quiet stillness of the cabin, a stark reminder of the storm's unyielding power. Debbie paused, her hand resting against the front door, as if she could somehow keep the storm at bay. She drew in a slow, steadying breath.

Outside, the world was vanishing into a swirling, unrelenting curtain of snow, heavy and unmerciful. Yet here, within the sturdy walls of their home, she still held onto a fragile sense of control, warmed by the steady crackle of the fire.

Kicking off her boots, Debbie set them neatly on the boot tray to dry, the snow melting into damp puddles beneath them. She shrugged off her coat, hung it in the entryway closet, and tucked her gloves and scarf onto the shelf with precision, the simple motions grounding her in the moment.

"All right," she said, mustering a smile as she wrapped an arm around each of the twins and steered them toward the living room. "Let's pick a movie. I'll make some hot chocolate—tonight feels like a double-marshmallow kind of night."

Danielle's face brightened instantly. "Finally, Mom! Now you're speaking my language. Extra marshmallows are non-negotiable."

Nathan rolled his eyes. He flopped onto the couch, grabbing the remote with an exaggerated flourish. "What's the plan? Do I go rogue and pick something random, or are we voting on this?"

Debbie chuckled, already heading toward the kitchen. "You two decide. Just... keep it light. No horror movies tonight, please."

Danielle threw herself onto the couch beside her brother, her grin full of mischief. "Don't worry, Mom. We'll stick with something safe. Although I can't promise, it won't be a rom-com."

Nathan groaned loudly, feigning dramatic agony. "Anything but a rom-com. Fine, but no musicals this time. My brain can only take so much suffering."

Their playful banter followed Debbie into the kitchen, their voices rising and falling in familiar, comforting tones. She smiled to herself as she filled a pot with milk, the rhythm of the moment almost enough to lull her into forgetting the storm outside.

The cocoa began to steam as she stirred, the rich aroma curling upward and mingling with the scent of wood from the fire. But her contentment faltered when her phone buzzed against the counter, its sharp vibration cutting through the calm coziness of her kitchen. Debbie glanced at the screen, her stomach tightening as she read the alert: STORM UPGRADED TO PHASE TWO. SNOWFALL RATE INCREASED.

The storm was intensifying faster than expected, and Debbie's thoughts immediately turned to her closest neighbors, Harold and Mildred Hughes, who lived just a mile up the road in their remote farmhouse. Worry gripped her chest as she thought of her patients scattered across the county, each vulnerable to the storm's merciless fury. But Harold and Mildred weren't just neighbors—they were family friends she'd cherished since childhood.

The elderly couple held a special place in her heart. Their wisdom and gentle kindness had been a constant in her life, and she treasured their presence in the community. Harold, however, was still recovering from a recent fall on the icy back steps of his home. The nasty cuts and scrapes on his thin, fragile skin required careful tending, as even minor wounds in someone his age could escalate quickly. Debbie had been keeping a close eye on him, ensuring the injuries healed properly, all the while marveling at the quiet strength Harold and Mildred exhibited despite their age.

Debbie cared deeply for all her patients, but Harold and Mildred were different. They weren't just part of her rounds—they were part of her heart, a living connection to her past and a reminder of the strength found in enduring bonds.

Through the kitchen window, the snow seemed to fall harder, faster, thickening the already impenetrable night. The wind howled against the cabin, its ferocity an almost living presence. For a moment, Debbie pressed her hand to the cold glass, watching as nature unleashed its wildest fury. The weight of her responsibilities pressed heavy on her heart, but there was nothing more she could do tonight except pray.

She closed her eyes, letting the warmth of the kitchen and the sound of her children's laughter in the other room anchor her. "Lord," she whispered softly, her voice nearly lost to the hum of the storm, "keep us safe. And please, watch over those who need You most tonight."

When she returned to the living room, balancing three mugs of hot chocolate, Nathan and Danielle had settled on a movie, their earlier bickering replaced with easy camaraderie. The fire cast a golden glow over the room, and the storm seemed a world away. For now, they had each other, their sturdy cabin, and the strength of faith to carry them through the night.

Chapter 2

Caleb Warren yanked the tarp tight over the stack of oak boards, the heavy fabric snapping sharply in the wind as he wrestled to secure it in place. Snowflakes clung to his weathered face, melting into icy trails that streaked down his skin before freezing into his beard in the bitter, biting air. His breath clouded in front of him, the metallic tang of snow sharp in his lungs as he worked. Around him, the lumber mill yard was deserted, the workers having long since hurried home to warm fires and waiting families.

He yanked the bungee cord with a sharp pull, securing it firmly despite the ache that shot through his gloved fingers. The storm had strengthened all afternoon, the snow now falling in thick, relentless sheets, and dusk had settled into an ominous bruise-colored twilight. The world around him was rapidly vanishing beneath a smothering white blanket.

"Caleb! You comin' inside?" John Warren's voice called out, breaking the stillness. It was familiar and steady, tinged with brotherly exasperation and concern.

"In a minute," Caleb barked, not looking up as he straightened from his crouch and stretched his back. His eyes stayed on the tarp, double-checking its hold as though it were the only thing keeping the storm at bay.

"That tarp's tighter than a drum," John said, stepping closer, arms crossed against the cold. "You've checked it twice already. Enough's enough."

Caleb exhaled through his nose, the puff of white curling around him as he finally turned. "It's better to be sure," he muttered, pulling off his gloves and giving them a sharp slap against his thigh to knock off the snow.

John's frown deepened, but his words softened. "So help me, Caleb, if you don't get your rear inside..."

"No need to fuss," Caleb cut him off, brushing past him with purposeful strides toward the main building of Warren Lumber Mill. Inside, the air was dry and tinged with the lingering scent of sawdust and pine. It was dim and utilitarian, but the quiet hum of the heaters and the shelter from the wind made it feel like another world compared to the swirling chaos outside.

"You're gonna drive home, aren't you?" John said, trailing behind him.

Caleb didn't answer immediately. His fingers absentmindedly traced the faint scar on his forearm, a leftover from an accident years ago, before he shrugged. "I've driven through worse."

John shook his head, his tone laced with a grin Caleb didn't have to see to hear. "You're as stubborn as ever. Look, why don't you just come over to my place tonight? I've got chili in the crock pot and cornbread from yesterday. David's stopping by, and we're gonna catch up on that football game from last weekend—I recorded it. Better than sitting alone in that cabin of yours, don't you think?"

Caleb hesitated, his jaw tightening as he bent to grab his bag from his office chair. It was a harmless offer, made with the easy warmth of family. Time at John's or David's houses meant shared meals, easy camaraderie, and the kind of conversation that pried open doors he preferred to keep closed. The closeness felt more like a challenge these days, a reminder of what he'd lost and the parts of himself he couldn't seem to piece back together.

"I need to get home," Caleb said gruffly, his strides deliberate as his boots echoed sharply off the cement floor of the dimly lit hallway.

John's heavier footsteps followed, his frustration audible in every word he spoke. "Great plan," he said, his voice dripping with sarcasm. "Drive twelve miles up a narrow, icy mountain road with no guardrails, in the middle of a blizzard. Brilliant."

Caleb tossed a glance over his shoulder, a fleeting acknowledgment that did little to deter John's persistence.

"Come on, Caleb," John pressed, moving to block his brother's path. "At least stay the night. You'll be snow-blind out there, and you know it."

John's tone softened as he placed a firm hand on Caleb's shoulder, his thumb brushing against the frayed patch on Caleb's coat. "Just stay at my place. You don't have to go home tonight."

"Back off," Caleb snapped, his eyes narrowing as his voice cut like a blade. He shrugged John's hand away with a sharp jerk of his shoulder.

John stepped back, his face a storm of frustration and concern, though his hands rose in a gesture of surrender. "Fine. Go, then. But listen—" He hesitated, his tone dropping to something steadier. "Dad's upstairs glued to the weather report. This storm's bad, Caleb. It's supposed to get worse."

"I'll be fine," Caleb said flatly, the finality in his voice closing the conversation. Without another glance, he strode past John toward his office.

Grabbing his bag, Caleb swapped his damp gloves for a dry pair, flipped off the light, and stepped back into the hallway. As he passed the office door beside his, he caught the faint sound of his father's voice—Howard Warren, ever meticulous, likely running through safety protocols with the night guard. Howard didn't take risks, not in this line of work and certainly not in his mill.

"Just be careful, all right?" John called after him, his voice quieter now, tinged with reluctant resignation.

"Always am," Caleb replied without looking back, his chin dipping in the barest acknowledgment. He pulled his coat tighter as he opened the mill's main door and stepped into the storm.

The full force of the blizzard hit him immediately, the wind clawing at his face and the snow swirling in suffocating waves. Darkness had almost completely swallowed the mill yard, the pale blue-gray remnants of evening fading into shadows. Caleb shoved his hands deep into his pockets, shoulders squared as he braced against the storm's icy grip.

"Forty minutes tops," he muttered under his breath, his words barely audible over the wind. "I've handled worse drives than this."

Reaching his truck, Caleb grabbed the door handle of his 1970 Ford pickup and gave it a sharp tug. The hinges groaned in protest. The door sticking stubbornly before finally giving way. He climbed into the cab, shaking snow from his hat and shoulders, and let the door slam shut behind him. The silence inside was a stark contrast to the chaos outside, but it was short-lived.

The engine sputtered before roaring to life, vibrating through the cab like an old friend shaking off sleep. Caleb let it idle for a moment, his hands rubbing the heat back into his fingers. His gaze dropped to the dashboard, where Bonnie's leather Bible rested, wedged securely in its usual spot. The cover was cracked and faded, its edges softened from years of relentless sun that had filtered through the windshield, leaving its mark on the once-pristine leather.

He hadn't touched the Bible since the day he put it there ten years ago.

Caleb shook his head, forcing the unwelcome memories back. No. He couldn't go there. Not now.

His lips pressed into a thin, grim line as his eyes fixed on the swirling storm ahead. The windshield wipers worked furiously but fruitlessly, the relentless snow battering the glass and reducing his visibility to mere feet.

"This drive's going to be rough," he muttered, tightening his grip on the steering wheel. Shifting the truck into gear, he eased forward, the tires groaning in protest as they carved through the thick blanket of snow.

The miles crawled by in agonizing slowness. The narrow mountain road wound like a snake, twisting through a dense curtain of white. Skeletal trees flanked the road, their bare branches drooping under the weight of heavy snowfall, looming like silent guardians over the treacherous path. The truck's headlights barely managed to cut through the storm's chaos, casting a dim, almost futile glow against the unrelenting swirl of snow.

Caleb leaned closer to the windshield, squinting against the blinding white, his dark eyes scanning the road ahead. The tension in his body was palpable, his shoulders hunched and rigid, his grip on the wheel iron-clad, as though his sheer determination could force the truck to stay on course. Every patch of ice sent a fresh jolt through his chest as the tires slipped before grudgingly regaining traction.

The truck's engine rumbled, struggling against the steep inclines and the increasing drag of the snow. Another vicious gust of wind slammed into the side of the vehicle, rocking it with enough force to send Caleb's heart pounding. Snowflakes swirled in relentless loops, blurring his vision and stealing the world beyond the windshield. The isolation of the mountain, usually a welcome reprieve, now felt ominous, edging dangerously close to the kind of solitude that could swallow a man whole.

A patch of black ice in a sharp curve caught him off guard, the truck sliding as his tires struggled for purchase. Caleb's knuckles whitened as he corrected the wheel, forcing the vehicle back on track. His breaths came heavier now, visible puffs of air that fogged the glass, even as the heater worked in vain to combat the cold creeping into the cab.

"This is bad," he muttered. "Real bad."

The glowing clock on the dashboard told him it had been thirty-five minutes since he'd left the mill. He wasn't even halfway home. The thought of his cabin, a sanctuary nestled deep in the woods at the top of this mountain, felt impossibly distant in this storm. The snow was winning, blanketing everything in a smothering white that erased all sense of direction.

Then it happened.

The truck hit a patch of black ice, and for a split second, everything felt weightless. The tires lost all grip, spinning uselessly against the frozen surface. Caleb's heart jolted as the rear end fishtailed violently, swinging the truck sideways. Instinctively, he eased off the accelerator and feathered the brakes, trying to regain control, but the vehicle ignored his efforts, sliding inexorably toward the edge of the road. His pulse thundered in his ears, breath catching in his throat as the steering wheel fought back against his grip, the truck teetering on the edge of disaster.

"No, no, no—"

The words broke from him, desperate and raw, but the truck had already lost the fight. The tires slid sideways, gravity dumping him down the embankment as the truck veered off the road. The front end crumpled with a sickening crunch as it slammed into the ground, snow exploding around him in a suffocating burst of white.

The jarring impact hurled Caleb forward, his chest slamming into the steering wheel, knocking the air from his lungs. His head slammed against the driver's side window, and a sharp, searing pain shot through his skull. For a moment, his vision blurred, and the world tilted into a chaotic swirl of snow, ice, and darkness.

The engine sputtered, then fell silent, leaving an eerie stillness in its wake. Snow continued to fall in thick, relentless waves, cocooning the wreck in a shroud of white. The wind howled like a living thing, rattling the truck as if trying to tear it apart.

Caleb groaned, the sound weak and hoarse as he fought to stay conscious. His chest heaved, the cold biting deeper, invading his coat and clawing its way to his skin. Pain radiated from his temple, sharp and unyielding, and his limbs felt sluggish, like they were weighted with lead.

Somewhere in the distance, the low rumble of thunder rolled across the mountains, a haunting echo that seemed to vibrate through the very ground. Caleb's lips moved, his voice barely more than a whisper, a name slipping past his trembling breath.

"Bonnie..."

The storm roared in answer, its fury drowning him in an unforgiving symphony of wind and snow. And then there was only silence.

Chapter 3

The soft pop of kernels bursting on the stove filling the cozy cabin with the scents of golden butter and popcorn. Nathan shook the pot vigorously, his focus intent on avoiding another culinary disaster. The sound of the storm outside—the howl of the wind battering the cabin walls—served as a stark contrast to the comforting hum of normalcy inside.

"You burned it again, didn't you?" Danielle called from the living room, her voice carrying a playful accusation. She was crouched by the coffee table, setting up their well-worn Scrabble board. Her hazel eyes sparkled with mischief as she glanced over her shoulder.

Nathan rolled his eyes but didn't turn around. "The burn adds flavor," he countered, his tone dripping with mock indignation. "It's called culinary artistry. You wouldn't understand."

Debbie smiled from her recliner by the window, tugging her thick quilt closer, the edges brushing her recently scrubbed hardwood floors. She kept one eye on the twins, soft amusement warming her heart, while the other stayed steady on the frosted-over view outside.

The storm's intensity had grown since she'd returned from work. The sound of wind, muffled yet powerful, battered the trees and walls, making the cabin feel both snug and vulnerable at the same time.

It was as though the world outside was losing itself in chaos, but here—this quaint cabin nestled at the edges of nowhere—there was nothing but contentment, popcorn, and the promise of a lazy night playing board games.

Danielle began laying out letter tiles, humming. "I hope you've got more in you than artistic charcoal popcorn, brother. 'Cause I'm about to crush you in this game."

Nathan scoffed. "Please. I'm going to let you think you're winning. It's called 'mental strategy'. You wouldn't get it."

The flickering porch light caught Debbie's attention, and her smile faltered. The erratic glow strained against the storm's relentless gusts, casting faint shadows across the snow-covered yard. A familiar knot of unease began to tighten in her stomach. She didn't want to admit it, but something about this storm unsettled her. It wasn't just the way it had rolled in faster than predicted or how the wind seemed intent on tearing through the mountain—it was something deeper, a whisper of foreboding that tugged at the edges of her thoughts.

Lord, keep us safe tonight, she prayed silently, brushing a strand of hair out of her face. There wasn't much use in worrying over what she couldn't control, and she knew better than to borrow trouble before it even arrived.

It was strange, Debbie thought, how a storm could make the world feel both snug and precarious. Within these walls, there was laughter, popcorn, and the promise of a quiet night filled with board games. Outside, the elements raged with unyielding ferocity, untamed and indifferent to the lives huddled within their fragile shelters.

Then, as if summoned by her unease, a bright flash illuminated the room. The thunderous crash that followed shattered the stillness, cutting through the cozy warmth like a blade. Debbie and Danielle jumped to their feet, eyes wide, as the sound reverberated through the cabin.

"What was that..." Nathan's voice trailed off, eyes wide as they darted around the room, trying to locate the source of the noise.

For a split second, the world seemed to hang in suspended confusion before Debbie's instincts kicked in. Her heartbeat thrummed against her chest, and the urgency she had learned to live with as a nurse took over in full force.

"Stay inside," she ordered, already moving to the front door.

Her words were practiced, steady, the quiet assurance of motherhood mixed with her years of training taking charge. Even though her heart had jumped into her throat, she didn't have time to let it distract her. Throwing on her thick coat and boots, she grabbed the flashlight from beneath the hall table.

"Mom..." Danielle started, worry etched across her face.

"I'll be right back," Debbie reassured her, flashing a quick smile she hoped looked more confident than she felt.

The moment Debbie opened the door, wind slammed into her, flinging snow into her face and stinging her cheeks. She blinked rapidly, her breath catching in shallow puffs as the cold gripped her. Each step through the yard was a struggle, the snow drifts knee-deep and unforgiving. The flashlight beam flickered against the swirling chaos, barely cutting through the dense wall of white.

She had a gut feeling telling her what the sound might have been, but in truth, it could have been any number of things. A tree finally giving in to the weight of snow and ice, a rogue piece of debris knocked loose from the roof. But deep down, something told her it was more than that.

Her boots crunched through the snow as she trudged across the yard, eyes narrowed against the gusting wind. Dim headlights flickered in the distance, barely cutting through the dense, swirling snowfall. Each step was a battle as the deep drifts resisted her progress, but she pressed on, fighting through the biting cold.

As she neared the edge of her front yard, she spotted it—a battered old pickup truck, its front end smashed, and the back end buried deep in a snowbank at the edge of her property below the road. The vehicle sat crumpled, a twisted remnant of impact entombed in snow.

"Mercy…" she breathed, quickening her pace, hoping against hope no one was seriously injured.

The wind howled louder, forcing her to think tactically with every step. She approached the truck and her stomach flipped, but she steeled herself and reached the driver's side door, shining her flashlight inside.

A man was slumped over, moving slightly, but clearly disoriented. A thin line of blood trailed down from a gash on his forehead. Without hesitation, she yanked the door open, her eyes scanning him swiftly as she began mentally cataloging his condition.

"Sir?" Debbie raised her voice over the howling wind. "Can you hear me? I'm a nurse. Where do you hurt?"

The figure inside shifted, and a low, gravelly voice emerged, laced with pain but steeped in stubbornness. "I'm fine… need to get home."

Debbie shook her head, already knowing she'd have to fight this one. "You're not going anywhere in this weather. Believe me. You've got two choices—either come inside my home willingly, or pass out from hypothermia out here. Your call."

A beat of silence, broken only by the wind and the sharp contrast of their breath against the ice-filled air.

Then, impossibly, a low chuckle. "Always this bossy with strangers who crash their trucks?"

Debbie cracked a small smile despite herself. "Only the stubborn ones." She glanced at him closer. "I'm Debbie Ferguson."

He finally turned his head enough for her to catch those deep, dark brown eyes beneath his brow. "Caleb Warren," he muttered. "And I... I'm fine."

Debbie narrowed her eyes, her trained gaze taking in his condition. The man could barely sit upright, his movements sluggish and pained. A gash on his forehead sent a thin trickle of blood down his temple, the icy wind freezing it into a faint, glistening trail that disappeared into the scruff of his beard. His hand was smeared with blood from another cut, though it was hard to tell how deep. She crossed her arms, her voice firm but not unkind. "Let me be the judge of that. Medical professional, remember? You'd be doing yourself a favor to listen."

Caleb blinked, his disoriented brain catching up with his situation. Pain flickered across his face when he shifted in the seat, his left arm clutching his side. "Seriously. I've got it." He grunted as he tried to move, wincing.

"No, you don't," she answered flatly, already stepping back from the truck to shout toward the house where the kids stood on the porch trying to see what was going on. "Nathan! Get out here!"

Within moments, a bundle of tall, lanky energy in a winter coat and half-zipped boots made its way toward the truck, slipping slightly as he marched through the snow, his brow furrowed with confusion. "Anyone hurt? Should I call someone?"

Debbie shook her head once. "Just help me get him into the house. Judging by his little self-diagnosis,"—she shot Caleb a knowing look—"I'd say, we've got a pretty banged up man on our hands with a mild head wound."

Caleb's face scrunched in aggravation, though whether it was from pain or pride—or both—was yet to be determined. "I can walk."

He stood to prove his point and immediately regretted it as dizziness hit. He dropped back on the truck seat with a rough exhale.

"Right. And I'm a circus trapeze artist," Debbie remarked dryly. "Come on, Nathan. Help me get him to the house."

Together, she and Nathan took hold of Caleb under each arm, no matter how much the man tried to brush them away. He stumbled, pain etched across hardened features more used to frowning than smiling. Ultimately, he had no choice but to let them lead him toward the house.

"I don't need—" Caleb bit out between shallow breaths, wincing in pain. The cold wind stung at his exposed cuts, and despite himself, he felt weak.

"You do need help, now hush," Debbie answered firmly. She turned her gaze, meeting his eyes. "I'm going to make sure you're okay. No arguments."

Caleb gave in, nodding silently as he allowed them to guide him toward the cabin.

Once inside, the warmth of the cabin wrapped around them, a welcome contrast to the biting cold outside. The relief, however, was short-lived. Caleb's heavy, unsteady frame wavered as they helped him through the doorway, and suddenly the fragile balance tipped.

"Whoa!" Nathan yelped as Caleb's weight shifted heavily against him, throwing them both off-kilter. In the scramble to steady themselves, Debbie was pulled into the fray, a startled grunt escaping her as the three of them tumbled into a tangled heap near the door.

Coats, boots, and scarves became a chaotic jumble, their snow-covered forms sprawled on the hardwood floor like the aftermath of an overly ambitious snowball fight.

The absurdity of the moment hung in the air, the firelight flickering warmly as if mocking their predicament. Caleb, tall and rugged, fumbled awkwardly with a pained expression, Nathan and Debbie pinned under the weight of the man they had just rescued.

Caleb's dazed eyes found hers, half-lidded with disorientation but also narrowed with a mixture of embarrassment and irritation. He looked like a man who had gone ten rounds with a bear and still wasn't quite sure who had won.

"Heavier than he looks," Nathan muttered dryly, grimacing as he tried to extricate himself from the pile of limbs. His breath was coming out in short bursts, every word highlighted by the strain of moving Caleb up and off him.

Despite the situation, Debbie couldn't suppress a small, wry smile, laughing softly at the sheer ridiculousness. "You alright there, big guy?" she teased Caleb, as she tried to get a grip on the situation.

Caleb, clearly trying to save face, grumbled, "I'm not that heavy."

Nathan couldn't resist. "Yeah, well, tell that to my lung capacity. You just knocked the wind right out of me."

Debbie shot her son an amused look, quickly examining Caleb for any signs of further injury. "Let's just focus on getting him to the couch before he bulldozes the rest of the house with him," she quipped, rising to her feet with practiced efficiency.

Still clearly woozy but determined to salvage the smallest bit of dignity, Caleb made a vain attempt to stand on his own. He planted both palms on the floor and tried to leverage his weight. As soon as he shifted, a grimace tugged at his features. "I've got it," he muttered.

"You don't got it," Debbie corrected with a knowing shake of her head, moving to his side to help brace him.

Nathan stepped in on Caleb's other side, wrapping one of Caleb's arms over his shoulder. "I've met bags of concrete lighter than you, dude," Nathan joked, managing the kind of light humor that seamlessly danced between concern for Caleb and giving his mother a bit of comedic relief.

"I'm not a dude, kid," Caleb grunted, a trace of amusement slipping through his discomfort, "but you can call me whatever you want if it stops you from dropping me."

Nathan gave him a sideways grin. "Deal."

Danielle, who had been hovering nearby, wide-eyed with both amusement and concern, jumped into action the moment she heard her mother's instruction.

"Danielle, get the first aid kit from the pantry," Debbie called.

"On it!" Danielle replied, her hazel eyes sharpening with focus as she dashed toward the kitchen.

With Nathan's help on one side and Debbie on the other, they slowly maneuvered Caleb into a more upright position. Despite his protest, it was obvious he needed the support, his breath hitching every time he moved. Together, mother and son helped guide him carefully toward the couch, where he collapsed with an exhale that was half-relief, half-aggravation.

"There," Debbie said, brushing a strand of hair from her face and standing back to assess him like she would any other patient. "No more playing Superman. Let's get you patched up properly."

Chapter 4

Debbie knelt beside Caleb, her hands moving with practiced precision, the calm, methodical demeanor of a seasoned nurse guiding her every action. Caleb leaned back on the couch, his body stiff and uncooperative, each movement eliciting a grimace, though he voiced no complaints. His face told the story of a man who was used to fighting his own battles—a hardened solitude that somehow softened now that he had no choice but to lean on others for a while.

None of Caleb's injuries seemed life-threatening, thank goodness. The cuts weren't deep, though the gash on his head and the one on his hand bled more than she liked. From the way he winced and the tension in his body, she suspected he had taken a hard beating inside the cab when his truck crashed. If he hadn't cracked a rib or two, he'd certainly feel like it tomorrow.

Danielle reappeared, clutching the first aid kit close to her chest. "Here, Mom."

"Thanks." Debbie smiled and nodded, taking the kit from her daughter and opening it on the coffee table. "Someone grab some towels and mop up the snow by the door."

Danielle ran to find towels and Nathan had the good sense to stay nearby, but not in the way. "Do you need anything else, Mom?"

"Could you grab a bottle of water for him from the kitchen? Then stick around in case I need an extra hand," she said, as she kept her focus on Caleb. Her movements were calm and deliberate as she treated his wounds.

She wiped gently at the blood on his skin, her touch deft and practiced, though her mind couldn't shake the wearied and dazed look in Caleb's eyes. It wasn't just physical exhaustion and pain; something deeper seemed to grip him. Even as he winced from the antiseptic sting, he managed to mask most of his discomfort, like a man too used to bearing life's hits without complaint.

"You're pretty banged up," she said.

"Not my first time," Caleb muttered, that dry mountain man tone creeping in as he turned his head slightly, the muscles in his jaw hardening. "Won't be the last, either."

His refusal to admit vulnerability wasn't lost on Debbie. She had dealt with stubborn patients before. Men who thought pain made them weak—who carried an invisible, almost unspoken responsibility not to show any cracks.

"You think you've got iron skin, don't you?" Debbie teased lightly, dipping the corner of the cloth into the antiseptic again and carefully working around the cut on his forehead. "Hate to break it to you, but even the toughest need a little fixing up now and then."

A ghost of a smile tugged at the corner of his mouth, fleeting but genuine. "Maybe," he said, his voice gravelly, "but I've never been keen on bein' fussed over."

"Too bad for you," she retorted cheerfully, barely missing a beat. "You're in the hands of a professional fuss-er. And I take that job seriously."

"Let's get this coat off," she continued, her voice softening with care. Debbie moved with deliberate gentleness, hoping to ease some of the pain she knew he must be feeling. Despite her best efforts, Caleb let out a low grunt as the thick fabric slid down his left arm.

She gently pushed up his flannel shirt to inspect the damage underneath, revealing a deep welt spreading across his left side and upper chest. The skin was an angry red, mottled with the telltale signs of impact from the crash.

Carefully, she unbuttoned it and slid it off his left arm, her movements deliberate to avoid causing unnecessary pain. Her gaze shifted to his arm, where similar bruising marked the aftermath of the collision, the darkening patches of skin mirroring the force his body had absorbed. Debbie's expression remained steady, but her mind raced, already cataloging the injuries and planning the steps she'd need to take.

"Well," he muttered dryly under his breath, "there went half my dignity."

She shook her head slightly, her tone firm but warm. "Relax, I have to check for any serious injuries," she said, her lips curling into a teasing smile. "If letting someone help takes a hit to your pride, we've got bigger problems." Her eyes softened as she continued, but her voice stayed steady, professional.

"You took a pretty hard hit, Caleb. Your chest and side are all red—there are welts," she explained, tipping her head briefly toward his arm. "See how banged up your arm is?" She waited until his eyes followed her gesture. "Your left side and chest look the same," she paused, her gaze sharp with knowing concern. "You weren't wearing a seat belt, were you?"

It wasn't a question that needed answering, and they both knew it.

"Here's a water bottle, Mom," Nathan said, handing it over with a glance toward Caleb, who was clearly still trying to mask the discomfort that rippled through him with every breath.

"Thank you, sweetheart." Debbie unscrewed the cap and offered it to Caleb, who accepted it with a small grunt of gratitude.

His hands trembled, a subtle sign betraying what his stoic front tried to deny.

"Drink up," Debbie said, her hand resting briefly on his forearm like a mother encouraging a reluctant child. "Fluids will help. You lost your fair share of blood out there from that head wound and the other cuts."

With effort, he tilted the bottle toward his lips, taking a slow sip while his eyes squinted with a trace of skepticism. "I wreck a truck, and suddenly, I'm a fragile porcelain doll now?" he asked dryly, a slight chuckle coming from the back of his throat, though there was no real fight left in his words.

"Honey," Debbie quipped back, her voice light but caring as she began to carefully wrap the small gash on his hand, "anyone that crashes during a storm like this, gets knocked unconscious, and still manages to walk is made of something far tougher than porcelain."

Debbie continued her work, making sure every wound was tended to properly. "You've got one job now—it's to rest. That means no arguing, no macho acts, and definitely no trying to walk it off while you're half-conscious. Got it?"

Caleb's laugh was a rough, low rumble from within. "Rest," he repeated, yawning despite himself. "Something I'm not all that good at."

"Consider it part of your rehabilitation plan, then. You'll be an expert by the time this storm passes." Smiling, Debbie stepped back, surveying her work with satisfaction.

"You'll be alright," she reassured, offering him a warm smile as she began gathering the medical supplies. "You got banged up pretty good, I'll say that. But nothing you can't come back from."

Nathan moved to the front window overlooking their front yard. "Mom, this storm... it's bad."

Debbie looked out the window at the swirling chaos beyond the front porch. The wind howled with fierceness, tossing snow in impossible spirals. Everything beyond their cabin was shrouded, disappearing into a vast white oblivion.

There was no chance of anyone leaving tonight. The storm had rendered the roads treacherous, and an ambulance wouldn't stand a chance of making it up the mountain in this weather. Debbie's focus returned to the man on her couch. She didn't know much about him, but she did know he lived farther up the mountain—an impossible journey given the relentless snow and ice outside. For now, he was staying put, whether he liked it or not.

Caleb shifted on the couch, letting out a low sigh. "You about done with me, nurse?" he muttered, his tone somewhere between humor and frustration.

"Almost," Debbie replied. "Just sit tight and let me think a minute."

He raised an eyebrow. "You're a bit bossy, aren't you?"

Debbie flashed him a playful grin. "I am." She stood, her posture firm as she pointed down the hallway toward the guest bedroom. "We're going to move you to the guest bedroom, where you can get some rest."

Caleb drew in a deep breath but winced halfway through as he attempted to rise from the couch. The flare of pain in his chest quickly reminded him that he was injured. With a grunt, he flopped back down.

"I think I'll stay right here," he muttered.

"Nah, you're not," Debbie said, a soft yet firm note in her voice. "That couch isn't going to cut it. Not with possible broken ribs and a banged-up arm and head. You'll thank me in the morning."

He stared at her, his eyes cutting sharp, as if assessing whether fighting her was going to be worth it. But something in her look—call it motherly determination wrapped in a layer of sharp attitude—made him reluctantly nod. "All right, you win."

"Good," Debbie said without missing a beat, her tone as decisive as ever. She turned to Nathan, her expression already conveying the plan. "Let's get him settled in the guest bedroom. We need to make sure he's comfortable."

"Nathan, you take one side," she added, gesturing with a nod in Caleb's direction.

Debbie caught Danielle's watchful eye. "Danielle, run and grab a quilt and pillow from the linen closet," Debbie said, her voice softening just a little. "And bring my medical bag from the kitchen. I'll stay in the guest bedroom tonight to keep an eye on him."

Danielle raised an eyebrow, curious, but she disappeared up the steps before asking too many questions. Nathan, meanwhile, stepped forward and shared an awkward glance with Caleb. The two exchanged a silent nod, both understanding that neither enjoyed this forced interaction, but Caleb wasn't in any state to argue.

"Ready?" Nathan asked.

Caleb sighed deeply, then extended one burly arm. "Guess so."

With Nathan on one side and Debbie steadying him from the other, they managed to help Caleb onto his feet. Caleb muttered something about the stubbornness of mothers into the collar of his jacket, but Debbie chose to ignore it as they led him down the hallway toward the bedroom.

"What kind of circus is this?" Caleb muttered, his voice soft but carrying a gruff humor.

"Only the best for stubborn patients," Debbie replied. "We specialize in reluctant mountain men who crash into snowbanks."

Caleb huffed out a breath—it might have been a laugh.

Chapter 5

Once they had helped Caleb into the guest bedroom, he let out a low, weary groan, his body sinking heavily into the mattress as though it had finally given him permission to rest. His eyes half closed, the tough exterior he had clung, crumbling under the weight of exhaustion. For the first time, he looked truly vulnerable, his sharp features softened by fatigue.

Nathan adjusted the pillows behind Caleb's head, then straightened up, glancing at his mother with a quiet concern lingering in his eyes. "You good here, Mom?" he asked.

She nodded. "Thanks, bud. Could you move the recliner from the corner up next to the bed?"

"Sure." Nathan said. "Want me to put on a pot of coffee too?"

"That'd be wonderful... and make it strong." Debbie responded with a smile.

Nathan flashed a quick grin as he moved the recliner from the corner of the bedroom, then slipped quietly out into the hallway.

Debbie turned her attention back to Caleb, gently removing his boots and draping a quilt over him. He made a feeble attempt to adjust his position, but a sharp jolt of pain quickly stilled him. Too exhausted to argue, he let out a resigned sigh.

"You really don't need to sit in here," Caleb said, his voice low but edged with stubbornness. "I've gotten by without help before. Don't see why tonight should be any different."

"Maybe because you crashed your truck over the hill and into a snowbank at the edge of my yard," Debbie replied, arching an eyebrow as she shook her head. "And because you're pretty banged up, whether you're willing to admit it or not."

There was a resigned quiet that fell between them as Caleb's gaze lingered on some invisible spot on the ceiling. "Always thought I was smarter than to let something like this happen."

"Even tough guys like you have off days," Debbie said as she sat down in the recliner and spread the quilt Danielle had brought her across her lap. "Give yourself a break—and remember, trucks can be replaced. You, on the other hand, can't."

Caleb let out a huff of air—not quite a laugh, but close. "That was a good work truck," he muttered, the faint hitch in his words betraying a trace of regret. Though his voice was quiet, it carried a surprising fondness, as if, for a brief moment, the truck's loss overshadowed the bruises and battered state he was in.

Debbie smiled, leaning her head back against the recliner. "I'm sure it was," she said lightly. "But hey, she earned a proper retirement. Going out in a snowbank's a lot more dignified than rusting away in some scrapyard, right?"

Caleb grunted, almost wistfully. "Guess that's one way to look at it."

"Still, can't say I'm thrilled about the idea of heading up the mountain without her. Dependable. Solid. Don't come by stuff built like that anymore. New trucks these days—" he paused mid-thought, the weariness seeping back into his words like it was too much effort to finish the sentence.

Debbie smiled as she playfully nudged at his brooding. "You're talking about that truck like it was a long-lost friend. You really pick favorites that easily?"

Caleb cracked a tired smirk from the corner of his mouth. "Better a truck than people." His words came out casually, but there was an edge of truth that lingered beneath.

Debbie watched him quietly, her thoughts drifting as she studied his weary expression. She understood that feeling all too well—the tendency to find solace in things that couldn't hurt you, couldn't let you down. Objects like trucks, tools, or even routines—they were dependable, predictable. People, on the other hand, were far more complicated.

With a soft sigh, she broke the silence. "Well, lucky for you, trucks don't have feelings, so they won't hold a grudge." Her voice was light, but carried a note of sincerity. "But people? If you give them a chance—" She hesitated, her gaze dropping briefly before meeting his again, her tone strengthening. "They don't always disappoint... not all of them, anyhow. Sometimes people can surprise you."

A long silence followed this time, Caleb neither agreeing nor disagreeing, his brow furrowing slightly as if he were weighing her words but too tired to commit to any answer. Eventually, his body relaxed further into the mattress, tension ebbing away as the weariness overtook him.

"I don't know about all that..." he muttered, the fight draining from his voice.

Nathan entered the room, carrying two steaming mugs of coffee, the rich scent filling the space. He handed one to his mother before taking a seat on the edge of the bed, his eyes flickering between Debbie and Caleb.

"Strong enough, Mom?" he asked, offering a tentative smile as he sipped from his own cup.

"Just the way I like it. Thanks."

Nathan nodded as he glanced at Caleb. "How are you holding up?"

Caleb gave a half-hearted chuckle, clearly still trying to mask the discomfort on his side. "I've been worse."

Nathan raised his eyebrows, his lips tilting into a crooked grin. "Give it a few hours. I have a feeling you'll feel like a human punching bag in the morning."

Caleb's eyes narrowed, but a hint of amusement tugged at the corner of his mouth. "Is that supposed to be comforting?"

Nathan shrugged. "Just setting expectations."

Debbie shook her head and laughed, taking another sip from her mug. "No need to scare the poor man, Nathan. He's had enough for one night."

Nathan grinned. "Fair enough." His gaze flickered back to Caleb, a touch of curiosity mixing with his concern. "Seriously, though... what were you doing out there in the middle of this storm?"

Caleb let out a slow breath, his eyes on the ceiling again, as if weighing his response. "Work." His voice was gruff but honest. "Tried to make it back home before the worst of it hit. Didn't exactly go as planned."

"You live far from here?" Nathan asked, his tone casual but probing. Debbie shot him a quick look—there was something in her son's voice. More than idle curiosity.

"About five more miles up the mountain," Caleb replied, his gaze shifting briefly to the window, where snow continued to swirl mercilessly.

Debbie frowned, setting her coffee down on the small bedside table. "You're lucky you didn't end up in worse shape. That road is dangerous in this kind of weather."

Caleb grunted, his breath heavy with exhaustion.

Nathan looked like he wanted to ask more, but Debbie gave him a gentle nudge on the arm. "Let's not poke the bear tonight, Nathan. Caleb needs rest." She turned her gaze to Caleb, her voice softening. "We've got plenty of time for conversation in the morning."

Caleb chuckled low in his chest, but the sound tapered off into a wince of pain. "Y'all are somethin' else."

Debbie smiled, brushing a stray lock of hair from her face. There was a brief moment of silence. The only sound was the wind howling outside and the crackling fire in the living room.

"Guess I owe you one," Caleb finally murmured, his voice softer, more vulnerable than before.

Debbie shook her head. "No debt owed here, Caleb. That's what neighbors are for."

Caleb's gaze lingered on her for a moment, something unreadable passing through his deep brown eyes, before he let his head rest back against the pillow. "If you say so."

Nathan finished his coffee and stood. "Well, if you need anything else, shout. I'm gonna head to bed."

As he moved toward the door, Debbie shot him a grateful glance. "Thanks again, Nathan. Get some rest."

"I will," Nathan said with a nod, just as Danielle stepped quietly into the room, her arms full of quilts.

"Everything okay in here?" she asked, her voice soft as she glanced between her mother and Caleb, concern etched in her features.

Debbie smiled, nodding toward the extra quilts in her arms. "Perfect timing, hon. Go ahead and drape one across the foot of the bed, just in case."

Danielle moved to do so, her movements precise but gentle. As she spread one of the quilts over Caleb's legs, she shot him an encouraging smile. "Cozy enough?" she asked, trying to lighten the mood.

Caleb opened one eye, his gruffness softened by exhaustion. "Depends. What's this service going to cost me?"

Danielle grinned and raised an eyebrow as she threw a glance at her mom. "Oh, we've got a great payment plan. First installment includes cleaning the porch off when the snow clears."

"Second installment is clearing the driveway once this storm's over," Nathan added from the doorway.

"Mmm... tempting," Caleb muttered, but winced as he adjusted his position. His tone was dry, but there was a thread of humor underneath.

Debbie chuckled, shaking her head in mild exasperation. "You two are relentless," she said, shooting a playful glance at her kids before turning her attention back to Caleb. Her tone shifted, softening with concern.

"How are you feeling?" she asked, her gaze steady. "Anything worse than before?"

"'Bout the same," he mumbled, tiredness starting to weigh heavy in his voice. "Thanks for this. Really... I appreciate it."

Debbie leaned back in her chair. "Don't mention it, Caleb. Just try to rest. We'll handle everything else."

Nathan and Danielle lingered for a moment, casting one last glance at Caleb.

"We'll be around if you need anything, Mom," Nathan said.

Debbie offered a warm smile and nodded, her eyes following them down the hall for a moment before turning back to Caleb, who was already drifting off. The rhythmic rise and fall of his chest gradually evening out with sleep.

"Rest well," she murmured, her voice almost a whisper as she settled deeper into the chair.

Chapter 6

The storm raged on, battering the windows of Debbie's cabin with relentless force. The thick glass muffled its howls, but the wind's persistence was a constant reminder of the chaos outside. Night had fully cloaked the world, burying it in a swirl of darkness and snow that seemed unending. Inside, the house creaked and groaned softly, settling against the storm's fury like an old ship riding out a squall.

In the guest room, Debbie sat quietly, her hands clasped in her lap, the only sound the low, steady rhythm of Caleb's breathing. Alone with her thoughts, she watched over her unexpected patient, the lamplight casting a warm glow around the room.

Caleb looked different in sleep. The hard, guarded lines of his face had eased, though a faint furrow remained between his brows, as though even unconscious, he couldn't fully let go of the tension. His chest rose and fell in a slow, deliberate rhythm, occasionally hitching when his bruised and tender ribs made their presence known. Debbie's gaze lingered, her nurse's instincts cataloging every detail, but beneath her professional concern was something else—a quiet curiosity about the man who had literally crashed into her life on this stormy night.

The storm might be relentless, but in this room, there was a fragile stillness, a moment of quiet amid the chaos outside.

Caleb stirred slightly, his face pinching with discomfort. "M'fine," he mumbled, still mostly asleep. "Used to... handling things... since Bonnie..."

Bonnie. The name hung in the air, heavy with meaning. She watched as Caleb's face tightened, even in sleep, at the mention of his deceased wife.

Debbie knew a little about Caleb Warren—a few scattered pieces of information gleaned through patient visits around the area and small-town whispers. In a close-knit community like Laurel Ridge, it was nearly impossible not to hear a name mentioned, especially a name like Caleb's, which lingered on the edges of gossip for years. She knew he lived a solitary life far up in the mountains, several miles beyond her cabin, tucked away where the wilderness reclaimed the land and snow could bury you for days without notice. Word was, he preferred it that way—a man who enjoyed his distance and guarded his privacy with quiet, almost fierce, determination.

Caleb Warren wasn't exactly what you'd call charming. He was gruff, always had been, and his conversations—if one could even call them that—rarely went beyond a few clipped words. Still, there was something about him that had always piqued Debbie's curiosity, though she'd never had a reason to dig deeper. What little she knew about his past made it clear he was a man full of heartache and regrets.

Caleb has suffered an immense loss years ago. Two, actually. His wife, Bonnie, had passed unexpectedly—a tragedy that rippled across the small community. Debbie remembered being told that Bonnie had died at home. It had been a brain aneurysm. Sudden and final. One moment there, the next gone—a thought that sent an unsettling chill through Debbie as she imagined the depth of such grief.

A few residents of Laurel Ridge had been close enough to witness Caleb's downward spiral after the tragedy. The small-town grapevine buzzed quietly behind closed doors, whispers weaving their way through coffee shops and church pews. When Caleb ventured into town, cautious nods and sidelong glances followed him, the kind of unspoken acknowledgment that said they knew but didn't dare bring it up.

It was as if some of the community had silently agreed to keep their distance, unsure of how to navigate his grief. Yet, despite the collective hesitation, many had reached out in their own ways—dropping off meals, offering prayers, or trying to pull him back into the rhythms of the community. Still, their efforts were met with polite refusal or quiet indifference. Caleb had been a man determined to shoulder his pain alone, and over time, people stopped trying, leaving him to wrestle with his loss in solitude.

Bonnie's death hadn't just devastated Caleb—it had utterly broken him. Debbie recalled hearing about how, in his grief, he had sold the lovely home he and Bonnie had once shared in town without even setting foot in it again. Instead, he had retreated to the mountains, living off the land and building a cabin of his.

Everyone in town knew about Caleb Warren's dark period—a shadow that had stretched from his teenage years after his mom had died and extended well into adulthood until the day Bonnie died. Caleb had been a storm in human form, a raging alcoholic whose pain and anger tore through him like a wildfire, leaving destruction in its wake. The stories were consistent, if incomplete: nights when the bottle seemed to take control, dragging him into a pit so deep he couldn't claw his way out until the last drop of liquor burned out of his system.

The rumors painted a vivid picture of chaos—fights that ended with bloodied knuckles and bruised egos, though no one could ever pin down the details. There were whispers of drywall punched through in fits of anger, chairs overturned in bars, and shattered glass littering the streets, remnants of bottles thrown in blind frustration. Caleb had been a force of nature, all raw suffering and unchecked fury.

Many had marveled at Bonnie's role in it all—how she had endured the tempest of Caleb's worst years and still stood by him. No one could quite understand why Bonnie had fallen so deeply in love with Caleb, or how she managed to stay by his side through it all. But she had, unwavering in her devotion. Sunday after Sunday, she'd sat in the church pews, lifting Caleb's name to the Lord in prayer, asking for mercy, for redemption, for strength. Despite everything, Bonnie had believed in him when few others could. And perhaps that belief had been enough to keep Caleb tethered to something greater than himself—until it wasn't.

And yet, the most enduring truth about him was one that baffled the entire town: Caleb Warren had quit drinking the very day Bonnie died. Not a drop since. The change was so sudden, so absolute, that it left people wondering how one man could bury such a monstrous habit overnight.

Most of what Debbie knew about Caleb Warren came from Martha Kincaid, the sharp-eyed owner of Martha's Diner. Over a cup of coffee years ago, Martha had shared the story of Caleb's abrupt end to drinking—a tale that had become part of the fabric of small-town gossip. Martha had a way of knowing everything that had happened in Laurel Ridge, her watchful presence like a constant hum beneath the sleepy rhythms of the town.

According to Martha, Caleb had woken up on the morning of his wife's death with a hangover from the night before. His head pounding, his body heavy with the aftermath of too much alcohol, he'd stumbled into the kitchen—and found Bonnie on the floor, lifeless. That moment had marked an unshakable turning point. From that day forward, Caleb hadn't touched another drop of liquor.

Some people doubted the story, of course. Skeptics whispered in low tones at the diner counter or after church services, questioning how a man like Caleb, with years of dependence and demons trailing behind him, could suddenly and completely abandon the bottle. It didn't seem possible—not after everything he'd been through.

But while the town speculated, Caleb rebuilt his life secluded in the mountains. Sober. Day after day, year after year, he carried on, the storm inside him seemingly quieted. Over the years, it was clear to everyone that Caleb Warren was a changed man.

Beyond the basic pieces of his grief-driven past, Debbie didn't know much more about the man now lying in her guest bed. Caleb kept to himself and managed to shift through life like a ghost no one could get close to. The cutting rumors of his drinking days were all but relics now, though traces of the hardened version of him could still be seen in the lines etched across his face—a testament to years lived under the weight of quiet pain.

And now, here he was—this man whom many in Laurel Ridge had deemed untouchable—resting under her roof. Debbie studied him, noting the tension that lingered even in sleep, the way his guarded demeanor never seemed to fully let go. There was more to Caleb Warren than the gruff, closed-off exterior he wore like a shield. She saw it in the way his eyes had flinched from her care, avoiding tenderness as though it might sting.

Beneath the rugged exterior and self-imposed solitude, Debbie sensed something deeper. He was a man who carried the weight of his beliefs, someone who had weathered life's storms and was quietly searching for calm—perhaps even forgiveness. Isolation had become his armor, distance his way of protecting himself from the world. But now, here in the quiet stillness of her home, Debbie saw the cracks in that armor, the faint glimpses of a fractured soul beneath the surface. It was a kind of pain she recognized all too well—the kind that came from trying to carry too much for too long.

As a nurse, it had become second nature for Debbie to read people—pain, whether physical or emotional, wasn't easily hidden when you knew the subtle signs to watch for. She had caught glimpses of the cracks in Caleb's armor—the fleeting vulnerability in his face when exhaustion claimed him. The unconscious winces as he shifted against his injuries. His silence spoke volumes, louder than any words could.

This wasn't just about the crash. Caleb was a man who had been fighting to hold himself together for far longer than anyone could imagine. The fractured pieces of him were still there, carefully held in place, waiting for someone to notice. There was undeniable strength in him—a resilience that demanded respect—but it was tempered by a weariness so deep it seemed as if it could drag him under without leaving so much as a ripple on the surface.

As Debbie sat quietly in the dim light of the guest room, the wind howling against the windows and snow piling in heavy drifts outside; she watched the steady rise and fall of Caleb's chest. The question she couldn't shake echoed in her mind: How can I help him?

A soft knock at the door drew her attention. Nathan and Danielle stood in the doorway, steaming mugs of coffee in their hands.

"Thought you might need this," Nathan said, walking into the room. He handed her one of the mugs, then glanced at the second one in Danielle's hands with a sheepish grin. "We brought one for him too, but I guess that wasn't the best plan."

Debbie, smiling at them both, accepted the coffee gratefully, inhaling the rich aroma. "Thank you, sweetheart. And hey, it's the thought that counts."

Danielle set the second mug of coffee on the nightstand, then leaned against the wall, studying Caleb with a mix of curiosity and concern. "He say anything interesting? Dad used to talk about fishing trips in his sleep when he was sick."

Debbie laughed. "Actually, he mumbled something about burnt eggs and mentioned his deceased wife Bonnie a little while ago."

"Burnt eggs?" Nathan's eyebrows shot up. "Well, that's... specific."

"Maybe he's a secret chef," Danielle suggested, her eyes twinkling. "Though, based on the evidence, not a very good one."

Nathan snorted softly. "Must be a guy thing." He paused, then added with a grin, "Present company included."

Their quiet laughter was interrupted by a low groan from Caleb. His eyes fluttered open, dark and disoriented, immediately locking onto Debbie's warm hazel ones.

"You're still here," Caleb murmured, his voice thick with sleep. His gaze swept over the room, landing on the twins. "The whole crew, it seems."

Debbie set her coffee aside and leaned forward, automatically checking his pulse. "Of course we are. Someone has to make sure you don't try to escape and crash another truck."

The corner of his mouth twitched. "Wouldn't get far in this weather, anyway."

"Exactly. So you might as well accept your fate, right?" Her fingers were gentle but professional as she checked the bandage on his forehead. "How's the pain?"

Caleb started to shrug, then winced. "Had worse."

"Ah, yes. The classic tough guy response." Debbie raised an eyebrow. "Care to try again with the truth this time?"

Nathan cleared his throat. "I'm gonna head back up to bed. Try not to let him escape, Mom." He gave her a quick kiss on the cheek, then headed for the door, calling over his shoulder, "Night, Mr. Warren. Don't let Mom boss you around too much."

"Too late for that," Caleb muttered, but there was a hint of humor in his voice.

"Goodnight, Mom," Danielle said, leaning in to hug her. As she turned toward the door, she offered Caleb a small smile. "Goodnight, Mr. Warren."

After Nathan and Danielle left, Debbie busied herself checking Caleb's injuries, her touch careful but sure. Years of nursing had taught her to be gentle and thorough.

"Thank you," Caleb said suddenly, the words seeming to surprise even him. "For... all this. You didn't have to..."

"Yes, I did," Debbie interjected, her tone soft but firm. "You crashed in my yard during a blizzard. This is what neighbors do—we help each other."

Caleb grunted, his face contorting with pain as he shifted on the bed.

"Feeling a bit sore, I take it?" Debbie asked, her voice calm but concerned. "How about I get you some ibuprofen to take the edge off?"

He didn't reply, just exhaled heavily, his silence conveying both fatigue and resignation.

Without waiting for an answer, Debbie reached for her medical bag. Pulling out a small bottle of ibuprofen, she shook two pills into her hand. "Here," she said softly, holding them out. "This should help.

And don't even think about arguing—I can see right through that stoic mountain man act."

A ghost of a smile touched his lips. "Yes, ma'am."

As she helped him take the medication, their fingers brushed briefly. Something electric and unexpected sparked between them, causing them both to pull back slightly. Debbie busied herself with adjusting his pillows, trying to ignore the way her heart had jumped at the contact.

Caleb let out a long breath as he settled back against the pillows and closed his eyes. "I could get used to this, you know," he muttered as he drifted back to sleep

Chapter 7

Debbie woke to the soft glow of morning light filtering through the windows that overlooked the front of her property. The gentle rays cast shifting shadows across the hardwood floor, painting the room in shades of quiet calm. Outside, the snow continued to fall in delicate flakes, blanketing the landscape in pristine white. The fierce winds of the night before had subsided, their howls now replaced by a faint whisper that brushed softly against the cabin's sturdy walls. The storm's fury had passed, leaving behind a serene stillness that seemed to cradle the world in quiet reflection.

Stretching carefully, she winced, her body stiff from a night spent in the recliner. Her gaze drifted toward Caleb, who still slept, his breathing deep and even.

Moving quietly, Debbie slipped out of her chair and approached the window, wrapping her arms around herself against the lingering morning chill. Outside, the world was buried under a thick, unbroken blanket of snow. The road had vanished beneath towering drifts. Caleb's truck was almost completely submerged, its shape barely discernible under the heavy mound of white. The sight confirmed what Debbie had already suspected—they weren't going anywhere, anytime soon.

She turned back toward the guest bed just as Caleb began to stir. His eyelids fluttered open, sluggishly blinking against the light streaming into the room. A flicker of confusion crossed his features, his strong, calloused hand shifting beneath the quilt, as though he were trying to orient himself. For a moment, he seemed caught between reality and whatever fractured dreams had lingered through the night.

Then his gaze met hers. Recognition slowly dawned, his expression relaxing as he took in his surroundings and her presence, the weight of uncertainty easing ever so slightly.

"Morning," she said, moving closer to the bed. "Looks like you survived the night without causing too much trouble."

Caleb let out a low, groggy chuckle that ended in a wince. "I've had worse nights. That chair you were in doesn't look fit for sleeping." He gestured to the recliner, his voice rough from sleep but already tinged with the dry humor she was coming to recognize.

"You're not wrong about that," Debbie admitted, rolling her shoulders with a smirk.

He shifted slightly, testing the boundaries of pain, before nodding. "How's the storm?"

"Still coming down, though not as bad as yesterday. Let me check you over before we talk about the weather." She moved over to his side, her touch deft and gentle as she checked his vitals. "How're you feeling this morning?"

Caleb's eyes darkened as he let out a slow breath, possibly from caution or just plain stubbornness. "Arms sore, my chest feels like I ran into a brick wall, but I'll live."

"This might surprise you, but I already had a hunch you'd live." She flashed him a quick, teasing smile before continuing to check his bruises. "Doesn't mean you're off the hook from taking it easy, though."

He grunted something in response, clearly not interested in an argument he was destined to lose. Instead, he laid there, slightly embarrassed by his wounded state, while she worked in silence, hands warm as they moved with surety, checking his bandages.

After a moment, Caleb cleared his throat, his brows drawing together. "I, uh… don't suppose anyone would be looking for me, but I should probably check my phone. It's probably in my coat pocket."

Debbie dabbed a bit of antiseptic on a small cut before she paused, tilting her head in question.

"I'm sure you most likely have plenty of people worried about you," she said.

Caleb's jaw shifted, his eyes avoiding hers now as they focused somewhere on the wall. "No. But I should at least check for messages, in case the mill's down a man or two."

"The mill?" Debbie raised an eyebrow, her voice gentle but firm. "Caleb, I don't think Warren Lumber Mill should be your top priority right now. Look outside—we're buried under snow, and I guarantee no one is braving this storm to keep any business running. I imagine most of Laurel Ridge is shut down completely." She paused, her tone softening slightly. "Besides, you need to focus on healing. That mill will still be there when the storm clears. Right now, I'm more concerned about getting you back on your feet."

Caleb grunted, his gaze drifting toward the window. "I've never been much good at sitting still," he muttered, his voice gruff with lingering exhaustion. "Things need tending, storm or no storm."

Debbie crossed her arms and smiled, both amused and exasperated. "I get that you're used to taking care of everything yourself, but right now, what you need to tend to is recovering. I don't think being snowed in with possible broken ribs is the best time to push yourself, do you?"

Caleb's fingers twitched against the quilt, his jaw tightening as if he wanted to argue, but knew she wasn't wrong.

"Listen," Debbie continued, her tone soft yet resolute, "I know letting someone else handle things can't be easy for you. But right now, you don't have much of a choice. The mill can wait. For now, how about focusing on getting through today?"

Caleb exhaled a slow, heavy breath. "You're not one to back down, are you?"

"Nope," Debbie said with a sly smile. "Guess you'll just have to get used to someone 'fussing' over you for a change. Besides, I've had enough stubborn patients in my time to know how to stand my ground."

A quiet chuckle rumbled through Caleb's chest, though it was cut short as he winced in pain. His voice softened, almost as if conceding defeat. "I've noticed."

Debbie smiled warmly. "Good. Now, how about some breakfast?"

"Speaking of breakfast," Danielle said, appearing in the doorway with a mischievous grin. "I'm thinking pancakes—how does that sound to you, Mr. Warren?"

"Just call me Caleb," he huffed. "Mr. Warren sounds like my dad."

Debbie smiled as her daughter entered the room. "Morning, Dani. Pancakes sound like a great idea. Is your brother up yet?" she asked, watching as Danielle made her way to the window, peeking out at the snow-covered landscape.

"Oh my gosh, Mom! Everything is buried out there," Danielle exclaimed as she peered out the window, eyes wide in disbelief. "I can't even see the road—or your car, for that matter. It's like the whole world just disappeared under the snow!"

"The last time we had snow like this, you and Nathan were probably eleven or twelve years old," Debbie said with a faint smile, glancing toward the window. "Guess we were overdue for a storm this fierce. And here it is."

"It's still coming down, Mom. Any clue how long this is supposed to last?" Danielle asked, her voice laced with curiosity and a hint of concern.

Debbie glanced out at the near-blinding whiteout conditions beyond. "Last forecast I caught said we're in for heavy snow until at least tomorrow night. Could be longer, depending on how the system moves."

Danielle's eyebrows shot up. "We're going to be buried alive."

Debbie nodded, her expression part serious, part bemused. "Wouldn't be the first time we've had to dig ourselves out."

She turned toward Caleb, who had propped himself up slightly against the pillows and headboard. "What about you?" she asked. "Did you catch any updates before... you know," her hand gestured vaguely toward the window, implying his unfortunate crash.

Caleb shook his head, his features hardening a little. "Don't bother much with the news," he said, his voice low and gruff. "My brothers wouldn't stop harping about the storm while we were at the mill yesterday, though. Guess I should've listened better."

Debbie smirked, folding her arms across her chest.

Caleb grunted. "I usually trust my gut more than the weatherman. Kept an eye on the clouds yesterday, figured I had more time than I did."

Danielle chuckled, shaking her head. "Well, next time, how about you and your gut listen to your brothers?"

For a moment, Caleb's eyes flicked up toward the ceiling, a faint smile ghosting his face. "Not sure I'll be telling them that," he muttered.

Debbie laughed lightly. "Smart man. But for today and the foreseeable future, at least, you've got us stuck with you. So, settle in and let the experts—meaning me—take care of things."

Danielle grinned as she headed toward the door. "I'll be in the kitchen prepping a pancake marathon. Yell, if you need some extra hands... I'll have Nathan bring y'all some coffee."

As she disappeared down the hallway, Debbie turned her attention back to Caleb, her gaze softening. "You should try to relax a little."

"I'm fine. Don't think my ribs are broken—doesn't feel like it did last time I cracked four of 'em. I'm just banged up, took a pretty good hit from the steering wheel to the chest. You know how it goes," Caleb said, his voice gruff but laced with an attempt at reassurance.

Nathan appeared, carrying two steaming mugs of coffee. He handed one to Caleb and then passed the other to his mom.

"Coffee," Caleb muttered almost reverently, as if the mug itself held the cure to his aching wounds. "Thanks, boy. I needed this." He took a long sip, the warmth easing some of the tension in his body.

Nathan smirked. "It's Nathan, by the way. If we're gonna be snowed in together for a while, you might as well get my name right. I won't call you dude if you won't call my boy."

Caleb looked up from his cup, a bemused expression crossing his face as he gave a small grunt. "Noted." He settled back into the pillows, the faintest hint of a smile playing on his lips.

Nathan turned to his mom. "Danielle's got a pancake assembly line going in the kitchen. Found some sausage in the fridge too—mind if I cook that up?"

Debbie grinned, appreciating her son's initiative. "Go for it. Pancakes and sausage sound perfect. Thanks for handling it."

"No problem," Nathan said with a quick wink as he headed toward the kitchen. Over his shoulder, he added, "We'll have breakfast ready in a few minutes. You sure you're up for eating with us, Caleb?"

Caleb raised an eyebrow, lowering the coffee mug. "Yes, I'm starving."

Nathan disappeared down the hall, leaving Debbie and Caleb alone in the quiet of the guest room.

"You have good kids. They don't seem rude or crazy like some of 'em do nowadays," Caleb said after a moment.

"I know. Both of them turned out pretty great, even if they give me gray hair some days."

Caleb cleared his throat and took another sip from his mug. "Haven't had breakfast with a bunch of people in a while," he admitted gruffly, his eyes distant.

"Well," Debbie said gently, "you're about to."

Chapter 8

The rich aroma of syrup, butter, pancakes, and sizzling sausage filled the air as Nathan and Danielle maneuvered into the guest room with trays carefully balanced between their hands.

"Hope you've got an appetite, Caleb," Nathan grinned as he set the first tray on the edge of the bed, then handed Caleb his plate. "We made enough to feed a small army. Well, a snowed-in one, anyway."

"You ready for the best pancakes of your life, Caleb?" Danielle asked with an exaggerated flourish, her tone bright and playful as she set the food tray on Debbie's lap. She grabbed her own plate and plopped down beside her mother on the floor, her wide grin making it clear she was enjoying the theatrics of her self-proclaimed culinary masterpiece.

"You do make good pancakes," Debbie said, glancing at her kids with an affectionate smile. "But we'll see how Caleb fares. Hopefully, we'll have a survivor on our hands."

Caleb grunted, eyeing the precariously large stack of pancakes in front of him as though it might try to swallow him instead. "You sure this isn't some kind of trap?" He sniffed the air, curiosity evident despite the gruffness. "Smells better than what I burn up at my place, anyway."

Nathan sat on the floor beside his sister, his long legs folding into a half-hearted crisscross position.

"We thought we'd give you the real Ferguson special today," Danielle explained with a grin, popping open the syrup bottle with a flourish. "This is Mom's secret syrup. Trust me, it'll keep you going through the apocalypse."

"What's so secret about it?" Caleb asked, raising a brow.

"Well, it's not store-bought," Debbie said, leaning slightly forward in her chair. "Homemade. Got the recipe from my mom." She paused, her smile softening. "It's a family thing."

Caleb hesitated for a moment, glancing at the three sets of expectant eyes around him. He reached for the syrup bottle, poured a generous amount over his pancakes and sausage, and handed it off to Debbie. He grabbed his fork with a smirk and settled into breakfast.

"These ain't half bad," Caleb finally admitted, his voice gruff. "Better than mine."

Nathan smirked. "That's practically a glowing review."

Danielle elbowed her brother playfully. "He's lucky he didn't end up with some of the burnt one from my first batch."

"Ah, nothing wrong with a little charcoal," Caleb said, surprising himself by the ease in which he joined in their banter, despite his awkwardness.

Nathan glanced at Caleb with a raised eyebrow. "So, you ever wrecked or been stuck somewhere in a snowstorm like this before?"

Caleb took another slow bite, chewing thoughtfully. "Yeah, I've wrecked a vehicle or two." His eyes drifted toward the window. "But I haven't been caught off guard by a storm like this in a long time."

"Well, we all get caught off guard sometimes," Debbie said.

"It happens," Nathan quipped with a grin. "I guess any of us can hope we could outrun a storm... right?"

Caleb let out a chuckle. "Well, I figure if you can't outrun it, you might as well plow through it. But," he admitted grudgingly, "guess I didn't plow through it too well this time."

"Still, you're made of tough stuff. Not many people would've walked away from that sort of crash, let alone made it all the way up here as far as you did last night." Nathan said.

Danielle pursed her lips, shaking her head as she drizzled more syrup over her pancakes. "Especially without a seatbelt," she muttered under her breath, though loud enough for Debbie to hear.

Debbie shot her daughter a stern but affectionate look. "Danielle..." she warned lightly. She turned back to Caleb, leaning in just slightly. "Accidents happen. But trying buckling up from now on."

"Lesson learned," Caleb grunted, though there was the faintest twinkle of amusement in his eye.

Danielle shot him a small grin. "Good. We're not planning on making this an annual thing, okay?"

"Noted. So, about that snow," he said. "Looks like we might be stuck here a while?"

"I'm not too worried," Debbie replied lightly. "Plenty of food in the pantry... And we've got plenty of hands to help shovel when the time comes."

Debbie winked in Caleb's direction as she said that, and Caleb let out a low chuckle, followed by a wince from the lingering ache in his chest. "I might be able to manage," Caleb said.

Danielle sat up straighter, the teasing gleam in her eyes sparkling. "Ah, so you've agreed to help once we break out the shovels, huh?"

"Hey, don't let him out of the deal," Nathan added, casting a mock serious glance at Caleb. "Verbal contracts are binding in this household."

Caleb raised his hands slowly, careful not to strain his sore side. "Alright, alright. Sounds like I'll be earning my keep after all," he said, a hint of amusement slipping into his voice.

The room filled with laughter, light and unguarded. It was the kind of friendly warmth Caleb hadn't experienced in years, the kind that caught him off guard. In that moment, he was simply present, surrounded by people who didn't seem to expect anything from him except his company.

The conversation flowed easily, marked by casual chatter and a few more well-timed quips from Danielle and Nathan. Eventually, Danielle cleared her throat, her playful demeanor shifting slightly. She leaned closer to Debbie, her movement subtle but intentional, before glancing Caleb's way with a look that carried both curiosity and caution.

"Uh... I know this may be a little late to bring it up, but..." Danielle offered a small, apologetic smile, glancing between her mother and Caleb. "Would it be okay if we said grace? We kind of forgot."

The word "grace" hung in the air, and Caleb immediately tensed. It wasn't something he'd thought about in years. Shared prayers, expressions of faith—they weren't part of his world anymore. He kept his gaze down, focusing on the plate in front of him as a wave of discomfort crept in.

But Danielle's tone wasn't forceful or judgmental. It was light, gentle—like she'd just remembered something ordinary and wanted to include everyone, not impose. Nathan, noticing Caleb's hesitation, shrugged casually. "We can go without it if you're not comfortable, but we usually—"

"No," Caleb cut in, shifting slightly against the pillows. He cast a quick glance at Debbie, who was watching him with a steady, quiet curiosity. Her expression wasn't pushy, just patient, as though waiting to see how he'd handle this moment.

"Go ahead," Caleb said, his voice low but steady. "I don't mind."

Danielle exchanged glances with Debbie, who nodded encouragingly.

With everyone gradually bowing their heads, Danielle kept her words simple, thanking God for the food, the safety of those inside the cabin, for shelter amidst the storm. She added a subtle plea for Caleb to heal quickly and praised the strength they'd all been given to care for each other.

Debbie, eyes closed, snuck a quick look at Caleb as Danielle ended the prayer. If Caleb had been uncomfortable, he did a good job hiding it.

Caleb's jaw tightened momentarily when the prayer ended. It wasn't that he didn't appreciate the sentiment behind it... but standing before God like this—it was a raw reminder of just how far he'd drifted over the years. Whatever belief system Debbie's family held onto, it was steady in a way his no longer was.

"You okay, Caleb?" Debbie asked.

"Yeah," Caleb muttered. "I'll be... alright."

The memory of Bonnie flickered in his mind—her bright laughter, her colorful Sunday dresses, and the way she would close her green eyes tight during prayers, like she meant every word whispered between her and God. It had been years—a whole decade—since he'd heard her pray.

"I'm lucky that storm laid me up here," Caleb mused, his tone light, though it was clear he was steering the conversation away from prayer—and the ache it stirred within him. "If it wasn't for you folks, I'd probably still be in that truck, half-frozen, by now."

Debbie, ever perceptive, caught the shift and offered him a reassuring smile. She took a sip of her coffee before speaking, her voice warm. "For what it's worth, I think having a little extra company while being snowed in is a good thing."

Nathan leaned toward Caleb, his grin wide. "We're not too shabby for a snowbound crew, don't 'cha think, Caleb?"

Caleb glanced at him, his lips twitching into a faint smile. "Yep," he said simply, his voice low but sincere.

Chapter 9

Debbie stood in front of her open closet, staring vacantly at the neat rows of sweaters, shirts, jeans, and uniforms. Her fingers absently grazed the soft fabric of a flannel shirt as her mind wandered back to the situation at hand. They were snowed in. She tried not to think about how long they were likely to be stuck here, how long Caleb, a stranger really, would be sharing her space. Her kids seemed to be handling it well enough, but for her...

It was an odd feeling, having someone else in the house. Especially a man. Particularly after everything with James. The memory of her ex-husband still left a bitter aftertaste, but she quickly brushed it aside.

Her eyes darted toward the window, watching as fat, lazy snowflakes piled relentlessly onto the windowsill. The silence outside was almost oppressive, the world swallowed whole by the storm. Just how long would they be stranded here? Would it be a couple of days, or longer?

"Lord, though the snow is beautiful," she muttered, "maybe ease up a little on us?"

She sighed, kneeling in front of her dresser and tugging open the bottom drawer. Her hands sifted through its contents, searching for anything that might work for Caleb to change into. The thought of him having to stay in his work jeans and flannel shirt for days was beginning to grate on her.

It wasn't just about practicality—sure, she could wash his clothes, but something more comfortable to lounge in would be better. *No one should have to sit around in stiff work clothes for days on end,* she thought, her determination growing as she dug deeper into the drawer.

Not that she had anything that would remotely fit a man his size. Debbie glanced helplessly at her clothes, the thought striking her as absurd the longer she considered it. A soft sigh escaped her as she closed the drawer partway, her mind still turning over ideas.

The creak of the door pulled her attention, and she turned to find Nathan and Danielle standing there, her twins framed in the doorway. Their expressions were a blend of curiosity and mischief, the kind of look that only came when they knew they were about to stir the pot—or at least offer commentary.

"What are you doing, Mom?" Danielle asked, elbowing Nathan as if daring him to intervene first.

"Yeah... what are you doing?" Nathan echoed, quirking an eyebrow. He folded his lanky arms across his chest, lifting a brow in amusement.

Debbie paused for a moment, pushing the drawer shut. "Looking for something Caleb can change into. I doubt he wants to spend several days in those dirty work clothes."

Danielle threw her brother a knowing look. "Good call. He looks like he's been through a wood chipper. But..." She tapped her chin in exaggerated thought. "You know who might have something that fits him?"

Debbie raised an inquisitive brow.

Danielle's eyes gleamed. "Grandpa." She snapped her fingers together like the idea had just hit her. "He's got clothes in the guest room where Caleb's staying, right?"

Debbie blinked. How had she not thought of that? "You're right." She smiled at her daughter. "I guess my mind is so busy with everything going on, I'm not thinking clearly."

Nathan chuckled from where he stood leaning against the door frame. "You think Grandpa's stuff'll fit him? Caleb's not exactly a small guy, and Grandpa's... well, Grandpa."

Debbie laughed. "Even if the pants are a little short," she said with a small grin, tossing a playful look at Nathan, "at least they'll be clean."

Nathan rolled his eyes but smirked in return.

"Alright." Debbie said, her tone shifting as she brushed past them and motioned for them to follow. "Let's go raid your grandpa's clothes and see what we can find."

They made their way downstairs toward the guest room, the old hardwood steps creaking beneath their feet. The door to the guest bedroom was partially open, and Caleb was sitting up in bed. His broad shoulders were propped against the headboard and his strong, weathered hands cradled the coffee cup Nathan had brought earlier.

As they entered, Caleb's gaze lifted, his dark eyes tracking their movements. A flicker of curiosity passed over his face, tempered by the wariness that seemed to come as naturally to him as breathing. He sat still, his posture straight despite the discomfort he was likely feeling, watching them with an expression that asked more questions than his lips ever would.

"We, uh," Nathan began, smirking, "we come searching for clothes."

Caleb's brow furrowed. "Beg your pardon?"

Debbie tried not to laugh as she motioned toward the guest room closet and then pointed to the dresser. "You've been stuck in those clothes for long enough. I figured you might want something else to change into. My parents leave some of their things here so they can travel lighter when they come for a visit. My dad's clothes might be close enough to your size. Maybe not perfect," she added quickly, noticing Caleb's skeptical expression, "but at least you won't be wearing the same thing for days."

Caleb set the coffee mug down on the nightstand, his brow furrowing slightly. "Your dad's clothes?" he asked, the skepticism in his voice clear.

Debbie nodded, her expression calm but resolute, her tone softening to reassure him. "Yes. He's practical, just like you. He wouldn't mind—not under the circumstances."

Caleb hesitated, his fingers brushing the edge of the quilt in a restless, unconscious motion. She could almost see the internal battle playing out behind his guarded expression. He wanted to refuse, to insist he didn't need anyone's charity. But at the same time, there was a quiet understanding in his eyes—a reluctance to offend or appear ungrateful. The silence stretched for a moment before he finally nodded, a small, almost reluctant gesture of acceptance.

"Caleb," Debbie said softly, meeting his gaze. "You've already been through enough. There's no shame in letting us help."

Nathan crouched down and yanked open one of the lower drawers on the dresser. He pulled out a pair of old khakis and a thick, mustard-colored sweater. "Check this out!" he declared, holding the sweater aloft like a prize. "Vintage Grandpa style."

Danielle snorted, already rifling through another drawer. She turned toward Caleb with a wide grin, holding up a brightly patterned Hawaiian shirt that had clearly seen better days—likely a relic her dad had left behind during a summer visit. "You could totally pull off the 'Vacation Grandpa' look," she teased, her tone light and playful.

Caleb's lips twitched into a faint smile, and he let out a deep chuckle. "Yeah, that's exactly what I need right now," he said, "something to make me look even more like a tourist stuck somewhere I don't belong."

Debbie, leaning against the doorway, couldn't help but laugh, her arms crossed as she watched the exchange. The banter seemed to cut through some of Caleb's guardedness, bringing a rare flicker of ease to his otherwise tense demeanor.

"Don't worry," Debbie said, moving toward the bed. "You won't look like a complete tourist in my dad's clothes. And besides, comfort counts more than fashion when you're snowed-in."

Caleb shook his head and sighed, though there was a glimmer of gratitude in his eyes. "I appreciate the, uh... effort."

"So," Danielle began, her tone deliberately casual, "you live all the way up this mountain by yourself, right? I think I remember someone mentioning you before."

Caleb's gaze flicked briefly to Debbie, then dropped as he shifted uncomfortably under the quilt. His broad shoulders tensed, and he seemed to draw inward, as though the spotlight had been turned squarely on him. "That's right," he replied, his deep voice quieter now, almost hesitant. "It's, uh... peaceful up there."

Danielle raised an eyebrow, her curiosity undeterred. "Don't you ever get lonely?"

The question hung in the air, and Debbie's breath hitched, freezing in her chest. She hadn't expected Danielle to tread so directly into Caleb's personal life. The room, which had been filled with light-hearted teasing moments ago, seemed to shift, the weight of the question settling over them. Debbie glanced at Caleb, unsure how he'd respond, bracing herself.

Caleb rubbed a hand over his chin, his eyes distant, as though sifting through the weight of the question and deciding how much of himself he was willing to share. "Been living by myself for a long time now," he said at last, his voice quiet but steady. His words were deliberate, each one chosen with care. "After Bonnie... well, I didn't see much reason to be around people."

The air in the room shifted, the easy banter of moments ago replaced by a stillness that felt both soft and heavy, like snow settling after a storm. Caleb's gaze remained fixed ahead, unfocused, as if he was looking at something far beyond the cabin walls, something only he could see.

"After Bonnie." The words lingered, unspoken but clear: *After his wife.* Debbie's heart tightened as she watched him, his face a portrait of grief too long held alone. Whatever memories he was wrestling with in that moment, they seemed to pull him somewhere deeper than the room they sat in, deeper than even the storm raging outside.

Danielle nodded, her expression thoughtful, though softened by empathy. "I can't imagine living alone. I'd get lonely."

Caleb shrugged, his shoulders lifting in a motion that seemed more habitual than genuine. "You get used to it," he said, his voice low and steady. "And then, after a while... you don't miss being around people. You don't miss the noise."

The words hung there, unchallenged, but as he spoke, Caleb's gaze flickered toward Debbie. It was a quick, almost involuntary glance, but it carried the weight of uncertainty—like he wasn't sure if he believed what he'd just said. The quiet in the room seemed to stretch as Debbie caught the flicker of something unspoken in his expression.

It wasn't defiance or stubbornness this time. It was doubt. A hint of vulnerability breaking through the cracks.

Nathan shot Caleb a playful grin, rescuing the moment from slipping too far into the solemn. "Okay, but the real question—can you actually get internet up there, or are you a total back-to-the-land mountain man?"

The faintest smile tugged at Caleb's lips again. "I've got internet. Cell service too."

As Debbie turned back to the dresser, sorting through the clothes, her thoughts wandered. The situation was far from ordinary—being snowed in with a complete stranger—but Nathan and Danielle were handling it with a grace that both surprised and reassured her. Their easy banter with Caleb filled the room with a warmth.

No matter how unusual the circumstances, they were all adapting, falling into an unspoken rhythm that fit better than she would have expected. Perhaps this storm, strange and disruptive as it was, had brought something good with it. Maybe, just maybe, it wasn't as burdensome or uncomfortable as it had first seemed.

Caleb's voice broke into Debbie's thoughts, low and almost hesitant. "It's been a while since anyone fussed over me like this," he admitted, his gaze following Danielle and Nathan as they wandered toward the window, their attention captured by the snow piling higher outside.

Debbie paused, her hand resting on the edge of the drawer as she considered her response. "It's not a big deal," she said gently, her tone warm and sincere. "In a situation like this, I think most people would offer a hand however they could."

Her fingers closed around a pair of her dad's flannel pants and a soft, long-sleeved shirt. She pulled them from the dresser and turned back to Caleb, offering the clothes with a small, reassuring smile.

"Why don't you change into these?" she suggested, holding them out to him. "I'll wash your things in the meantime."

Caleb hesitated, his hand brushing lightly over the fabric before finally taking the clothes. A flicker of emotion passed across his face—gratitude, perhaps, or maybe the faint unease of someone unused to being cared for so openly. Either way, he gave a small nod. "Thanks," he said quietly, his voice low and gruff, but carrying a sincerity that didn't need embellishment.

"You really don't need to go through all that trouble, washing my clothes for me," Caleb added after a moment, his tone touched with discomfort, as though the idea of accepting yet more help unsettled him. His gaze dropped briefly before lifting again, uncertainty flashing in his eyes.

Debbie met his protest with a soft, easy smile, unfazed by his reluctance. "Caleb, it's no trouble at all," she said warmly. "I probably do laundry in my sleep at this point—comes with the territory of motherhood." She gave a light shrug, her voice turning playful. "Besides, I wouldn't want you stuck wearing the same dirt-streaked clothes when it's finally time for you to head home. Let me help—it's really not a big deal."

Her words carried a quiet reassurance, and Caleb didn't argue.

He looked down at the clean clothes in his hands, his fingers absently brushing over the worn but soft fabric. His hesitation lingered, a quiet tension that hung in the air. Debbie recognized it instantly—it was a familiar resistance, one she'd seen in countless patients before. That reluctance to lean on someone, as though accepting help, might somehow chip away at their strength or independence.

"You know," Debbie said gently, her tone softening, "letting someone help doesn't make you any less capable. Besides," she added with a light smile, "you're doing me a favor by letting me fuss. Keeps my mind occupied." She tossed him a playful look, hoping to lighten the weight she sensed pressing down on him.

Caleb shook his head, the barest hint of a smile tugging at the corners of his mouth. "Reckon I'm gonna have to get used to you fussing over me for a few days, aren't I?"

Debbie chuckled, crossing her arms as she leaned against the doorway. "Oh, you better believe it. But don't worry—I'll try not to overdo it. Much."

His smile lingered for a second longer before fading, but the air between them felt a little less heavy now, a small victory in the quiet warmth of the room.

Nathan and Danielle exchanged a quick glance, the kind of silent communication siblings mastered over the years. Though their eyes sparkled with the usual mischievous curiosity, there was something deeper in the look they shared—an unspoken understanding as they quietly observed the dynamic unfolding in front of them.

Their mom, usually so composed and focused, was talking with Caleb, a man who had been a stranger just hours ago. Yet there was a surprising ease in her tone, a warmth that softened the edges of their interaction. Nathan and Danielle exchanged a glance, their silent sibling connection speaking volumes.

Maybe it was the way Caleb's guarded exterior had started to show cracks, or perhaps it was the way their mother's voice carried a softer, almost instinctive kindness when she addressed him. Whatever it was, something in the room felt different—a subtle shift, a quiet vulnerability in their mom that neither twin was used to seeing.

Nathan flashed Danielle a knowing smirk, and she pressed her lips together, fighting the grin that threatened to break free. Neither said a word, but their shared look said it all: something was changing, and they were both curious to see where it would lead. This snowstorm was turning out to be a lot more interesting than they'd imagined.

"Guess there's no fighting the weather... or you," Caleb said, his tone carrying a trace of reluctant humor as he glanced at the swirling snow outside. He shifted his gaze back to Debbie, his expression softening slightly.

Debbie met his eyes with a knowing look. "You're a smart man," she said, her voice warm but firm. "I think you can manage walking to the bathroom down the hall, but take it easy. Nathan will follow behind you, just in case." She gestured toward the door, her tone shifting to gentle reassurance. "You're definitely going to feel sore and stiff, but I don't think there's anything too serious—just a few good bumps and bruises."

She paused, offering him a small, encouraging smile. "There are fresh towels in the tall cabinet in the bathroom, and shampoo and soap on the shelves by the sink. Take your time, get cleaned up, and then join us in the living room. No need to stay cooped up in here all day. A little change of scenery might do you some good."

Caleb's lips twitched, the barest hint of a smile tugging at the corner of his mouth. "Alright," he said gruffly, clearly resigned but not entirely displeased with the arrangement.

As Debbie turned to leave, Danielle trailing close behind, Caleb cleared his throat. "Debbie?"

She paused at the door, glancing back over her shoulder, her hand resting lightly on the frame. "Yeah?"

"Thanks..." he said, his voice rough around the edges, but the sincerity in it was unmistakable. It wasn't just about the clean clothes or the space to recover—it was deeper, a gratitude he didn't quite know how to put into words.

Debbie's smile softened, a warmth lighting her eyes. Her voice was steady but gentle as she replied, "Anytime, Caleb."

Chapter 10

Debbie glanced over at Danielle, who sat cross-legged on the couch beside her, hands wrapped around a steaming coffee mug. The warm amber light of the fire in the hearth cast flickering shadows across the room's rustic log walls, the crackle of the flames a soft, steady rhythm in the background. Outside, the wind murmured through the trees, occasionally gusting hard enough to push fresh drifts of snow across the porch and against the windows, the sound a faint reminder of the storm's persistence.

For a few moments, they sat quietly, wrapped in a silence that felt peaceful rather than awkward. Debbie let herself sink into the stillness, savoring the rare pause from the usual chaos of life. It wasn't often she found herself free of the endless whirl of work shifts, her kids' schedules, or the long list of things needing her attention. Here, in the snowbound cabin, the world outside felt far away. No errands to run, no work to tend to, no homework to help with.

Danielle took a sip from her mug, a faint smile tugging at the corners of her mouth. She looked at her mom, her eyes glimmering with quiet humor. "Feels weird to sit and have nothing to do, doesn't it?"

Debbie chuckled. "Weird, but nice. I'm enjoying this."

Danielle's eyes sparkled mischievously. "You do realize there's an actual mountain man in our house, right?"

Debbie chuckled, adjusting the edges of the fleece blanket draped over her legs. "Hey, he's a human like the rest of us. Plus, it's a bonus when he growls?"

Danielle laughed, her dimpled smile lighting her face. "I'm pretty sure he hasn't technically growled yet, but he's getting close. And seriously, Mom, you should totally set him up with an Instagram account. 'MoodyMountaineer90,' coming soon to the internet near you."

Debbie shot her a playful eye-roll, settling back into the cushions, her mind wandering briefly to Caleb's gruff demeanor, bruised chest, and quiet hesitations.

"You have to admit," Danielle said, her tone shifting suddenly from lighthearted to serious. She glanced at her mom, her fingers tracing the rim of her mug as she fidgeted with it. "He's kind of..." She paused, her brow furrowing as if she was searching for the right words. "Quiet. Different."

Her gaze dropped to her lap, and she hesitated before continuing. "I mean, it's sad, right? How he lives up there all by himself. I can't imagine being that lonely." Her voice softened, her usual playful spark replaced by a genuine thoughtfulness.

Debbie tilted her head slightly, watching her daughter carefully. Danielle had always been perceptive, noticing things most people overlooked. "It's hard to say what he's feeling," Debbie replied gently, her voice low, as though not to disturb the fragile weight of Danielle's reflection. "But it's definitely a different way of living. Not everyone chooses it, though sometimes life leaves you with little choice."

Danielle nodded slowly, her lips pressing together in thought. "I just... I hope he's okay, you know? Like, not just his injuries, but... everything else."

Danielle bit her lip, her brows drawing together in thought. "I've heard bits and pieces—just gossip, really. About how his wife, Bonnie, died." She shrugged, her voice trailing off. "He's a mystery. No one sees him around much anymore."

Debbie's gaze drifted to the flickering flames in the fireplace, the warm light playing across her face. "It's not hard to see how that kind of loss could change someone," she said quietly, her tone steady but tinged with something deeper.

Danielle nudged her with a gentle elbow. "I know that look."

"What look?"

"That look you get when you're worried about someone—but not in the just doing my job kind of way." Her daughter smirked, but her eyes were soft. "You're fussing over him more than you admit. Don't think I haven't noticed."

Debbie snorted, though her cheeks warmed at the quiet but accurate accusation. "I'm just being a good nurse, Dani. The man had a rough night."

"Oh, sure," Danielle said with a teasing wink, the playful glint in her eyes unmistakable. "But, hypothetically speaking, isn't this just the kind of cozy, homey movie scenario where a gruff lumberjack could discover love and rediscover the joys of small-town life?" She tilted her head dramatically, as if setting the perfect stage, her grin widening with every word.

Debbie shot her a sharp but playful look. "Danielle Marie Ferguson, you are officially banned from watching anymore rom-coms."

"I make no promises." Danielle raised her cup in mock salute before sipping. "But seriously, Mom. I mean, he is kinda cool in that mysterious mountain man sort of way. He's not as scary as I thought when he first fell into our house... literally. Kinda feels sad, though, having no one. Do you think..." she trailed off, eyes thoughtful. "Do you think he's alright? Not just with his bruises and cuts and stuff, but...you know. Emotionally?"

Debbie paused, contemplating her words. "Honestly? I think Caleb's dealing with a lot more than just his minor recent injuries. He's carrying a whole decade of hurt. It's obvious. You can see it in his eyes whenever he thinks no one's watching."

Danielle let the thought hang in the air for a moment before speaking again, her voice quieter this time. "Do you... feel sorry for him?"

Debbie's response was immediate, her tone firm but thoughtful. "No. I don't feel sorry for him. I think he's resilient. He's strong; anyone who's been through what he has would have to be. Besides, pity doesn't help people. What they need is space—space to heal, to breathe. Sometimes, people just need time to figure out how to fit into a world that doesn't make sense to them anymore."

Danielle gave a small nod, her gaze fixed on the flickering flames in the fireplace. She was quiet for a moment, chewing on her mother's words, before she spoke again. "Yeah," she murmured. "But... do you think he even wants to heal, Mom?"

The question struck a chord deep within Debbie, stirring thoughts she hadn't fully allowed herself to confront. Danielle's words lingered, pulling at something unspoken, but before Debbie could form an answer, the sound of footsteps broke the stillness, drawing both women's attention toward the hallway.

Nathan appeared with his usual easy grin, his green flannel shirt haphazardly half-tucked and half-untucked, a signature look for a teenage boy who cared little for such details.

"All clear," he announced with an exaggerated flourish, striking a mock-heroic pose. "Caleb is safely in the bathroom without any major disasters. I'm officially considering a career in physical therapy now. Or maybe personal training. Strength training with grumpy mountain men—any takers?"

Danielle burst out laughing, leaning back into the couch cushions and crossing her arms. "Bet you got an earful the whole way."

"He grumbled the entire time," Nathan confirmed, his smirk growing wider. "He's about as talkative as a brick wall when he doesn't want help. But credit where it's due—he toughed it out."

Debbie nodded toward the recliner beside her. "Come sit. I want to chat with you two before Caleb gets out of the shower."

Nathan arched an eyebrow but didn't argue, dropping into the recliner with his usual relaxed sprawl. "What's up?" he asked, his tone casual, though his curiosity was clear.

Debbie glanced between her two kids, her gaze softening as she took them in. For a moment, she didn't speak, her heart tugging at the sight of them. She'd raised them to be good, kind-hearted people, and now, on the cusp of adulthood, they were proving themselves more than capable of handling life's unexpected twists. She was proud of the way they'd adapted to having Caleb in their home, their empathy shining through in how they treated him, even when it might have been easier to keep their distance.

But being a parent wasn't just about celebrating the things they got right—it also meant checking in, digging a little deeper into the thoughts and feelings they wouldn't always share on their own. Especially now, with a stranger under their roof and the storm amplifying everything, Debbie knew it was important to make space for those quieter conversations.

"I know he seems... well, a bit rough around the edges," Debbie began, her words measured and careful. "But I think Caleb's been through a lot more than we can even imagine."

Nathan, ever the pragmatist, gave a casual shrug. "Yeah, but lots of people go through hard stuff, right? I mean, we don't have to treat him like he's about to break or anything."

Debbie nodded, a small appreciative smile curving her lips. "True. And I'm not saying we should tiptoe around him. But people handle pain in different ways. Sometimes, it's not about breaking—it's about retreating because the world feels like too much." She paused, her thumb brushing lightly over the rim of her coffee cup. "I just think we should be patient. Let him open up in his own time. Don't push or ask too many questions if he's not offering answers. Let him steer the conversation, okay?"

Danielle, leaning her head back against the sofa, considered this, her expression thoughtful. "That makes sense," she said finally. "I get the feeling the last thing he wants is people poking around in his business."

Debbie's eyes lingered on her daughter for a moment before shifting back to Nathan. "Exactly," she said gently. "It's not about treating him differently, just giving him room to breathe. Sometimes just being there is enough. But that doesn't mean he doesn't need people. Whether he admits it or not, Caleb's been alone for a long time—longer than most of us could bear."

Nathan shifted in his seat, his brows knitting together in thought. "Do any of the other nurses you work with, or your patients, ever talk about him?"

Debbie raised a curious brow. "Why do you ask?"

He shrugged, looking a little sheepish. "Just wondering. I mean, I've heard a couple of things here and there. Nothing bad, though. Everyone seems to respect him. They just say he likes his space, and it's better not to cross the lines he draws. I've also heard he's a good supervisor at his dad's lumber mill."

Debbie's lips curved into a soft smile. "Well, it's important to respect people's boundaries—in work and in life. But I also think sometimes people need someone to reach out, even just to remind them they're not alone. It doesn't have to be intrusive, just... kind."

Nathan nodded slowly, absorbing her words. "Yeah. I guess even someone who wants space might need to know that people care."

"Exactly," Debbie said, her smile deepening. "It's a delicate balance, but it can mean the world to someone."

Nathan nodded, his usual teenage bravado giving way to a rare moment of sincerity. "Noted. We'll behave. But I can't promise I won't slip in some sarcasm now and then. Sacrifice too much, and what's left of me?"

Debbie chuckled, reaching over to ruffle his hair affectionately. "Fair enough. Sarcasm's one of the finer points of communication. I'll give you that. Just maybe don't overdo it with Caleb—ease him in slowly."

Nathan grinned, swatting her hand away. "No promises, but I'll try not to scare him off."

Danielle snorted from the couch. "Yeah, Nathan's sarcasm is totally subtle. You're practically a diplomat."

Debbie shook her head, laughing softly as the warm banter filled the room.

Just as the conversation was winding down, Caleb appeared in the hallway, his presence immediately shifting the room's energy. He looked slightly awkward, as if unsure how to navigate the warmth and easy banter of a family dynamic he wasn't accustomed to. The flannel pants and shirt fit well enough—though they were a bit short in the legs and sleeves—but they served their purpose. In his hands, he carried a bundle of crumpled work clothes, his grip on them almost hesitant.

"Where should I put these?" he asked, his voice low and uncertain. His gaze flickered toward Debbie, as though seeking direction, his discomfort palpable.

Debbie stood, stepping toward Caleb and gesturing for him to hand over the bundle. "There's a basket in the laundry room," she said gently, her tone leaving little room for protest. She took the crumpled clothes from his hands before he could argue. "I'll toss them in the wash. No sense letting them sit all dirty."

Caleb shifted his weight, clearly uneasy with the ongoing kindness being extended his way. His hands moved to his sides, then back to his pockets, as if unsure what to do. After a moment's hesitation, he muttered, "Thank you," his voice quiet but genuine.

"You're welcome," Debbie replied with a soft smile, her eyes meeting his briefly. The warmth in her voice was unmistakable as she added, "Just settle in. You're not really a guest anymore—you're practically family after the number of pancakes you put away this morning."

Nathan grinned from the recliner, his amusement clear, while Danielle, never one to pass up a chance to tease, chimed in. "Yep, you've officially survived the Ferguson crash course in hospitality. It's all downhill from here."

To everyone's surprise, Caleb let out a low chuckle, his lips curving into a faint smile. "Not sure that's good news."

"No one is," Nathan shot back with a playful wink. "But hey, at least now you're prepped for the full Grandpa Wardrobe Experience. Perfect timing, since it looks like we're stuck here for a while."

Caleb glanced down at the flannel pants and oversized shirt he was wearing, a faint smirk tugging at his lips. "Figured I should blend in with the environment. Stealth mode."

Danielle burst into laughter, her head tipping back as she clutched her mug. Nathan, ever quick with a quip, threw a playful arm over the back of his chair. "Careful—next thing you know, we'll be offering you a part-time gig on the driveway shoveling team."

Caleb's wry reply came without missing a beat, sparking another round of chuckles. "Pretty sure I'm already signed up for that one, remember?"

The room filled with easy laughter, the kind that felt natural and unforced. It was small, but the shift in Caleb was undeniable. The tension in his shoulders had loosened, and the guarded edge in his expression seemed to soften, just enough to let the surrounding warmth in.

Danielle gestured to the open seat at the far end of the couch. Caleb hesitated for a moment before lowering himself into the cushions. His fingers fidgeted absently against his knees, betraying the internal debate he seemed to be having about whether sitting there was the right choice.

Debbie returned moments later, stepping quietly into the room after putting Caleb's clothes in the wash. She paused, her gaze softening as she watched him settle onto the couch.

Crossing the room, Debbie offered him a fresh cup of coffee, her voice calm and reassuring. "Here you go," she said with a warm smile. He accepted the cup with a nod of thanks, the heat from the mug working its way through the lingering coolness in his hands.

"There's plenty more where that came from," she said as she reclaimed her own spot on the couch.

Just as Debbie sank into the cozy warmth of the couch, the familiar chime of her phone broke the quiet moment. She didn't need to check the screen to know who it was—that particular ringtone meant only one thing: her parents were calling.

Chapter 11

Debbie glanced at the photo flashing on her phone screen, a familiar image of her parents standing on their front porch. Her dad had one arm slung around her mom, his favorite red flannel with the patched elbow standing out against the soft backdrop of their yard. Her mom's silver-streaked hair shimmered in the sunlight, making her look effortlessly elegant, like she belonged in an old black-and-white movie. They were both smiling broadly, a picture of contentment, as though the world beyond their porch didn't have a single problem worth worrying about.

A smile tugged at the corners of Debbie's mouth. Their predictability—the way they always seemed to know when to check in—was a steady comfort, especially on days like this. Even through the phone, their presence felt like a warm hug, a grounding reminder of everything stable in her life. With a soft sigh, she swiped to answer, already anticipating her mom's concerned tone and her dad's calm reassurance.

"Hey, Mom. We're snowed in, but we're doing fine." Debbie said.

Her mother's lively voice crackled through the phone. "Well, that's good to hear, sweetie. We just saw the weather report down here, and your dad nearly had a heart attack, seeing how much snow you're getting up there. Honestly, Debbie, I know you love it there, but part of me wishes you'd move down here by us."

Debbie chuckled, her gaze drifting to the snow piling up on the windowsill. "Yeah, well, these mountains are home. I'll never leave," she said warmly, her voice carrying the kind of certainty only rooted in a deep love for a place.

On the other end of the line, she could hear the faint hum of background noise—probably the TV in her parents' living room, playing a news report or an old sitcom. "Well," her mom replied, her tone light but knowing, "good thing you're always prepared for this kind of weather. Nathan and Danielle staying out of trouble?"

Debbie smiled, a soft laugh escaping her. "Yes, you know how they are—always keeping themselves busy with something. Never a dull moment with those two."

Her dad's familiar, warm voice cut in. "Now, don't go making things too easy for them. Gotta let them feel like they're putting in some work."

Debbie chuckled softly, shaking her head. "Oh, don't worry. They'll have plenty to do once we can get outside and start shoveling our way out."

"Well," her dad said with a hint of nostalgia, "a bit of snow's nothing new in the mountains. You and your brother and sister were always out there building snow forts whenever we had a big storm."

"I remember those days," her mom chimed in, her voice bright with warmth. "Being snowed in as a family... we always had such a good time."

Debbie smiled, the memories of those childhood storms flashing through her mind. Long days spent outside in the snow, cheeks flushed with cold, followed by cozy nights by the fire. Those moments had shaped her love for the mountains, for the sense of home that snowstorms always seemed to bring.

"Well," Debbie began, keeping her tone casual as she tried to find the balance between truth and not over sharing. "There's actually someone here with us. A visitor... of sorts."

There was a brief pause on the other end before her mom's voice chimed in, curiosity unmistakable. "Oh? Someone from town?"

Debbie sighed, the awkwardness settling over her like an ill-fitting sweater. "Not... really from town, exactly. It's Caleb Warren."

"Oh!" her mother exclaimed, the recognition in her tone immediate. "The Caleb Warren? From the mill? The one who lives further up the road?"

Before Debbie could reply, her dad cut in, the amusement in his voice unmistakable, even over the crackle of the line. "That rugged lumberjack from the Warren family? Can't imagine he's just out there trimming trees in this kind of snow."

Debbie let out a soft laugh, shaking her head. "Not exactly. He had an accident going home last night. Slid off and crashed his truck down the embankment into the yard. He's fine—just banged up a little. We brought him inside to wait out the storm."

There was another pause, her parents' processing silence almost palpable through the phone, before her mom spoke again, a mix of concern and intrigue in her tone. "Well, I hope you're making him comfortable. Poor man. I've always thought he seemed a little... distant, but kind."

Her dad chuckled. "Guess he's snowed in whether he likes it or not, huh? Sounds like he landed in good hands."

"Is he alright?" her mom asked, concern edging her voice.

"Nothing too serious," Debbie replied quickly, her tone calm and reassuring. "A few bumps and bruises, but nothing major. He's staying in the guest bedroom."

There was a brief pause, and Debbie could almost feel her mom processing the unexpected situation. Then her mother's voice came through again, light but tinged with that knowing tone Debbie recognized all too well. "Well, isn't that something? God does have interesting ways of putting people together, doesn't He?" Debbie could practically hear the smile in her mom's words. "He's okay, though? You're taking good care of him?"

"Yes, yes," Debbie said with a slightly awkward laugh. "We're doing our best."

"Well, good," her dad chimed in, his voice more reflective now. "You know, sweetheart, God doesn't leave anyone out in the cold—not even those who've stumbled through life, caused trouble, or fought their own battles. Sometimes He guides them right where they need to be—even if it takes a storm to get them there."

Debbie smiled softly, her heart warmed by her dad's steady faith and reassuring words. His ability to find God's hand in every situation never failed to bring her a sense of calm, even when life felt uncertain.

Before she could respond, her mom's voice broke in again, lighter now, carrying that playful, teasing tone Debbie had inherited from her. "Well, sounds like Mr. Mountain Man has landed himself in the best hands. Just don't let him stay underfoot too long, or you'll have more than a house guest to deal with."

Debbie laughed, though she could feel the warmth creeping into her cheeks. "Mom."

"I'm just saying!" her mom replied in that sing-song tone. Debbie knew all too well.

"Mom!" Debbie protested, her voice firm but betrayed by the laugh bubbling up despite her best efforts to sound serious.

Her mother chuckled softly before her tone shifted to one of affection. "Alright, honey. You all stay safe, and give those grand babies a big squeeze for us. We'll check in again soon!"

"Yep, love you guys," Debbie said quickly, ending the call with a practiced swipe.

"What was all that about?" Danielle asked, her brows arched in playful suspicion, a knowing smile tugging at her lips.

Debbie shot her a sideways glance, her own lips curving slightly. "Oh, you know, your grandparents," she said with a light shrug. "Always checking in. Always making sure everything's okay."

She shook her head slightly, brushing away the flood of thoughts that threatened to linger, and set her phone down on the table. As she did, she glanced over at Caleb. His eyes were steady, his expression unreadable but filled with a kind of subdued curiosity. Debbie held his gaze for a beat longer than she intended before turning her attention back to the room, the moment passing like a gentle ripple in still water.

"Everything alright?" Caleb asked, his voice low and steady, cutting through the lingering quiet.

"Yeah, just a check-in from the parents," Debbie replied casually, her tone light but natural.

"So, who's up for a game?" Danielle asked, her eyes lighting up with mischief. "Pictionary, anyone?"

"Pictionary?" Caleb asked, his brow lifting skeptically. "That doesn't involve trivia about pop culture, does it? 'Cause if it does, you're on your own."

Danielle burst out laughing, shaking her head. "No pop culture, I promise. Although," she added, narrowing her eyes in exaggerated seriousness, "we might have to endure some of Nathan's killer jokes, so… proceed at your own risk."

Nathan scoffed, leaning back in his chair with a dramatic flourish. "I'll have you know my jokes are a gift to this household. You're welcome for the free entertainment."

Debbie rolled her eyes, the affection clear in her expression. "It's just Pictionary—nothing too dangerous," she said, her voice warm and inviting. "You up for it, Caleb?"

Caleb hesitated, glancing around the room at the eager faces. For a moment, it seemed like he might decline, but then a faint smirk tugged at the corner of his mouth. "Sure," he said, his tone gruff but agreeable. "Why not? Just don't expect me to draw anything fancy."

Danielle clapped her hands together in mock seriousness. "Oh, don't worry, Caleb. Stick figures are a perfectly acceptable medium in this household."

The kids teased Caleb gently, suggesting simple drawings to start with—"log cabins" and "mountains" thrown out with exaggerated seriousness. Caleb's gruff responses slowly wove into the rhythm of the game, as he became more involved in the lively back-and-forth.

"She's doing it again!" Nathan suddenly exclaimed, pointing an accusatory finger at his sister. His tone was equal parts outrage and delight. "She's drawing a stick figure!"

Danielle let out a dramatic yelp, clutching her paper to her chest as though hiding state secrets. "It's abstract!" she protested, her wide eyes feigning innocence.

"Abstract, my foot!" Nathan shot back, crossing his arms and narrowing his eyes in mock indignation. "That's the same stick figure you've been drawing since third grade!"

Even Caleb laughed, a deep, rumbling sound so unexpected from him that Debbie's heart stilled for a moment. It was rare, and it transformed his face, softening the sharp lines into something almost unrecognizable. The smile that followed—small but genuine—spread across his features, surprising her even more.

Later in the game, as Debbie reached for a pen at the same moment Caleb did, their fingers brushed briefly. The contact was fleeting, yet it carried a spark—subtle but undeniable—that sent a jolt through Debbie's chest. Her eyes widened slightly, the moment catching her off guard.

Caleb, for his part, paused for the briefest fraction of a second. His expression didn't betray much, but the slight pull of his hand, slow and deliberate, hinted at something unspoken. The moment passed quickly, like the flicker of a flame, leaving them both a little quieter than before. Debbie turned her focus back to the game, but the touch lingered faintly in her thoughts, hovering just out of reach.

Chapter 12

After another half-hour of drawing, guessing, and lighthearted banter, the energy in the living room began to settle into something quieter, more mellow. The game had wound down, leaving a cozy sense of calm in its wake. Nathan sprawled lazily across the floor, twirling a pen between his fingers, while Danielle curled up on the armchair, a satisfied smile tugging at her lips. Caleb, now more at ease, sank back into the couch with a low, comfortable sigh.

In the stillness of that moment, Caleb's brow suddenly furrowed, as though a thought had abruptly surfaced. He leaned forward slightly, his elbows resting on his knees, and asked, "Where's my coat?"

Debbie glanced toward the coat closet, her tone casual. "It's hanging up in the closet."

"I think my phone's in there..." Caleb said, already pushing himself up from the couch. His movement was slow and stiff, a sharp wince flashing across his face as his bruised body reminded him of its limits.

"I'll get it!" Danielle called, springing to her feet before Caleb could even think to protest.

Debbie raised an eyebrow in Caleb's direction as he rubbed the back of his neck, the roughness of his calloused hand a testament to years of hard work. "I forgot you mentioned your phone earlier," she said.

"I should probably let my brothers or dad know I'm safe," Caleb muttered, a wry smile tugging at the corner of his mouth.

Moments later, Danielle strolled back into the room, holding his coat with a flourish. "Here you go, Mr. Mountain Man," she teased, a playful grin lighting her face.

Caleb accepted the coat with a faint smile, his hands moving automatically as he patted the pockets with practiced efficiency. But as his fingers brushed over the empty fabric, his expression shifted. His brow furrowed, and the warmth in his features faded, replaced by a darker, more serious look.

"It's not here," Caleb muttered, his voice tinged with unmistakable frustration. "Must've fallen out in the truck when I wrecked."

He trailed off, his frown deepening as the reality sank in. His phone, likely buried somewhere in the wreckage of his truck, now sat under a thick pile of snow outside. The ease he'd started to settle into seemed to vanish, tension creeping back into his shoulders as though losing the phone had yanked him out of the warm cocoon of their evening and dropped him right back into the chaos of the storm.

Debbie caught the shift immediately, her eyes flicking to Nathan, who didn't need her to say a word. He straightened from his lazy sprawl on the floor, nodding subtly, his expression sharpening into readiness.

Caleb gave Nathan a small nod of thanks, his expression tight, before he disappeared into the swirling snow outside, the sound of his boots crunching softly on the icy ground. For a moment, Caleb stood motionless, his eyes fixed on the door. There was a tension in his posture, as though he wasn't entirely comfortable letting someone else take charge on his behalf. It was a dynamic that felt foreign to him—unusual for a man who had spent over a decade relying on no one but himself.

From her spot on the couch, Debbie watched him silently, her gaze tracing the weariness etched into his face. He looked like a man who had spent years building walls high enough to keep the world at bay, his isolation carved into every line and shadow of his features. And yet, here he was—standing in her living room, drawn into proximity and forced to accept the help he hadn't asked for.

Debbie sank back into the cushions, her gaze steady but warm as she studied Caleb. A crooked smile tugged at the corner of her mouth, breaking the lingering silence with a natural ease. "So," she said casually, tilting her head slightly toward him, "tell me about that truck of yours. She looks like she's been through a storm or two—figuratively and literally."

Caleb glanced at her, momentarily startled by the shift in tone, but something about her easy grin softened his usual instinct to retreat. He rubbed the back of his neck, a habit Debbie had already come to recognize, and for a brief moment, the faintest hint of a smile played at the corners of his mouth.

"She's old," he admitted gruffly, as he sat back down on the couch. "A '70 Ford. Runs better than she looks... most of the time, anyway."

Debbie raised her eyebrows, amused at the way his tone shifted when talking about the truck—gruff but tinged with pride, almost like he was describing an old friend. "I bet she's got a story or two."

"Plenty," Caleb replied, his lips quirking ever so slightly. "Most of them involve me under the hood, cursing at some part that decided to quit."

Debbie chuckled. "Sounds like you know your way around an engine."

He shrugged. "Enough to keep her running," he said. Then, with a wry grin, he added, "She wouldn't win any beauty contests, but she was always dependable. That's all that matters."

Debbie smiled at his pragmatic answer. "Dependable is a pretty attractive quality these days. Seems like she's served you well."

Caleb nodded. "She has. Gotten me through a lot of winters, a lot of miles." His gaze dipped to the floor.

Debbie leaned forward, resting her elbows on her knees. Her tone, though still light, was threaded with genuine interest. "Do you work on her yourself, or does someone from town give you a hand?"

His response was immediate, almost reflexive. "I handle it myself." Then, catching her expression, he smirked faintly and added, "Easier that way."

Debbie regarded him thoughtfully, turning his words over in her mind. "Easier, huh," she said after a moment. "Or just what you're used to?"

Caleb didn't answer right away. His head tilted, and his brow furrowed ever so slightly in thought. Finally, he met her gaze, his dark eyes locking with hers for a brief yet searching moment.

"Both," he admitted. "When you're used to fixing things on your own, asking for help feels... like admitting defeat."

"Maybe," she said gently, her tone inviting but not pushing. "Or maybe it's just a self-induced habit."

Something unspoken flickered in his dark eyes—an unsteady dance between vulnerability and resistance. He didn't argue, but he didn't agree either. Instead, a chuckle escaped his lips as he shifted on the couch, his posture echoing the unease of a man caught in the delicate push and pull of surrender and self-preservation.

"You know," she said, "my dad always said working with his hands kept him grounded. Gave him something tangible to focus on when everything else felt overwhelming."

A long pause followed, and for a second, Debbie wondered if she'd said too much. Caleb's jaw tightened, but then he gave a slow nod.

"There's truth in that." His voice was quieter now, more thoughtful. "Fixing things... it forces you to stop thinking about... things, at least for a little while. Can't get lost in your own head when there's work to be done."

Debbie smiled gently. "I get that. Guess we all find our own ways to deal with the noise in our heads."

"Yeah," he murmured, almost to himself. "I reckon we do."

The rhythmic sound of boots on snow announced Nathan's return. He swung open the door with one gloved hand and bounded through the doorway, shaking loose a dusting of snowflakes from his coat.

"Found it!" Nathan proclaimed, holding up the cell phone triumphantly. "No surprise, it slid under the seat."

Relief flickered across Caleb's face, like a man finally granted back a small token of stability. He took the phone from Nathan's open hand, checking quickly over it for damage.

"Thanks for going and getting it Nathan," Caleb said

Nathan kicked off his boots and walked into the living room.

"You're welcome," Nathan said as he held up a small, tattered book. The leather cover was worn and faded, its edges fraying with time and use.

"Found it on the floor on the passenger side," he explained, extending the book toward Caleb. "Looks like it's been through a lot."

Caleb's expression froze. The Bible. His hands twitched as if to reach toward it, then stilled.

He didn't move.

"Caleb, are you okay?" Debbie asked.

Caleb didn't answer right away. His jaw worked silently, as if he were chewing on words that didn't quite want to come out.

"I'm fine," Caleb said, but his voice was hoarse, unconvincing.

Nathan shifted awkwardly.

Debbie cleared her throat. "Why don't I take it?" she offered, her voice soft but steady. She reached out her hand to Nathan, giving him a reassuring nod. Nathan handed her the Bible with a glance toward Caleb.

"Thanks," Caleb muttered, though he still avoided both their eyes.

Debbie cradled the worn book in her hands for a moment. The leather was cracked and faded, as if years of life and hardship had etched themselves into its skin. She glanced at Caleb, his large hands clasped firmly in his lap as if to anchor himself.

"Looks like it's been with you a while," Debbie said.

"Yeah," Caleb said, his voice distant. "Belonged to my wife."

The room fell quiet again. Danielle moved to busy herself in the kitchen, the clatter of mugs and spoons a polite barrier against the heavy silence. Nathan, too, shifted uncomfortably before murmuring an excuse to step outside and check on the snow.

Debbie stayed, her presence steady but unobtrusive, holding the Bible in her lap. She wasn't about to pry. But she could feel it, this storm that Caleb carried inside him, as wild and unrelenting as the one that had trapped them all together.

"I keep it in the truck... it's always on the dashboard to remind me," Caleb said.

His voice was low, as though the words cost him something heavy to speak aloud. Debbie remained quiet, her eyes attentive but soft, not probing—just listening. Caleb ran a hand through his hair.

"To remind you of what?" she asked gently, her tone careful, like one would use when coaxing a frightened animal to trust.

Caleb exhaled, the sound weary but resigned. His gaze moved to the fire, its flickers casting shadows across his face. "Of her," he answered simply. Then, after a pause, he added, "And of what I couldn't fix."

Debbie's heart ached at the raw honesty in his voice, and she instinctively clutched the Bible a little tighter.

"It was Bonnie's." His thumb rubbed absently across his palm, as though tracing the grooves of time. "She kept it on the side table by her chair in our living room. Always reading it, always jotting notes in the margins. She... she tried to get me into it, tried harder than I deserved. But back then..." He shook his head.

"Back then, I had other priorities," he continued after a moment, his voice brittle. "I was too busy running the mill, or fixing things around the house, or... drinking." The last word came out a little sharper, like it had been caught in his throat. "And then one morning, she—" He stopped abruptly, his eyes narrowing as he stared into the fire. "I woke up, and she was gone."

Debbie stayed silent, the stillness between them thick yet not uncomfortable, as though the room itself was holding space for Caleb to find his footing.

"I keep that Bible in the truck as a reminder," Caleb admitted, his voice barely louder than a whisper. "Figured... maybe if it was close by, it'd remind me every day to never pick up another bottle of booze."

Debbie turned the Bible over in her hands, running her fingers along the faded edges, tracing the grooves worn into the leather.

"It takes strength to walk away from something like that and stay away. It's not easy," Debbie said.

Caleb's brow furrowed, his gaze still fixed on the dancing flames in the hearth. "It's not strength," he said after a beat. "It's—" He sighed, his broad shoulders sagging. "It's fear. Fear of becoming the man I used to be again."

Debbie wanted to reach out, place a hand on his arm, offer a gesture of comfort—but something told her that this moment, this confession, wasn't meant to be interrupted. Instead, she placed the Bible gently on the coffee table between them, the movement slow and deliberate, as though setting down something sacred.

"If it were just fear," she said, her gaze meeting his, "you wouldn't still have this Bible. You wouldn't carry it with you, keep it close. Fear might have pushed you to stop drinking, but what keeps you going? What keeps you moving forward?"

Caleb's jaw tightened, and for a moment Debbie thought he might not answer. Then he leaned forward, resting his elbows on his knees, his hands clasped tightly together.

"Guilt," he admitted.

Debbie watched him quietly, her heart aching at the rawness in his voice. "Guilt from drinking?"

"That and..." Caleb began, drawing in a deep, unsteady breath, as if steeling himself to continue. "Bonnie died alone," he said, his voice cracking under the weight of the admission. "That morning, she'd made breakfast—like she always did. She had fixed a plate for me and had it waiting on the table." He paused, his brow furrowing as his gaze fixed blankly on the fire. "I imagine she was probably on her way to wake me and tell me it was ready. But that never happened."

He swallowed hard, his Adam's apple moving visibly as his jaw tightened. "I was upstairs, passed out, too hungover to even lift my head off the pillow. The night before, I'd been out drinking again—like a fool. And because of that—because of me—I wasn't where I should've been. I wasn't sitting at that kitchen table, eating the breakfast she made for me... and I wasn't there when she needed me most."

His knuckles whitened as his hands clenched into fists before releasing again. The repetition was like a futile attempt to wrestle back control over something no longer within his grasp. "She collapsed... just a few feet away from that table," he continued, his voice trembling now, thick with anguish. "Right there on the kitchen floor. And I didn't hear her. I didn't come for her. I didn't... save her." His shoulders sagged as the words fell out, each one heavier than the last.

"If I hadn't been drinking..." Caleb's voice splintered, barely above a whisper now. His head dipped, eyes closed, as though the weight of his own regret pressed too heavily. "If I'd just gotten my act together, if I'd... been the man she deserved, I would've been downstairs. I could've... done something. Anything. But instead..." He trailed off, unable—or unwilling—to finish, his regret filling the silence like a raw, unhealed wound.

For a moment, the crackling of the fire was the only sound in the room, but it did nothing to drown out the echoes of Caleb's pain.

"Caleb, that's a heavy burden to carry all these years," Debbie said gently, her voice soft but steady. "What happened to Bonnie..."

"Brain aneurysm," he said sharply.

"A brain aneurysm," she repeated, her voice wrapped in compassion. "Caleb, that's... that's something you couldn't have stopped. Even if you'd been sitting right there next to her, there's no guarantee—"

"I should've been there," Caleb interrupted, his voice sharp and laced with bitterness. He shook his head, clenching his fists on his knees. "I wasn't. That's what it comes down to. She was alone because I wasn't the man I promised her I'd be. I wasn't the husband she needed. I... failed her."

Debbie hesitated for only a moment, choosing her words carefully, her tone firm yet tender. "You didn't fail her, Caleb," she said, her voice steady but warm. "You loved her. That much is clear, even now. You're human—you made mistakes—but you loved her. And whether you know it or not, I believe she knew that. She knew you loved her."

Caleb gave a bitter laugh, shaking his head. "Love didn't save her, though, did it?"

"You're right," Debbie said quietly, her words deliberate. "Love doesn't always keep bad things from happening. And guilt? It won't fix the pain. But Caleb, punishing yourself, locking yourself away from the world, it won't bring her back. It won't erase what happened."

He fell silent at that. His hands unclenched, though they still hung heavily on his knees, as if held down by invisible chains.

"You've been carrying this guilt for so long, as if it's the price you have to pay for something you couldn't control." She paused, her gaze gentle but unwavering. "But guilt isn't your burden to bear—not like this. It doesn't honor Bonnie. It doesn't honor her memory or the life you shared together. If anything, I think it would break her heart to see you like this."

Caleb's expression shifted—a flicker of something raw and un-guarded, like a crack in the armor he'd built around himself. He rubbed a hand over his face, his rough palm dragging across his beard as he exhaled heavily.

"I believe she's in heaven right now, and she's already forgiven you," Debbie said softly after a pause, her voice barely above a whisper. "The real question is... can you forgive yourself?"

Caleb's eyes lifted to hers, dark and searching, as if her words were something foreign, something he wasn't sure how to grasp. He didn't speak or move, his stillness heavy with the weight of emotion. His gaze held hers, a mixture of disbelief and uncertainty flickering across his features, like he was wrestling with a truth he wasn't ready to face.

"You've got to let it go, Caleb," Debbie said, her voice tender yet resolute. "Not for her—she's already at peace—but for you. You have to let God take that pain and regret you're clinging to and replace it with grace. That's the beauty of grace—it's not something we earn; it's a gift. And whether you believe it or not, Caleb, you deserve it."

He shook his head slightly, his jaw tightening as though he wanted to argue, but no words came. Instead, he leaned back into the cushions of the couch, his hand lifting to cover his mouth as his gaze drifted upward to the wooden beams of the cabin ceiling. His chest rose and fell in uneven breaths, the weight of her words settling over him like a tangible force, heavy and unrelenting.

Debbie knew she couldn't make him believe—not with a single conversation or even the most heartfelt plea. Faith wasn't something she could hand him; it had to come from within. But she also understood that, in the quiet of his own heart, Caleb would have to face the truth for himself. All she could do was plant the seed and hope it would take root in time.

Finally, he broke the tension, his voice thick and gravelly as he spoke. "You make it sound so... simple," he murmured, his gaze still fixed upward.

"It's not simple," Debbie said softly, leaning in slightly, her lips curving into a bittersweet smile. With quiet resolve, she shifted closer to him on the couch, her presence steady and unhurried. Gently, she reached out and placed her hands atop his, stilling the faint tremor in his fingers where they rested on his knee. Her touch was light but anchoring, a silent reminder that he didn't have to carry the weight alone.

"It's hard. It's messy. Sometimes it feels impossible," she continued, her voice steady and filled with quiet conviction. "But that's where faith comes in, Caleb. You don't have to figure it all out before you take the first step."

Her words hung in the air between them, a bridge she hoped he might dare to cross.

He didn't respond right away, but there was a subtle shift in his expression—small, almost imperceptible, yet unmistakable. The hard edges of his guarded demeanor seemed to soften, and the heavy weight of his self-reproach seemed to ease, if only slightly. It wasn't full acceptance—he wasn't there yet—but something flickered in his eyes. It was fragile, like a tiny ember just beginning to glow, but it held the quiet strength of hope.

His gaze dropped to her hands resting gently on his, the warmth of her touch grounding him in a way he hadn't expected. For a moment, the silence stretched between them, saying more than either of them could in words. Then, his voice broke through the stillness, low and steady, carrying a weight that gave it more meaning than mere gratitude.

"You're a good woman, Debbie," he said simply, the words carrying a depth that went beyond simple gratitude.

Debbie slowly drew her hand back from his, her gaze drifting to the weathered Bible resting on the table in front of them. Her fingers lightly traced the cracked leather cover, the years of wear speaking to its long journey. When she spoke, her voice was soft, steady, but filled with unmistakable conviction.

"You know," she began, her eyes lifting briefly to meet his, "this isn't just a piece of your past or something to carry the weight of your guilt. It's more than that. It's a path forward, a reminder that grace isn't something you've lost. It's still here—within reach. Not just for the man you were back then, Caleb, but for the man sitting here right now."

Her words lingered in the quiet, her touch on the Bible a silent testament to the power it held—not in the book itself, but in the hope and redemption it promised.

Chapter 13

Debbie gave Caleb's knee a gentle pat, her touch warm and steady, before rising to her feet with her usual quiet confidence. "I'm going to start dinner," she said with a soft smile. "You can stay here if you need more time to think—or you can join me in the kitchen and help chop vegetables. The choice is yours."

The corners of Caleb's mouth twitched into a faint smile. "Vegetables, huh?" he said, leaning back slightly. "You sure you trust me with a knife?"

Debbie chuckled as she headed toward the kitchen, her tone light and playful. "You work with saws and axes, don't you? I'd think a carrot would be no problem for you. But no pressure—help if you want to, or just sit and relax."

Her footsteps echoed in the quiet cabin, the sound blending with the soft crackle of the fire. Caleb sat where he was for a moment, his gaze drifting to the Bible still resting on the table. The worn leather reminded him of all the times he'd purposely ignored it, kept it close but unopened—as if proximity alone might absolve him of his guilt. He rubbed a hand over his face, then let out a low sigh.

Before he could let his thoughts spiral further, he pushed himself to his feet with a quiet groan. His bruised ribs protested, a sharp twinge reminding him of the crash, but he decided moving was easier than sitting alone with the weight of his mind pressing down on him.

Stepping into the kitchen, he paused for a moment, his eyes lingering on Debbie as she moved with practiced ease. Her hands worked deftly, her movements unhurried and purposeful, as though she'd repeated this routine countless times before. The soft hum of an old hymn floated from her lips, quiet and absentminded, yet undeniably comforting. It filled the warm space like a gentle melody, adding to the homey atmosphere.

The aroma of simmering broth drifted through the air, rich and inviting.

Danielle, perched casually on the counter with her phone in hand, glanced up when she caught sight of Caleb stepping into the kitchen. Her face lit up with an easy smile, the kind of warm, effortless friendliness that seemed to come naturally to her.

"Hey," she greeted lightly, her tone as casual as if they'd known each other forever.

Danielle swung her legs off the counter, landing lightly on the floor with practiced ease. "Mom's got it all under control," she teased, throwing a knowing glance toward the pot bubbling gently on the stove. A playful grin spread across her face as she turned her attention back to Caleb. "Good luck surviving her world-famous dinner routine. You're in for a treat."

Caleb raised an eyebrow, a faint smirk tugging at the corner of his mouth, but before he could respond, Danielle was already making her exit. With an amused wave, she padded softly out of the kitchen, leaving Caleb alone with Debbie amidst the quiet hum of her culinary rhythm and the cozy warmth of the space.

Caleb cleared his throat lightly, drawing Debbie's attention. She glanced up, a spark of surprise mingling with the warm smile already on her face. "Decided to take me up on my offer?"

"Figured I'd see if you could actually put me to work," he replied with mock seriousness, leaning casually against the counter.

Debbie raised an eyebrow, her grin turning playful as she reached for a chopping board. "Oh, trust me, I can." She set the board down in front of him and slid over a handful of vegetables. "Here. Chop these."

Caleb looked at the pile, his lips twitching into a faint smirk. "Any specific way, or am I free to use my creative license?"

"As long as it doesn't look like it's been through a wood chipper, I'll take it," Debbie shot back, her tone light and teasing.

Caleb nodded, setting to work with a quiet determination. At first, the small knife moved through the vegetables with an uneven rhythm, the cuts slightly jagged and unsure. But as he focused, his movements became steadier, the blade biting cleanly with each slice. His hands, rough and calloused from years of repairing machines and shaping wood, adjusted to the smaller, more delicate task with surprising ease.

"So," Debbie said, her hands busy peeling potatoes. "Is this the first time you've played sous-chef, or did Bonnie keep you in the kitchen now and then?"

The question made Caleb pause mid-slice. The knife hovering over the cutting board. "Bonnie," he repeated softly, his brow furrowing.

After a brief pause, he resumed chopping, his voice low and measured. "She... uh, she was the cook. Always insisted on making everything from scratch. Said it tasted better that way."

Debbie glanced up at him. "Sounds about right. Was she a good cook?"

"She was," he admitted, a faint smile tugging at his lips. "Especially around the holidays. She made this cranberry orange bread every Christmas... made the house smell like heaven."

"You're lucky," she said, her tone conversational but laced with genuine warmth. "Good memories and good food have a way of making hard times feel bearable."

"I guess it does," Caleb murmured, his voice low, almost as if the admission cost him something he wasn't used to giving. His hands stilled, the carrot he'd been chopping rolling slightly on the cutting board.

"So," Debbie said, her tone light but with an edge of curiosity, as she deftly peeled another potato. "If you were at home during this blizzard, what would you be making yourself to eat? What's your specialty? Any go-to recipes you've perfected over the years?"

Caleb let out a low, husky laugh. "Specialty? Can't say I've got one of those. Back home, meals are... let's just say, pretty straightforward."

Debbie arched an eyebrow, a playful smile tugging at her lips as she glanced up at him. "I don't buy it. Come on, even the most rugged mountain man has a go-to dish—a comfort meal or something you can whip up without thinking twice. Spill it."

Caleb smirked at her persistence, adjusting his grip on the carrot he was chopping. "Alright, if you're pressing me, I'd say scrambled eggs and toast." He looked over at her, his tone dry but teasing. "Does that count as a specialty?"

Debbie laughed, the sound warm and unguarded, filling the kitchen with its easy lightness. "Eggs and toast? That's it? Sounds like we've got some work to do on expanding your culinary horizons."

"What can I say?" Caleb replied with a deadpan tone, a smirk tugging at his lips despite the flicker of vulnerability in his eyes. "I'm not exactly running a gourmet operation. Some nights, cracking open a can of chili and pulling out a sleeve of crackers feels downright fancy."

Debbie's laughter bubbled up again, light and genuine. She shook her head, her grin widening. "Well, I'll give you points for honesty. At least you're not out here claiming to secretly run a five-star kitchen from your cabin."

Caleb set the knife down, leaning his weight on the counter as he met her gaze. "Not much need for that when it's just me," he said, his tone even but carrying a trace of something deeper. "I make what gets the job done. Efficient, practical—kind of the theme of my life, I guess."

She looked up at him then, her expression soft, her eyes thoughtful. "Nothing wrong with practical," she said gently. "But don't you miss the joy of it? Food can be simple and still be something to look forward to—something more than just fuel." She paused, her gaze steady. "Take Bonnie's cranberry orange bread, for example. I bet that wasn't practical, but it meant something, didn't it?"

"Yeah," he said quietly, his voice carrying a weight that softened the air between them. "It wasn't just bread. It was... something she loved doing." He paused, his gaze drifting to the side as a flicker of hesitation crossed his face, clouding his tone for a moment. Then, almost reluctantly, he continued. "She always said cooking was her way of loving people."

Debbie felt her heart tug at the quiet vulnerability in his voice, but she kept her response gentle, measured. "Sounds like she had it all figured out," she said softly, a small, encouraging smile touching her lips.

Then, with a slight tilt of her head, she added, her tone thoughtful but light, "Maybe it's time to carry a little of that forward. What do you think?"

Caleb's brow furrowed, his knife resuming its slow, deliberate rhythm against the cutting board. "Carry it forward?" he repeated, the words sounding foreign as he tested them out loud.

"Sure," Debbie replied, setting her own work aside for a moment to meet his gaze. Her tone was steady, but there was a softness behind it. "You don't have to bake her recipes or try to fill her shoes. But maybe… finding joy again, even in small things like cooking, could be a way to honor her memory. A way to start making peace with the past."

Caleb didn't respond immediately, his focus remaining fixed on the carrots beneath his blade.

"Maybe," he said at last, his voice low and contemplative. "I wouldn't even know where to start."

Debbie's smile softened, warm and encouraging. "Lucky for you, you've got a few willing understudies right here," she said with a playful lift of her brow. "And don't worry," her tone turned teasing, "we've got a little more to work with than just eggs and toast."

Caleb huffed a quiet laugh, the sound rolling out unexpectedly, rough but genuine. "Guess I might need all the help I can get," he admitted, the faintest trace of humor mingling with the vulnerability in his voice.

Debbie picked up another potato, the blade of her knife gliding smoothly along its surface. "Good thing you found yourself snowed in with an expert, then," she quipped, her eyes twinkling. "By the time this storm's over, you might just walk out of here with a dish or two you can actually call a specialty."

He glanced at her, his expression softening with something that felt suspiciously like gratitude. "I guess we'll see," he said, his lips twitching into a faint smile.

"Well," Debbie said with a playful shrug, "it's either that or let Danielle take over the kitchen. And trust me, you don't want to risk her creating something 'abstract.'"—she winked, repeating Danielle's earlier excuse during Pictionary.

Caleb laughed—a real, genuine laugh this time. It was warm and unguarded, the kind of laugh that reached his eyes and softened the sharp edges of his demeanor.

The sound of shuffling footsteps broke through the moment, and both turned to see Danielle standing in the doorway, her face lighting up as the savory aroma of the kitchen reached her. "What's going on in here? I heard my name," she asked, her eyes darting playfully between her mom and Caleb. A grin spread across her face as she added, "Wait a second... is Mr. Lumberjack actually chopping veggies?"

Her tone was teasing, her amusement clear as she leaned casually against the refrigerator, clearly relishing the sight.

"Isn't it a miracle?" Debbie teased, her eyes sparkling with amusement. "He hasn't even lost a finger yet."

Danielle crossed her arms. "Huh. His skills are expanding from cutting timber to the fine art of chopping vegetables."

"Funny," Caleb muttered, though there was no bite in his tone.

"I try," Danielle replied, grinning widely.

Nathan appeared next, his nose in the air like a bloodhound. "What smells so good in here? Mom, please tell me it's stew. You know that's the best."

Debbie smiled, tossing him a glance. "Yes, it's stew—and if Mr. Mountain Man here keeps chopping, we might actually have enough to feed the both of you."

Danielle stepped closer, peering dramatically around Caleb's shoulder. "Hmm. Not bad," she said with an exaggerated air of critique. "Not great, but not bad."

"Don't let her faze you," Nathan chimed in, his tone mock-serious. "Mom's a perfectionist in the kitchen, and Danielle's her apprentice."

The comment earned him a playful swat on the arm from his sister, though her grin only widened in response.

"You two are a riot," Caleb said with a chuckle, shaking his head at the banter.

Chapter 14

Dinner was ready just as the last traces of daylight slipped behind the snow-covered horizon. The dining room table was set, the large pot of steaming stew taking center stage alongside a crusty loaf of bread ready to be torn into.

As they gathered around, Debbie instinctively reached for Danielle and Nathan's hands, the gesture so familiar it required no words. Both kids bowed their heads immediately, their actions fluid and natural, waiting for their mom to lead them in prayer.

Caleb, however, hesitated. His hands hovered uncertainly just above the table, his brow furrowing slightly. He glanced at the others, unsure whether to join in or remain apart. After a moment, he settled for clasping his hands loosely in his lap, his gaze lowering without fully bowing his head. The movement was subtle, but the effort didn't go unnoticed.

"Lord, we thank You for this meal, the warmth of this home, and the chance to share this moment of peace together. Please bless the food, and guide us through our challenges, reminding us that we're never alone. Amen."

"Amen," Danielle echoed, diving immediately for the bread.

Caleb sat quietly, his gaze drifting over the table as he took in the easy rhythm of the surrounding family. Bowls were passed with practiced ease, and the soft murmur of casual conversation filled the space. Debbie moved with natural grace, her hands steady and practiced as she ladled hearty portions of steaming stew into each dish. The simple scene felt intimate in a way that caught him off guard—warm and unassuming, yet deeply inviting. For a moment, he felt like a spectator to something private, something he hadn't realized he missed until now.

"Caleb?" Debbie's voice gently pulled him from his thoughts. He blinked, looking up to find her watching him, her hand outstretched with quiet patience, waiting for his bowl.

"Oh, right—sorry," Caleb said quickly, fumbling slightly as he handed his bowl to Debbie.

As she filled it, Nathan leaned forward, his curiosity clearly piqued. "So, Caleb," he began, "what exactly do you do at the mill? What's it like?"

Debbie shot her son a quick look, a subtle warning not to bombard their guest with questions, but Caleb didn't seem to mind. Instead, he gave a small nod of thanks as Debbie handed him the steaming bowl of stew.

"I'm a crew supervisor," he said. "Mostly, I oversee the operations—make sure the guys stick to safety protocols, that the machines are running smooth. Dock work, checking incoming and outgoing shipments. It's not glamorous, but it keeps things moving."

Nathan's eyes lit up with genuine interest. "Do you get to work with the machines a lot? Like, fixing them and stuff?"

"Sometimes," he admitted. "Most of the time, I just make sure everything's running how it should. But when something breaks, yeah, I'll roll up my sleeves and get into it. Beats sitting behind a desk all day."

"That sounds... intense," Nathan said, clearly not deterred. "So, are you like the boss out there, telling everyone what to do?"

Caleb smirked, the corner of his mouth quirking up. "More like the guy reminding them not to lose a hand," he said dryly, though his tone carried a good-natured edge. "It's not always easy. Some of the guys don't think much about safety until it's too late."

Debbie caught the flicker of something in his tone—responsibility, maybe, or a quiet pride he didn't often let slip through.

"You ever think about doing something else?" Danielle asked, her voice softer than her brother's, curious yet careful.

Caleb paused. He hadn't really thought about it—not in a serious way. The mill was what he knew, what his family had done for generations. It wasn't a question of liking it or not; it was just... what was.

"I don't know," he said eventually, picking up his spoon. "The mill's been in my family for decades. My dad owns it, my brothers work there—it's just part of who we are, I guess."

Danielle nodded thoughtfully, satisfied with his answer.

"So you're a legacy," Nathan said, clearly impressed. "That's cool."

Caleb shrugged. "It's work. Honest work."

"What about you two?" Caleb asked, turning the conversation back to them. "What do you want to do after high school?"

The twins exchanged a glance, their sibling shorthand kicking in as they silently debated who'd speak first. Finally, Danielle nudged Nathan with her elbow.

"I want to go into engineering," Nathan said, his voice steady but carrying a hint of nervousness. "Mechanical, probably. I like figuring out how things work—taking them apart, putting them back together. It just... makes sense to me."

Caleb nodded, impressed. "That's a good field. You'll always have work if you're good at it."

Nathan smiled shyly at the praise, his hands fidgeting slightly with his napkin. "Thanks. I'm working on a car right now—well, sort of. I mean, it's my friend's dad's car, but he's letting me help rebuild the engine. It's been pretty cool."

"I'll bet," Caleb said, his approval clear. "If you ever need an extra set of hands, I might know a thing or two about engines."

Nathan's face lit up. "Seriously?"

"Sure," Caleb said, his tone casual but genuine. "I'm no expert, but I've kept my truck running long enough to know my way around an engine."

Debbie's heart warmed at the exchange, watching the way Nathan seemed to relax under Caleb's quiet encouragement. It wasn't often her son connected with male role models in such an easy, natural way.

"And you, Danielle?" Caleb asked, shifting his attention with a gentle smile. "What's the plan for you?"

Danielle sat up a little straighter, her confidence shining through. "I want to be a physical therapist," she said proudly. "I love working with people and helping them heal, you know? Plus, I've always been into sports, so it feels like a good fit."

"That's a solid choice," Caleb said, nodding in approval. "Takes a lot of dedication, though. You ready for that?"

"Absolutely," Danielle replied without hesitation. "I mean, it'll be hard work, but I'm used to that. And besides, I've got a pretty good example to follow." She glanced pointedly at her mom, a warm smile crossing her face.

Debbie reached over to squeeze Danielle's hand briefly, her heart swelling with pride.

"So, Caleb," Nathan began, his curiosity shining through as he stirred his stew. "What's your cabin like? Do you enjoy living so far up in the mountains? I heard you don't have any neighbors for miles."

Debbie shot her son a quick, subtle glare—a clear warning not to push too hard.

Caleb took a moment before answering, stirring his stew thoughtfully. "It's... quiet," he said finally, lifting his gaze to meet Nathan's. "Real quiet. That's the part I like most about it."

"Quiet? I'd probably lose my mind," Danielle chimed in, tearing off a piece of her bread. "I need noise—music, chatter, something. Doesn't it get... lonely?"

Caleb leaned back in his chair, his lips twitching faintly in what might have been the ghost of a smile. "Sometimes. But after a long day, peace and quiet can be a good thing. The cabin's nothing fancy—just a four-room place I built from timber on my land. Solid enough to handle storms like this, though."

"Wait, you built it yourself? Like, all of it?" Nathan asked, his tone a mix of admiration and disbelief.

"I did," Caleb said with a small nod. "The walls, the roof—every bit of it. I've always liked working with my hands, building things. When I built the cabin, I was going through a time in my life where I just... needed something to focus on. It gave me purpose when everything else felt like it was slipping away."

"That's pretty impressive," Nathan admitted, sitting up straighter. "That's next level."

"It wasn't easy," Caleb said with a shrug. "Made a lot of mistakes along the way." He paused for a moment before continuing, his tone thoughtful. "Takes a certain kind of stubbornness to cut logs, mill them down by hand, and stick with it when things don't go the way you planned."

"That's where I'd fail," Danielle interjected, grinning. "No patience. If it doesn't work the first time, I'm out."

"Don't let her fool you," Nathan teased. "She'll stick with something if it involves beating me in the end."

Danielle shot him an exaggerated scowl, and Caleb huffed out a deep chuckle, the corners of his mouth lifting just slightly. "Well, stubbornness ain't all bad," he said, his tone easy.

"So, Caleb," Debbie began, her voice warm and inviting, "what do you do to keep busy out at your place? I imagine it's not all chopping wood and fixing things all day."

Caleb's spoon paused halfway to his mouth, and he seemed to weigh the question for a moment before responding. "Well, between work at the mill and keeping the place running, there's not a lot of downtime," he admitted. "But when I do get a minute, I'll fish, hunt, hike some trails, or tinker around in the barn. There's always something that needs fixing or attention."

"It sounds... peaceful," Nathan ventured, his tone softening. "But... also hard."

Caleb's gaze shifted toward Nathan, his expression unreadable. Then, with the faintest curve of a smile, he nodded. "It is. Both, I guess."

"I'm not trying to pry, Caleb," Debbie said gently, her hazel eyes steady and kind. "I'm genuinely curious. Don't you miss being part of the community? I faintly remember you used to always take part in the town festivals and other things going on." Her tone was soft, free of judgment, only carrying genuine curiosity.

Caleb's lips pressed into a thin line, his gaze dropping to the table as though he was weighing whether or not to respond. For a moment, it seemed like he might deflect her question. But then he exhaled deeply, leaning back in his chair as his dark brown eyes finally met hers.

"After Bonnie died," he began slowly, his voice quiet but steady, "I didn't feel like I belonged anywhere anymore. Being out there... it was easier. Didn't have to talk about what happened, didn't have to answer questions, didn't have to... face people who meant well but didn't know what to say. And I didn't have to deal with their judgments. I mean..." He hesitated, his jaw tightening briefly before he added, "... it was no secret in this town that I was a drunk."

His words hung in the air, unfiltered and heavy, exposing the weight he had carried silently for so many years. Debbie's heart ached for him, the depth of his pain so evident it felt almost tangible.

The room grew still, the soft crackle of the fire in the living room hearth the only sound breaking the silence. Danielle shifted in her seat, her usual cheer dimmed by the gravity of Caleb's admission. Nathan cleared his throat, glancing toward his mother, his expression uncertain, as if silently asking how to respond to a moment so raw and unguarded.

"People care about you, Caleb," Debbie said, her voice steady and filled with compassion. "Even if they don't always show it the right way. The church community is always here with open arms. None of us are perfect—we all carry scars and burdens."

Caleb's jaw tightened, his gaze dropping to the table as her words settled between them. Finally, he spoke, his voice low and measured, each word carrying the weight of years spent alone. "My burdens were best dealt with alone. I needed to face them head-on... in my own way, in my own time."

His words, though quiet, held the weight of years of self-imposed isolation. Debbie watched him closely, her heart heavy with understanding. She could see the strength it took for him to admit even that much, to share a piece of himself after so long.

Gently, she reached out and placed her hand over his, her touch light but grounding. "I admire you, Caleb Warren," she said, her voice warm and unwavering. "You're a good, strong man."

Chapter 15

The television flickered with images of snowplows carving paths through towering banks of snow, their headlights cutting through the hazy twilight. On the screen, a weather forecaster stood bundled in a bright red coat, snow falling down as she reported. Her voice was buoyant and optimistic—a stark contrast to the dire warnings issued just days ago.

"Though many secondary roads remain impassable, major arteries are being cleared, and power is holding strong across the county with only a few areas without electricity. The worst of the storm has moved east, and as temperatures rise slightly tomorrow, we expect conditions to improve significantly."

Caleb leaned back into the couch, his long frame looking almost too big for the cushion beneath him. His hands were wrapped loosely around a steaming mug of coffee.

"Looks like I won't be a stranded lumberjack for much longer," he said, his voice low and a little wry.

"You say that like it's a relief," Debbie countered, a teasing lilt in her voice. "I thought you were just starting to enjoy the fine culinary experience of chopping carrots in my kitchen."

Debbie smiled softly from her spot on the opposite end of the couch, her legs tucked beneath her as she cradled a steaming mug in her hands. The warm glow of the firelight danced across her features, softening the sharper angles of her face and giving her an air of quiet serenity.

Caleb smirked. "Enjoy's a strong word. Pretty sure I got a blister from that knife."

Debbie laughed, soft and melodic, and Caleb found himself glancing over at her. There was something about seeing her like this—relaxed, unguarded—that tugged at something deep in his chest. He looked away quickly, taking a sip of coffee to busy himself.

"It looks like we'll finally be able to start digging our way out tomorrow," Debbie said, glancing toward the frosted windowpane. "Clearing a path to the road's going to take a while."

Caleb followed her gaze, his mug of coffee warming his hands as he let out a low hum of agreement. "Snow this deep? Yeah, it's not going to make it easy. I'll get out there first thing in the morning and help with the heavy lifting."

Debbie gave him a wry smile. "You sure you're up for it? You're still recovering, remember?" Her voice was light, but there was an undertone of motherly concern tucked beneath the teasing.

"I'll be fine," he replied, a touch of stubbornness sneaking into his tone. "Can't sit around twiddling my thumbs while you do all the work. Not exactly my style."

Debbie arched an eyebrow playfully. "Twiddling your thumbs, huh?"

A low chuckle escaped Caleb as he shook his head. "Guess I'm not built for idle hands."

"Well, in that case," she said, setting her mug down on the coffee table, "you might just earn yourself some bonus points."

He smirked, raising his mug slightly in mock toast. "That a threat or a promise?"

"Depends on how good you are with a snow shovel tomorrow," she shot back, the corners of her mouth twitching into a grin.

Caleb's gaze drifted toward the window, the snow still falling softly beyond the glass. The gentle crackle of the fire filled the pause in their conversation, the silence between them warm but thoughtful. After a beat, he spoke, his voice quieter, almost as if he were testing the waters of his own curiosity.

"I have to ask... how do you manage to always stay so upbeat and positive?" He hesitated, his brow furrowing slightly as he added, "You don't strike me as someone who falls apart when life throws a wrench your way. I mean, raising two kids on your own... I can't imagine that's been easy."

Debbie blinked, momentarily caught off guard by the unexpected sincerity in Caleb's tone. She tilted her head slightly, studying him for a moment before responding. "It's not always as together as it might look," she admitted, her voice soft but steady. "Some days, I wonder if I'm doing enough—or if I'm doing it right at all. For the kids, for myself... for everything."

Caleb's brows drew together faintly, his fingers tightening slightly around his mug as he absorbed her words. He shifted in his seat, his voice quiet but firm when he finally spoke. "From what I can see, you're doing pretty good."

A flicker of gratitude passed across Debbie's face, and she couldn't help but smile. "That means a lot," she said sincerely, her voice wrapping around the words like a quiet thanks. "I guess I've just learned to focus on what I can do in the moment. The rest... well, it's out of my hands."

"Where's their dad?" Caleb asked, his voice low, almost hesitant, as if he wasn't sure he should be treading into such personal waters.

Debbie paused mid-motion, her hand halting where it rested on the edge of the couch. For a moment, the gentle crackle of the fire seemed louder than anything else in the room.

"He's... around," she said carefully, tucking a loose strand of hair behind her ear. "He still lives in town, our old house, in fact, but he's not really part of their day-to-day lives anymore."

Caleb nodded slowly, sensing the restraint in her words. He glanced down at his mug, rolling it slightly between his hands. "I see," he murmured, his tone gentle but inquisitive. "Is that by his choice? Or... yours?"

Debbie let out a soft sigh and leaned back against the couch, her shoulders relaxing into a slouch that made her look more vulnerable than she usually allowed herself to be. "I'd say it's a little of both. After the divorce, he tried to stay involved for a while, but... well..." she trailed off, her lips pressing together in thought before she continued. "Let's just say his priorities shifted, and I didn't press the fact that he needed to be involved in his kids' life."

Caleb tilted his head slightly, watching her with quiet curiosity. "Shifted how?"

She offered a small, almost bitter smile. "He's engaged to someone that could be the twins' slightly older sister. My ex seems to be going through a midlife crisis and his mind is on his new friend rather than being focused on his children."

Caleb frowned, the lines of his face deepening. "That's tough," he said simply, his voice rough with sincerity.

"It is," Debbie admitted, her hazel eyes reflecting a flicker of the hurt she usually kept tightly locked away. "I try to remind myself that you can't force someone to be the parent you think they should be. And in the end, my job is to love them enough that they don't feel that void too deeply."

Caleb's grip on his mug tightened, and for a moment, he said nothing. The firelight danced off his deep brown eyes, which glimmered faintly with something unreadable. "Seems like you're doing a pretty good job of that," he finally said, his voice low but firm. "From what I can see, those two are smart, grounded, and closer to you than most kids their age are to their parents. That doesn't just happen on its own."

Debbie's lips curved into a soft, grateful smile. "Thank you," she said, her tone sincere. "It's not always easy, but I've learned to lean on faith and trust that God fills in the gaps where I can't. And honestly, they're good kids—they've handled everything with more grace than most grown-ups I know."

Caleb nodded again, digesting her words. After a pause, he asked carefully, "Do they... see him much?"

"Not really," Debbie admitted. "He's called them on their birthday and the big holidays, but it's always a bit... strained. I don't think he knows quite how to connect with them anymore. And they're old enough now to see the cracks in the relationship for what they are. It's painful to watch, but I remind them that their dad does still love them, in his own way."

Caleb leaned back against the couch, his gaze somber as he considered her response. "You're stronger than most, you know that?" he said at last, his tone almost reverent.

Debbie chuckled softly, though the sound carried a tinge of self-deprecation. "I don't know about that. I think it's more stubbornness than strength. You push forward because... what other choice do you have? Giving up isn't an option, not when you've got people depending on you."

Caleb's lips lifted into a faint smile, but there was no humor in it. "I get that," he said quietly. "Sometimes it feels like life doesn't give you much room for anything else—just... surviving."

"Exactly," Debbie agreed, her gaze steady as she met his eyes. "But I don't want it to always be just about surviving. For me or for them. I want them to see that even when life is hard, there's still room for joy, for love, and for hope. Even if it takes time to find."

She paused, then leaned forward slightly, her tone softening as she asked, "What about you?"

Caleb blinked, clearly caught off guard. His brows furrowed as he looked up at her. "What do you mean?"

"What do you want for yourself, Caleb?" she continued, her voice gentle but direct. "Beyond surviving?"

He opened his mouth, as if to respond, but then closed it again, the weight of the question settling over him. Finally, after a long silence, he spoke, his voice almost hesitant. "I... don't know. I'm not sure where to even start."

"Well," Debbie said gently, leaning forward slightly, "maybe it's time to start thinking about it. Just because the storm outside's clearing doesn't mean the storm inside has to go on forever."

Caleb's eyes flicked to hers, her steady hazel gaze meeting his own with an openness so disarming it stirred something in him he hadn't felt in years—a faint glimmer of possibility.

The television caught Debbie's eye, drawing her gaze to the news segment showing snowplows forcing their way through towering drifts, their yellow lights flashing rhythmically against the darkened backdrop. Tilting her head slightly, Debbie appeared absorbed in the footage, but the distant look in her hazel eyes made it clear her thoughts were elsewhere.

"You still feeling okay? No new aches or pains anywhere?" she asked, her voice gentle.

Caleb ran a hand through his hair, his gaze fixed on her. "Been better. But I'll be fine, just sore."

"Feel like watching a movie with me?" Debbie asked, her voice light but carrying just enough warmth to break the lingering tension in the room.

Caleb blinked, surprised by the casualness of the offer. His brow furrowed in thought as his gaze shifted toward the TV mounted above the mantle of the fireplace, then back to her.

"I don't know," he said, rubbing the back of his neck. His hesitation hung in the air, more out of uncertainty than rejection.

"Come on," she coaxed gently, "nothing serious. Just something easy to pass the time. Maybe a comedy?"

His lips quirked upward, a hint of dry humor flickering to life. "Not too sure I'm in the mood to laugh," he muttered, shifting in his seat like a man who wasn't quite used to being invited in.

Debbie chuckled softly as she folded her arms. "Well, that's precisely why you need to. Besides,"—she tipped her head playfully and looked at him—"last I heard, laughter's better than any medicine."

Caleb exhaled a quiet, reluctant laugh. He rubbed his chin thoughtfully, his eyes briefly flicking over her face, as though weighing the costs of letting a little more light in.

"What've you got?" he asked, the words slipping out before he could second-guess himself.

Debbie's smile widened slightly, a gentle victory glimmering in her eyes. "I was thinking something old school," she said with a casual shrug. "Maybe *Planes, Trains, and Automobiles*—you can't get more classic than Steve Martin and John Candy."

Caleb raised an eyebrow. "That the one about two guys trying to get home for Thanksgiving?"

"Yep."

"Alright," he finally agreed, his gruff voice softening as he surrendered to the idea, "but don't go judging me if I fall asleep halfway through."

Debbie grinned. "Fair warning. I'll totally make fun of you for snoring."

Chapter 16

Caleb woke in the middle of the night, his foggy mind unable to make sense of the biting cold seeping into every inch of his bones. He blinked groggily, lifting his head just enough to notice the fire had completely died down. There were only faint glowing embers left, little more than dots among the charred wood.

The movie had ended long ago, and Debbie's head rested against the arm of the couch, her breathing slow and even. She looked so peaceful, curled up under a blanket at the far end of the couch, her hand loosely holding onto the edge of the fabric, as if it anchored her to sleep.

Caleb didn't want to disturb her. He laid there, unmoving for a few moments, legs stiff from the cold. But when the chill finally became too unbearable, and a small shiver ran up his spine, he knew he had no choice.

He sat up slowly, wincing as his muscles resisted the movement. Debbie stirred slightly but didn't wake. Not about to let her freeze,

Caleb stood and walked over to the fireplace. His breath puffed in the air like it did on frigid days outside.

With a quick look around, he noticed something hadn't clicked into place in his mind yet: the power had gone out. That would explain the pervasive darkness—no humming from kitchen appliances, no faint light from the outside floodlight. He rubbed a hand over his face, feeling the stiff scratch of his beard.

Kneeling beside the fire, he stared at what little life remained in the logs. Maybe he could salvage it before it went completely cold. Caleb grabbed the iron poker, shifting the remnants of the logs to add new kindling.

As he reached for a piece of firewood from the dwindling stack by the hearth, his hand bumped into something, sending it clattering to the stone floor. Caleb flinched, muttering under his breath. The last thing he wanted was to wake Debbie, especially considering the kindness she'd extended him.

But the sound was enough to tug her from sleep. Debbie blinked, her eyebrows furrowing as she roused. "Caleb?" Her voice was thick with grogginess, eyes searching the room for his shadow.

He froze for a millisecond, feeling a strange heat rise to his cheeks before he quickly spoke. "Sorry. Didn't mean to wake you. Power's out... I'm trying to get the fire going again."

Debbie sat up, pushing the hair from her face. "What time is it?" she muttered.

"I'm not sure," Caleb admitted.

One glance toward the window, now frosted so thickly with snow that it hardly showed anything but darkness outside, told Debbie everything she needed to know. "We're low on firewood, huh?" she said, shivering as she reached for her blanket and wrapped it tighter around her.

"Yeah," Caleb said gruffly. "I need to get some more wood or this room's gonna feel like the north pole after these last few logs burn down."

Debbie rubbed her eyes and nodded. "I'll help," she said, pushing herself up from the couch. Before Caleb could protest, she was already heading toward the front hall closet, moving with purpose despite the thick fatigue clinging to her movements. She swung the closet door open and rummaged briefly, pulling out flashlights. Flicking one on, she placed it on the fireplace mantel to cast a soft light over the room. She handed the other to Caleb and kept one for herself.

"We've got a stack of wood on the back porch under a tarp," she said, her tone brisk but steady. "That should get us through until tomorrow. Once that's used up, we'll need to clear a path to the woodshed in the backyard and bring more closer to the house." She switched her flashlight on and gave Caleb a determined glance, a silent indication that this was non-negotiable.

"I can bring the firewood in. You don't need to—"

"Caleb, stop," Debbie interrupted, her tone kind but firm. "I know how to fetch firewood. Besides, you're still recovering, and you're my guest—which should mean I take care of this. But, knowing you..." She eyed him with amusement. "You're not the type to sit back, are you? So, grab your boots and coat, and let's get this done."

Despite himself, Caleb couldn't help but chuckle softly. Of course, she was right.

He nodded, giving up any attempt to argue, knowing full well she wouldn't stand for it. Together, they donned their coats, hats, and gloves and headed out the back door.

The cold wind hit them like an icy wall the moment they opened the door. Snow swirled around them in thick tufts, barely letting them see beyond a few paces. As Caleb squinted at the stack of wood on the back porch, a sharp gust sent snow flying down the collar of his coat. He shook his head at the bitterness of it and muttered, "Well, this is one way to wake up."

Debbie pulled her scarf tighter around her lower face, raising her voice to be heard over the howling wind. "Could've gone for coffee instead."

Debbie stepped onto the back porch, the icy wind nipping at her cheeks as she moved toward the neatly stacked firewood. Her boots hit the frost-slick boards, and before she had time to react, her feet slipped out from under her. With a startled gasp, she toppled backward. The flashlight flying from her hand as she hit the porch with a dull thud. The impact knocked the wind out of her, leaving her frozen for a moment, both from shock and the biting chill of the snow covered wood beneath her.

"Debbie!" Caleb's sharp voice cut through the swirling wind as he instinctively lunged forward, his arm shooting out in an attempt to catch her. He missed by a fraction of a second, his gloved hand swiping through the empty air as she went down.

"Hold still," he said, his boots crunching against the icy porch as he closed the short distance between them. She was already trying to sit up, her brows furrowed, breath puffing visibly in the frigid night.

"I'm fine... I think," Debbie managed, her voice tight as she placed her hands on the porch, testing her ability to move. But before she could hoist herself up, Caleb crouched beside her, his large frame blocking some of the wind and giving her a moment to catch her breath.

"Don't move yet," he said firmly, his tone gruff but laced with concern. His eyes searched her face intently, then flicked down to her legs and arms, as if checking for any obvious signs of injury. "You hit pretty hard. Did you twist anything?"

Debbie shook her head, her breath still uneven but growing steadier. "No... no, I don't think so. I just slipped. My pride might be bruised, though."

Caleb huffed a low, relieved sound. "Your pride'll survive. It's the rest of you I'm worried about." He extended a hand, his palm open and steady. "Here—let me help you up."

Debbie hesitated, her independent streak urging her to refuse. But as she glanced at Caleb, his brow furrowed with genuine worry, she gave in with a faint smile. "Alright, but if I drag you down with me, don't say I didn't warn you."

"I'll take my chances," he said.

She reached for his hand, his grip strong and firm as he effortlessly hoisted her to her feet. Debbie winced slightly as her back straightened, pressing a hand to her lower spine where the impact had left a dull, throbbing ache. Caleb's eyes narrowed, catching the small gesture.

"You sure you're okay?" he asked again, his voice softer, tinged with a seriousness that left no room for casual dismissal.

Debbie rolled her shoulders tentatively, testing her range of motion. "I'm sure. Just sore. Really, I'm fine." She gave him a reassuring smile, though her cheeks burned faintly—not from the cold, but from the unbidden awareness of how steady and solid his presence felt in that moment.

Caleb didn't look entirely convinced, his gaze lingering on her before he finally relented with a quiet grunt. "Alright. But if anything starts feeling worse, let me know. No toughing it out, got it?"

Debbie laughed despite the lingering ache in her back. "Yes, sir," she teased.

Caleb bent to retrieve the flashlight she'd dropped, dusting off the snowflakes clinging to its surface before handing it back to her. "Careful where you're stepping. Porch is slicker than it looks."

"I figured that out the hard way," she quipped, taking the flashlight and clicking it back on to illuminate the stack of wood nearby. "Thanks for the assist. It's nice having someone to look out for me for a change."

"Anytime," he said, his voice low but steady. Without another word, he turned and grabbed a few logs from the pile, tucking them neatly under his arm.

Debbie followed suit, her movements more cautious this time as they worked in a rhythm to quickly finish the task.

When they stepped back into the cabin, the warmth of the fire greeted them like a welcome embrace. Debbie set her armful of wood down beside the hearth and turned to Caleb with a small, lopsided grin.

"Any chance we can pretend that didn't just happen?" she asked, gesturing vaguely toward the porch.

Caleb glanced at her, his deep brown eyes glinting with faint amusement. "Not a chance. That one's going into the category of unforgettable moments."

Debbie groaned playfully, but her smile lingered. "Great. Just what I needed—another unforgettable moment starring me as the clumsy damsel in distress."

"You're not a clumsy damsel in distress," Caleb said evenly, his expression calm but resolute. "Not by a long shot."

Caleb shifted, adding another log to the fire, his movements as unassuming as ever, as if he hadn't just said something that sent warmth flooding through her for reasons she couldn't quite name.

"Well," Debbie said after a beat, her tone lifting lightly as she tried to ease the tension rising in her chest. "Lesson learned: no more late-night firewood runs without a buddy. Besides, seeing you in action was worth the price of admission."

Caleb chuckled softly, shaking his head as he stood and dusted his hands off. "Glad I could entertain."

Debbie laughed as well, the sound light and genuine.

They quickly made another trip, hauling armfuls of wood into the cabin. The cold bit at their cheeks, and their breath mingled in the air like puffs of steam as they worked together silently, the wind whistling its lonely tune around them. By the time they were inside once more, both were shivering but satisfied with their efforts.

"That should be enough to last us for a little while," she said, glancing at the pile of logs neatly stacked beside the hearth. "The kids can help us bring in more tomorrow. One silver lining—they've got plenty of energy to burn."

Caleb stretched his hands toward the flames, his tall frame casting shadows that danced across the walls. "Good plan," he said with a low grunt of approval. "Though, knowing teenagers, they'll probably want to turn it into some kind of competition."

Debbie shot him a sidelong glance, her lips quirking up in a playful smile. "And you're saying you wouldn't turn a simple task like wood-hauling into a competition if you were their age?"

Caleb chuckled softly, the sound warm despite his gruff exterior. "Who says I wouldn't do that now? I'd still win, though."

Debbie raised an eyebrow, folding her arms as she leaned against the back of the couch. "Oh, would you? Bold claim, considering you'd be up against two very competitive teens and... well, me."

One corner of Caleb's mouth curved upward. "I might have a few tricks up my sleeve. Don't count me out yet."

"Oh, don't worry," Debbie quipped, tilting her head with a mock-serious look. "I'd never underestimate someone who just survived a truck crash, hauled firewood in a blizzard even though he's banged up pretty bad, and still has the gall to think he can outwork a team effort."

The smallest laugh escaped him then, genuine and unrestrained. "Fair enough. But if there's a prize involved, don't expect me to hold back."

She grinned, her teasing tone mellowing into one of camaraderie. "Well, if we manage to make it through this storm without losing toes to frostbite, I'll gladly put together a trophy for 'Most Helpful Truck-Crashing Guest.' You'll win by default, don't worry."

Caleb huffed out another laugh—short but full of humor—and shook his head. "Wouldn't want to take home that kind of glory, but thanks for the offer."

A beat of comfortable silence passed between them, the fire crackling softly and starting to reclaim the room's warmth. Debbie sighed contentedly and rubbed her hands together, the last traces of chill leaving her fingertips.

"Honestly, though," she said, her voice softer now, "I think we make a pretty good team."

Caleb glanced at her, the faintest touch of surprise crossing his face before his features settled into something quieter, almost contemplative. "Yeah."

"Alright," she said, her practical tone returning as she motioned to the couch. "Now that we've saved the fire, I think it's time we both got some rest. I'm going to run upstairs and wake the kids up and have them come down here to the living room to stay warm."

Caleb nodded, standing and stretching with a quiet groan. "Sounds like a plan."

Chapter 17

A faint crackle from the dying embers in the fireplace greeted Debbie as her eyelids fluttered open. The quiet stillness in the room wasn't unwelcome; it reminded her of the early years with the twins, when the house would finally fall silent after their bedtime chaos. Except now, instead of baby monitors and lullabies, there was snow and wind to reckon with.

She shifted on the couch, careful not to disturb Danielle, whose head was nestled against her shoulder. Nathan lay sprawled on a makeshift bed of blankets on the floor in front of the fireplace, his rhythmic breathing evidence that he was still blissfully unaware of the morning cold creeping into the cabin.

The fire had burned low, and she could feel the cool chill in the air. Pushing herself up, Debbie tucked the blanket snugly around Danielle before tiptoeing across the room to add more wood. Once she had a steady fire going again, she quietly moved toward the kitchen. Her movements were second nature—quiet and deliberate, the way only a mother knew how to glide through a house full of sleeping people.

Her phone was waiting for her on the counter, the screen lighting up her face in the dim room as she checked for updates. The news apps confirmed what she already suspected—the storm was moving off, leaving heavy drifts in its wake, with power outages affecting much of the county now. No immediate restoration was expected.

Her gaze flickered to the coffeemaker on the counter, its lifeless presence mocking her. She winced, her craving for caffeine suddenly sharper than the cold. A soft sigh escaped her lips as she mentally sized up the task ahead: the generator.

Debbie slipped her arms into her coat. The gloves she always kept tucked into the sleeves were a little chilly against her fingers, but she didn't mind. Coffee would fix that soon enough. Her plan was simple: haul out the generator, get it running, brew a pot of coffee, and then check in on a few of her elderly patients nearby, who, she assumed, were also dealing with the lack of power.

She was shoving her feet into her boots when a voice startled her.

"And where exactly are you sneaking off to?"

Debbie spun around. Caleb's frame emerged slowly into the dim light, his hair disheveled, his dark brown eyes narrowing suspiciously. He didn't look entirely awake yet, but the questioning arch of his brow suggested he was alert enough to protest whatever plan she'd just concocted.

"Oh, good grief, Caleb," she hissed in a whisper. "You scared me half to death."

"Sorry," he said, though there was a trace of humor in his low voice.

"I'm going out to start the generator," she said, shaking her head as she bent down to lace her boots. "It's not a big deal."

"You're going to start the generator?" His tone was skeptical as he folded his arms across his chest, leaning against the door frame like a man who had no intention of being left out of this conversation.

Debbie stood upright again, crossing her arms with an amused expression. "Did I stutter? I'm perfectly capable of handling it, thank you very much. The generator's stored right on the back porch in a cabinet in the far corner to keep it handy for moments like this—we lose power here with every other gust of wind, it seems. And besides, that generator isn't going to start itself, and I want coffee." She paused, exaggerating her emphasis with a pointed look. "No... let me correct that—I need coffee. Right now."

"Coffee's that important?" His smirk deepened, though he was already moving toward the coat rack.

"Do you really want to know the answer to that? Because I'll stand here and explain the beauty of coffee until you turn around and fall back asleep."

"I'll go," he said, brushing past her to pick up his gloves from the table where he had left them last night.

"Excuse me?"

"You heard me," he replied evenly, rubbing a hand through his sleep-tousled hair. "I'll get the generator started."

"Caleb—"

"This isn't up for debate."

Debbie's protest stuck somewhere between her throat and her pride. There was a stubborn set to his jaw as he turned to grab the flashlight from the counter.

"I didn't ask for help, you know."

"That makes two of us," he replied, his tone as dry as winter air.

Caleb stepped outside, the cold biting at his skin as he made his way toward the storage cabinet at the far end of the back porch. As he pulled the cabinet doors open, he couldn't help but feel a pang of admiration. Built with care and precision, the inside of the cabinet housed shelves perfectly fitted around the generator, each one holding five-gallon containers of fuel.

"Impressive," Caleb muttered under his breath as he ran his hand over one of the shelves. With careful rationing, he guessed they'd have enough fuel to last several days.

Determined to get things running, Caleb pulled the generator out and positioned it, so the fumes blew away from the cabin. He crouched down by the generator to inspect it. The oil level was good, and he topped off the gas with practiced efficiency. Satisfied, he wrapped one hand around the starter cord and gave it a sharp pull. The generator roared to life, the sound breaking through the stillness of the morning air, a welcome hum of progress against the quiet wilderness.

From the lower shelf of the cabinet, Caleb retrieved a bundle of extension cords, carefully unraveling one. After plugging one end into the generator with practiced ease, he stretched the cord toward the house, its length uncoiling neatly as he went. Opening the back door, he stepped inside, the warmth of the cabin greeting him as he rubbed his gloved hands together, chasing away the lingering bite of the cold.

Debbie was waiting for him in the kitchen, her smile as bright as the flames flickering in the fireplace. "Well," she said, hands perched on her hips as she surveyed him with amusement, "looks like my knight in flannel has saved the day."

Caleb smirked, tipping his head toward her in quiet acknowledgment. "Generator's up and running. That coffee's calling your name."

"Thank you," she said, her eyes meeting his. "You didn't have to do that, you know."

Caleb shrugged. "Didn't seem right letting you do it when I'm quite capable."

Debbie nodded, plugging the coffee maker into the extension cord. She glanced at Caleb, a hint of a smile quirking her lips. "I have to say, I could get used to this—someone else handling the heavy lifting while I get to do the fun stuff, like waiting for caffeine to brew."

Caleb chuckled, leaning one shoulder against the door frame, his hands slipping into the pockets of his coat. "Well, I wouldn't call starting a generator the heavy lifting, but if it means I get some of that coffee, consider it my morning workout."

"Morning workout?" Debbie raised an eyebrow teasingly, her tone light but playful. "Does that mean you're not charging a fee for your service?"

"Coffee's a fair trade," Caleb said with a low drawl, the faint trace of a smirk quirking his lips. He tipped his chin toward the container of baked goods resting by the coffeemaker. "But if we're really sealing this bargain, you might want to sweeten the pot with one of those blueberry muffins."

Debbie's laugh was soft, the sound warming the room as much as the rekindled fire. "Ah, so now we're negotiating. Alright, fine. Coffee and a muffin it is—payment rendered in full."

"Deal," Caleb replied smoothly.

He shrugged his coat off before removing his boots and gloves. Crossing the room with an easy, unhurried stride, his tall frame seemed to shrink the cozy kitchen, making it feel smaller.

"Thanks," he said as Debbie handed him a cup of coffee.

Debbie leaned back against the counter, cradling her own cup as she blew gently across its surface. After taking a cautious sip, she glanced at him, her expression more contemplative now. "You know, for someone who's all rough edges and brooding silences, you're not half bad at being helpful."

Caleb's eyes narrowed faintly, though the ghost of a smile lingered on his lips. "Was that... a compliment?"

"Yeah," she teased, "don't get used to it."

"I'll keep that in mind," Caleb said, his voice dry but tinged with a faint trace of humor. "That cabinet where you keep the generator? Pretty impressive."

Debbie looked up from her coffee, a smile tugging at the corners of her mouth. "Oh, thanks. That was one of my post-divorce projects after we moved into this house."

Caleb raised an eyebrow, genuine surprise flickering across his face. "Wait... you're telling me you built that cabinet?"

Debbie met his steady gaze. "That's right."

He blinked, clearly caught off guard, his features softening just enough to reveal a flicker of admiration beneath his usually guarded demeanor. "A project like that? I've got to admit, I'm impressed." His voice was low, steady, but there was a hint of genuine curiosity woven into it. "So, was that your only post-divorce project, or are there more hidden talents I should know about?"

Debbie laughed, brushing a strand of hair back behind her ear as she leaned against the counter. "Oh, there were plenty of projects," she said. "Some are more successful than others. Let's just say I've got a very... eclectic skill set now. Everything from tiling a bathroom to unsuccessfully trying to reupholster a chair. Spoiler alert—fabric glue is not as forgiving as YouTube made it look."

Caleb's mouth twitched into a reluctant grin, his brow lifting slightly. "Sounds like you really threw yourself into projects."

"Oh, I did," she said, her hazel eyes lighting up with the memory. "At first, it was less about actually fixing things and more about proving that I could. You know that I was capable of running a household on my own and making it a home for me and the kids. But somewhere along the way, I started to enjoy it—well, most of it. Except for plumbing. My skills there can be questionable, but I can usually rig anything up and make do."

"Make do…" Caleb said with a faint chuckle. "I like that."

Her smile softened, her gaze drifting briefly to the fire crackling in the hearth. "I think it was about reclaiming pieces of myself, too," she admitted thoughtfully. "Everything in my life had felt so out of my control for so long. The projects… they were my way of taking something broken or neglected and making it whole again. It was satisfying in a way I didn't expect. And it felt… good. Like I was proving to myself and the kids that we'd get through it. One step—one repair—at a time."

Caleb nodded, his eyes never leaving hers. "Sounds like something more people should do," he said. "But sometimes it's easier to focus on fixing what's outside than dealing with what's inside."

Debbie studied him for a moment, the openness of his words surprising her. "It is," she agreed. "So, what about you? Got any hidden handyman talents? Or do you stick to chopping down trees, milling your own lumber, building a home, and crashing into people's front yards?"

Caleb huffed out a short laugh, shaking his head. "I'm not too bad at carpentry," he said. "Built the cabinets and some of the furniture in my cabin myself."

Debbie arched an eyebrow, her grin widening. "Oh, so you do have more hidden skills. Cabinet and furniture building, huh? That's impressive. Let me guess—rustic and sturdy, right? Functional over flair?"

"Something like that," he admitted, his tone light but tinged with sincerity. "I like working with my hands. Always have. Nothing fancy, though. Just solid pieces that do what they're meant to do."

"Hmm," Debbie mused, tilting her head. "I can see that. You strike me as the type that prefers straightforward over flashy. Let me guess, no Pinterest inspiration boards for you?"

"I have no idea what a Pinterest inspiration board is," Caleb said.

Debbie laughed, the sound warm and unguarded, and Caleb found himself leaning into the moment more than he intended. It had been years since he'd felt this ease with someone—this give-and-take that sparked humor and understanding in equal measure.

"Well," she said lightly, her voice full of teasing warmth, "the next time I decide to tackle a project that involves furniture repair—or reupholstering, heaven forbid—I'll know who to call."

"Fair warning," he replied, his voice dipping into a low, playful rumble, "I don't do fabric glue."

"Noted," she said, her grin lingering.

Their conversation eased into another silence, the rhythmic crackle of the fire filling the air. Caleb glanced out the window, where the faint light of dawn was creeping through the frost-covered glass.

"I'd better start clearing a path to the woodshed," he said, his voice low as he pushed away from the counter.

"If you think I'm letting you do that alone, think again. Team effort, remember?"

Caleb turned to look at her, his deep brown eyes meeting her hazel ones with something unreadable, though not unwelcome. For a moment, he seemed like he might argue, but then he simply nodded and said, "Alright. Team effort it is."

"I'll be out there in a few minutes. I just need to check on a couple of my patients who live nearby," Debbie said, her voice tinged with both determination and care.

Caleb nodded, his gaze steady as warmth flickered behind his dark eyes. "Take your time."

Chapter 18

Debbie watched Caleb methodically shovel a path through the snow to the woodshed from the kitchen window. Each stroke of the shovel was smooth and practiced, his tall frame cutting an impressive figure against the swirling snow. Even bundled up against the morning chill, there was a quiet strength about him that struck her, and not for the first time. He didn't complain, didn't hesitate; he just did what needed to be done.

She cradled her coffee mug, feeling its warmth seep into her palms. Though the fire had taken the edge off the cabin's chill, she still felt the echo of winter in her bones and wondered how much worse it might be for someone without a crackling hearth to huddle by. Her thoughts drifted naturally to Harold and Mildred Hughes, a sweet elderly couple she loved dearly. Harold had just started to recover from a nasty fall, and with the storm roaring across the mountain, and now the power outage, she couldn't stop thinking about him and Mildred.

Placing her half-empty mug on the counter, Debbie picked up her phone and dialed their number. When Mildred's familiar voice finally came through, it sounded cheerful but tired.

"Oh, Debbie, honey, I wasn't expecting to hear from you! I'm sorry it took me a second to answer—I had to remember which button to press on this contraption," Mildred said with a faint chuckle.

"No need to apologize, Mildred," Debbie said, leaning against the counter. "I just wanted to check on you two, with the snowstorm and all. How are you both holding up?"

"Oh, we're fine," Mildred replied breezily, though there was a strain in her voice Debbie didn't like. "Harold and I are bundled up under quilts on the couch. It's actually kind of cozy if you think about it."

The image of the elderly couple huddled under blankets while snow piled against their home tugged at Debbie's heart. "Mildred," she began, her tone sharper now, "do you have enough firewood? And have you checked Harold's bandages this morning?"

There was a noticeable pause on the other end of the line.

"Well," Mildred hedged, "we haven't gotten to his bandages yet. It's just been so cold, and I figured it was better to keep him warm with the quilts than to be fussing with that right away."

Debbie's nursing instincts immediately screamed at her that something was wrong. "Mildred, be honest with me. Is Harold okay? Is there anything else you're not telling me?"

"Oh, he's hanging in there," Mildred said, almost as if she were trying to convince herself. "He's just... tired, you know? The cold takes a lot out of him. But with the power out, we're doing the best we can."

"Mildred," Debbie said, her voice firm but gentle, "that's it—I'm coming over."

Mildred gasped, "Oh no, Debbie, you don't have to do that! It's too dangerous out there, with the roads and all."

Debbie shook her head, already pulling her thick socks from the laundry basket nearby as she spoke. "Don't argue with me about this. Your family to me, and I won't sit here worrying when I can lend a hand. I'll be there in a few minutes."

She ended the call before Mildred could protest further and immediately started yanking on her boots, adrenaline pumping. She barely registered Nathan and Danielle as they shuffled into the kitchen, bleary-eyed and wrapped in blankets.

"Mom?" Nathan asked, rubbing at the wisps of dark brown hair that flopped messily onto his forehead. "What's going on?"

"Harold and Mildred need help," Debbie said briskly, grabbing her coat and medical bag from the hooks near the door. "Their power is out too, and I think they're out of firewood. Harold hasn't had his bandages changed, either. I need to get there now."

Danielle, more awake now, straightened, concern flashing in her hazel eyes. "What do you need us to do?"

Debbie paused just long enough to give her twins a hug. "I need you to stay here. Make sure the fire stays fed and maybe start clearing snow off the front porch if you're up to it. I'll feel better knowing you're both here at home."

Nathan's gaze flickered toward the window. "Are you sure it's safe to go out there, Mom?"

"It's nothing the snowmobile can't handle," she assured him, slipping on her gloves. "You two will be fine here—think you can keep the place running without me for a couple of hours?"

Danielle smirked, pulling her hair into a haphazard ponytail. "We've got this. Just be careful, okay?"

Debbie gave her daughter a grateful nod before pushing out the back door. The cold was immediate and biting, clawing through her coat like icy needles. She moved quickly down the porch steps, her boots crunching against the snow.

Caleb turned as she approached. "Debbie?"

"Harold and Mildred need help," she called back, her voice muffled slightly by the wind. "I think they've run low on firewood. I've got to go."

Caleb frowned, but his movements were already decisive. "Hang on. You're not going out there alone," he said, dropping the shovel against the porch railing before striding toward the pole barn to follow her.

"You don't have to—"

"I know I don't have to," Caleb pulled open the barn door with a determined stride, and the two hurried inside to escape the biting wind. Without wasting a moment, he moved to the snowmobile and unscrewed the gas cap. Grabbing the nearby fuel can, Caleb refilled the tank with practiced efficiency. Once the machine was topped off, he tightened the cap, gave a firm tug on the starter cord, and the engine roared to life.

Debbie climbed onto the back of the snowmobile as Caleb mounted the driver's seat.

She grabbed onto the back of his coat as the snowmobile lurched forward, cutting its way through the yard and up the treacherous snow-covered mountain road. The wind stung as it whipped against her face.

By the time they reached the Hughes' farmhouse, Debbie and Caleb were both stiff and chilled to the bone from the bitter cold. The small, snow-draped home stood quiet against the backdrop of the storm, its stillness filling them with a renewed sense of urgency.

Caleb barely waited for Debbie to climb off the snowmobile before striding toward the front porch. He grabbed the snow-covered shovel leaning against the house and immediately began clearing the heavy drifts piled high against the front door. His movements were quick and efficient, the scrape of the shovel cutting through the silence, while Debbie waited, her breath forming clouds in the icy air.

Within minutes, Caleb had cleared enough of the snow away from the front door. His movements were swift but purposeful, driven by a sense of urgency.

Debbie didn't hesitate, pushing against the reluctant door until it swung open with a small puff of cold air. The sight inside tugged at her chest. Mildred was huddled on the couch, layered in quilts, her small frame barely visible. Harold lay beside her, pale and still, his breathing shallow but steady.

"Debbie!" Mildred exclaimed, her relief palpable as she struggled to sit up straighter. "You really didn't need to come all this way—"

"Hush now," Debbie said gently, already moving toward Harold. She removed her gloves and knelt beside him, her nurse's instincts taking over as she quickly assessed his condition.

Behind her, Caleb entered, shaking snow off his boots. "Firewood?" he asked.

"In the shed out back," Mildred said, her voice trembling slightly. "It's under a tarp... but with all that snow..."

"I'll find it," Caleb said simply, disappearing out the door again.

As Debbie finished her initial assessment of both Mildred and Harold, ensuring they were stable for the time being, she caught the sound of Caleb's purposeful footsteps moving in and out of the house. Each rhythmic thud was followed by a blast of cold air as he returned with armloads of firewood. Moments later, the satisfying whoosh of flames catching in the old hearth filled the quiet farmhouse, the crackle of burning logs breaking through the lingering chill. Caleb worked with an efficient determination, never lingering too long before disappearing back into the storm, seeking to replenish the couple's firewood supply.

Debbie could see the color returning to Mildred's cheeks as the room gradually warmed, but for Harold, still pale and bundled beneath layers of blankets, the warmth was taking longer to work its way to him. She didn't want to risk exposing him to the cold air just yet, which meant holding off on changing his bandages until the room was a little more hospitable. Deciding to make herself useful in the meantime, Debbie made her way to the kitchen, where the wood stove Caleb had stoked to life radiated a welcome heat.

Scanning the shelves above the kitchen counter, Debbie's eyes landed on row after row of neatly labeled jars of soup that Mildred had clearly canned herself at some point. Selecting a couple of jars, she quickly emptied their contents into a pot and set it on the wood stove. The familiar scent of home-cooked broth began to waft through the room, mixing pleasantly with the aroma of burning wood.

Spotting the percolator on the counter, she sighed in relief. "This'll do," she murmured, reaching for it with one hand while rummaging for coffee grounds with the other. As the pot began to bubble faintly atop the wood stove, Debbie felt warmth beginning to creep back into the bones of the house.

"Looks like you've got that under control," Caleb's voice rumbled from nearby, startling Debbie slightly. She turned to see him brushing snow from his jacket, his boots leaving wet prints in their wake on the old wooden floor. He carried another heavy armload of wood, his cheeks ruddy from the cold, hair damp beneath his knit cap. Without a word, he crossed to the hearth and began building a neat stack of logs beside it, ensuring there was plenty of fuel within easy reach for a few days.

"If you give me a few minutes," Debbie said, half-turning from the stove as she stirred the soup. "I'll help bring in more firewood."

Caleb arched an eyebrow, his movements steady and calm. "You've got enough to deal with. Just keep doing what you're doing," he replied in his low drawl.

Debbie nodded in agreement.

As Caleb headed back out again for another load of firewood, Debbie glanced toward the staircase. A thought struck her. She walked back into the living room to where Mildred sat wrapped in a cocoon of quilts. "Mildred, do you have extra blankets or quilts around? Maybe ones we could use as makeshift curtains?"

Mildred tilted her head in thought, her silver hair catching the light from the fire. "Oh, yes, of course. There's a whole stack of old quilts in the hall closet upstairs."

Debbie nodded, already halfway across the room. "Perfect. I'm going to grab them."

Upstairs, she found the hall closet Mildred had mentioned. As she opened it, a faint aroma of lavender drifted out—Mildred's old sachets tucked among the neatly folded layers of fabric. Debbie quickly selected several thick quilts and blankets, hefting the stack into her arms before heading back downstairs.

She scanned the downstairs layout quickly, assessing where the warm air from the fire was being lost. The staircase was a natural culprit, funneling heat upward into the unused spaces. The narrow hallway downstairs to the right of the staircase, leading to the back bedroom and bathroom, pulled warmth away from the living area. Both areas would need to be blocked off. Digging through one of Harold's junk drawers in the kitchen, Debbie found an old tin of push pins. Between makeshift engineering and a little creativity, she began tacking up the quilts and blankets over the door frames leading to the hallway and across the open space at the base of the stairs.

With both makeshift curtains secured, the house seemed to wrap itself tighter in coziness, the warm air slowly but surely being trapped within the living spaces.

By the time she returned to the kitchen, Caleb had come back inside. He stood beside the wood stove, adjusting the placement of the soup pot, stirring its contents carefully with a wooden spoon. The percolator beside him had already finished brewing, and the rich, nutty scent of coffee filled the small farmhouse kitchen.

"Well, look at you," Debbie said, a hint of teasing warmth in her voice as she grabbed mismatched bowls from one of the cabinets.

"Figured you seemed busy enough, so I thought I'd pitch in." He handed her the spoon as she approached.

"It's Mildred's," Debbie replied with a wink. "Home-canned... and it smells and looks so good."

"It'll do the job," Caleb said simply, stepping aside to let her take over.

He held the bowls while she ladled the steaming soup. He placed the bowls on a cookie sheet he had found in a cabinet, and then poured freshly brewed coffee into mismatched tin coffee cups.

Debbie carried the baking sheet into the living room with steady hands.

Harold stirred as Debbie set the baking sheet on the coffee table. The warmth in the room had clearly begun to revive him, and his eyes fluttered open as Mildred patted his head.

"Well now," he murmured, his voice hoarse but filled with faint amusement, "what's all the fuss about? A man can't even nap through a snowstorm without being waited on hand and foot?"

Debbie chuckled softly as she helped Harold sit up, then carefully placed a warm mug of coffee in his hands. "Nothing wrong with a little pampering, Harold. Just let us fuss—Mildred and I have things under control."

Caleb stood nearby, arms crossed, watching.

Harold raised an eyebrow as he noticed him and grinned. "Well, well, guess Mildred and I must be more important than I thought."

Caleb simply smiled.

"You two go ahead and enjoy this soup and coffee," Debbie said. "It'll warm you up and give you some strength. Mildred, is there anything else you need? Anything at all we can take care of while we're here?"

Mildred shifted slightly on the couch as she cast Debbie a grateful but hesitant look. "Oh, Debbie, honey, you've already gone above and beyond just by getting here in this mess. We've got most of what we need, I think. Between you and this young man,"—she nodded toward Caleb—" we're more than looked after."

Debbie wasn't convinced. She could see the weariness etched into Mildred's normally lively features, the subtle tremor in her hands as she held her coffee cup. Decades of independent living had made Mildred proud and self-sufficient, but this storm was testing even her mountain-hardened resilience.

"We're here now, Mildred," Debbie pressed gently, her nurse's intuition kicking in. "Let us help. What about getting your kitchen restocked? I saw all of your canned foods, but if there's anything fresh you're running low on, I can bring it over if I have it."

"And I'll come check on you both and bring more firewood in until the power is restored," Caleb added, his voice steady and grounded as he tossed another log onto the fire. The flickering orange glow danced across his features, softening the edge of his ruggedness.

Mildred glanced between the two of them, her blue eyes glistening just enough to betray her emotions. "You two... I don't even know what to say. Harold and I don't have much family left, and our kids are hours away. It's just... a comfort, knowing you care enough to come all this way to help us."

Debbie smiled, crouching beside her to gently adjust the quilt on her lap as she spoke. "We're family, whether we share blood or not. You've always been there for me and the twins, with your advice and prayers... It's just our turn to give back."

As if on cue, Harold stirred, his voice hoarse but laced with his trademark humor. "Well now, if I didn't know better, I'd think we'd won the lottery of good neighbors." He glanced at Caleb. "And what might this fellow's name be?"

Debbie let out a small laugh, relieved to hear Harold's spirit reemerging despite his weakened state. "This is Caleb Warren," she said, glancing over her shoulder. "He's—well, he's been quite the lifesaver since he crashed into my life a couple of days ago."

"Technically, I slid off the mountain and down into your yard," Caleb corrected dryly, though his lips twitched in amusement. He extended a hand toward Harold in a firm but careful grip. "It's good to meet you, sir."

Harold gave a nod of approval, his sharp eye clearly sizing Caleb up before settling back against the couch with a faint grin. "Well, if you're the type to dive headfirst into storms to help folks, you'll do just fine."

Mildred cleared her throat, drawing their attention as her kind, weathered face shifted into a grateful smile. "I think you both have done more than enough for us. Harold and I... we're truly thankful. I don't know how we would've managed without you today."

"Hush now, Mildred," Debbie replied gently, her tone filled with warmth but firm enough to dismiss the idea of receiving praise. She crouched beside Harold, who had begun to sip his steaming bowl of soup, the color gradually returning to his cheeks. "You don't need to thank us. This is what neighbors do for each other."

Looking up briefly at Caleb, who stood quietly leaning on the doorway, watching over the scene with his typical understated presence, Debbie gave him a small nod before turning her attention back to Harold. "While you work on that soup, Harold," she said, her tone as cheerful as the flickering firelight, "I'm going to check your leg and change your bandages. Then we'll get out of your hair and let you two rest properly."

"Oh, don't rush off on our account," Harold said in his usual teasing way, though his words carried an edge of weariness. He gestured vaguely toward the front window. "Doesn't seem like the kind of day you want to go traipsing back out into."

Debbie patted his arm gently, her smile soft but resolute. "We'll be fine, Harold. Just let me take care of this, alright?" Without another word, she carefully peeled back the layers of quilts covering his injured leg, her fingers deft but gentle as she began her inspection.

The bandages were damp from condensation caused by the layers of quilts he'd been covered in, but fortunately, the wound itself looked stable, albeit in need of cleaning. Debbie moved with practiced efficiency. She worked in calm, measured silence, only breaking it to ask Harold occasional questions about his pain levels or stiffness.

Mildred, for her part, watched on with a mix of gratitude and worry. Her thin, work-worn hands gripped the edges of her quilt tightly, her brows knit together. "You're sure he'll be alright?" she asked softly, directing the question as much to herself as to Debbie.

Debbie cast her a reassuring glance, the corners of her mouth lifting in a small but confident smile. "He's doing just fine, Mildred. The wound is healing nicely. It still needs monitoring, and I'll call and check on you again later. You've taken good care of him."

The tension in Mildred's posture eased slightly, and she nodded, reaching out to run a gentle hand over Harold's arm. "Well, having you here... it's a blessing, Debbie. That's what it is."

"Blessing or not," Harold grumbled good-naturedly, wincing just slightly as Debbie dabbed antiseptic on his wound, "this leg of mine's got no business making such a fuss over a little fall."

"A little fall?" Debbie said, raising an eyebrow. "Harold, you fell off the back porch steps."

Harold's eyes lit up with amusement as a deep chuckle rumbled from his chest. "Oh, it was just a little tumble," he said with a wave of his hand, as though brushing off the severity of the incident.

Debbie shook her head but couldn't help the smile that tugged at her lips as she finished securing the bandage. "Alright, all done," she announced, standing up and stepping back to inspect her handiwork. "You're all set for now, but you need to keep it elevated as much as possible, alright?"

"Yes sir, Doctor Debbie," Harold teased, giving her a playful salute before taking another sip of his soup.

Debbie grinned as she packed away her supplies, zipping up her medical bag with practiced ease. She gave Mildred a light, playful tap on the shoulder, her tone conspiratorial. "Now, it's your job to make sure he actually listens, alright?"

"Oh, don't you worry about that," Mildred said, her sharp blue eyes sparkling with mischief. "If I have to sit on him to make him behave, I surely will."

The room erupted in warm laughter. The sound filling the small farmhouse and chasing away the weary stillness that had greeted Caleb and Debbie upon their arrival.

Caleb cleared his throat, his low, steady voice cutting gently through the moment. "I've stacked enough firewood to last a few days," he said, his gaze shifting between Harold and Mildred. "You've got a good stockpile within reach now."

Mildred looked at Caleb, her expression softening into something almost maternal. "You're a good man, Caleb Warren."

Caleb shifted slightly, clearly unused to such direct kindness, but he nodded in acknowledgment. "Just doing my part," he said simply.

Debbie placed a quilt around Harold's shoulder before stepping toward the door. "You two get some rest now, alright? You've got enough supplies and firewood to keep you comfortable, but if anything changes—anything—you call me, okay?"

"We will, sweet girl," Mildred promised, her voice gentle yet firm. "But you make sure to get home safe. Those sweet kids of yours need you, too."

Debbie pulled her coat tightly around herself, bracing against the chill that waited beyond the door. She paused by the entryway, her hand resting lightly on the door frame. "Take care," she said warmly. "We'll check in soon."

As Debbie and Caleb stepped outside, the icy wind lashed against them, sharp and unrelenting. Caleb moved ahead with purpose, starting the snowmobile in a matter of seconds. He turned, offering his hand to help Debbie climb on before settling into his own seat.

Debbie wrapped her arms tightly around his middle, bracing against the cold. She pressed her face into the back of his coat, seeking refuge from the biting wind as they set off. Around them, the world blurred into a swirl of white as they pushed forward, heading back toward the warmth and safety of home.

Chapter 19

The hum of the snowmobile's engine echoed softly through the snow-laden trees as Caleb steered the machine down the steep, snow-covered road toward Debbie's cabin. The storm had left the world cloaked in bone-deep cold, yet Caleb felt a warmth that defied the frozen landscape. It wasn't from the pale winter sun or the layers of his coat—it came from the quiet, undeniable presence of Debbie, her arms wrapped around him, a reminder that even in the coldest moments, something deeper could thaw the edges of his guarded heart.

As they neared the cabin, Debbie's heart swelled with pride at the sight of Nathan and Danielle. Bundled in coats and scarves, their cheeks flushed from the cold, the twins worked together, clearing a path in the driveway.

Caleb guided the snowmobile smoothly around the cabin to the pole barn, cutting a neat path through the thick drifts of snow. Once inside the barn, shielded from the biting wind, Caleb turned off the engine, and silence rushed in to fill the space.

Sliding off the snowmobile, he reached out, his gloved hand steady and sure as he extended it toward Debbie. His dark eyes met hers. "Need a hand?" he asked.

Debbie hesitated for just a beat before slipping her hand into his. As he helped her down, the world around them seemed to still, their closeness amplifying the charge in the crisp winter air. This abrupt awareness left her cheeks warm, though she wasn't sure whether to blame the chill fading from her skin or the sparks Caleb seemed to leave in his wake.

She tightened her grip on his hand and didn't let go. Caleb noticed his gaze shifting downward to their hands before slowly lifting back to her face.

"Thank you," she said.

His brow furrowed slightly, not in doubt but in curiosity. "For what?" he asked.

Debbie searched his face, reading the quiet humility beneath his patience.

She let go of his hand and gently placed both of hers on either side of his face, as if to ensure he truly felt the weight of the words she was about to speak—the undeniable truth of who he was.

"For being the kind of man who shows up when it matters," she said. "For being you."

Caleb blinked. He opened his mouth as if to reply, but words failed him. There was humility there, but also something deeper—something wounded and uncertain, like a man unaccustomed to praise so genuine.

"I don't... think I'm all that special," he said, his words quiet but layered with a hint of self-deprecation.

"I think you are, Caleb," Debbie replied with a small, reassuring smile. "And I think you need to know that."

Her words hung in the air between them, fragile yet resolute, like snowflakes that refused to melt.

"You are so much more than you give yourself credit for, Caleb," Debbie said, her hands still cradling his face. Her hazel eyes searched his, warm and steady. "I'm glad the storm brought us together. You've made a difference in my life—one I won't forget."

Clearing his throat, Caleb glanced toward the barn doors. "We'd better get inside before you catch cold," he said, the practicality in his voice softening the weight of what had just passed between them.

Debbie smiled and nodded, turning toward the cabin. As she walked ahead, Caleb lingered a few steps behind, his gloved hands tucked into his coat pockets. His eyes followed her, captivated by the easy grace in her movements. Her laughter carried back to him, light and warm, as she called out to Nathan and Danielle, who had resumed shoveling the path from the back porch where he had left off earlier. In that moment, Caleb felt an unshakable truth settle over him: she was everything he hadn't realized he was searching for—steady, resilient, and filled with a quiet, unyielding strength.

He watched as Debbie grabbed a shovel and seamlessly joined her twins. Snowflakes clung delicately to her hair, glinting like silver threads, but the glow of her warmth outshone the winter's chill. Nathan and Danielle's laughter rang out, bright and uninhibited, weaving together with Debbie's own chuckles in a harmony that was both effortless and infectious. The trio worked together in a quiet, instinctual rhythm—clearing paths through the snow with a shared determination, punctuated by playful quips and affectionate nudges. What could have been a grueling task became almost cheerful, transformed by their connection into something lighter. They didn't complain or hesitate; instead, they found ways to embrace the moment, savoring small glimmers of joy amid the cold.

Life could be like this, Caleb realized—a little chaotic, a little uncertain, but undeniably good. It didn't have to be a solitary march of routine, day after day, burdened by silence and self-reliance. There could be connection. There could be warmth. The notion felt unfamiliar, almost distant, nudging gently but persistently at the edges of his guarded heart, daring him to let it in.

He stood motionless in the snow, captivated by the moment unfolding before him. Debbie glanced back over her shoulder, her hazel eyes locking onto his. They shimmered with warmth, but it was her smile that stopped him—the kind of smile that needed no words. It wasn't laced with pity or weighed down by expectation. It was simply grace—quiet, unassuming, and utterly genuine.

"Are you planning to grab a shovel, or should we expect the supervisor treatment from you?" Debbie teased, her voice dancing with a light humor that carried just a touch of playful challenge.

Caleb's lips tugged into the faintest smirk. "Supervising looks like the easier job."

Nathan's head popped up as he rested an elbow on his shovel, his grin as wide as his mother's. "Easier, maybe, but not as satisfying. C'mon, Caleb."

"Yeah, we could use some strong arms over here!" Danielle chimed in.

Caleb lingered for a moment, his gaze sweeping over the yard, not because clearing snow was foreign to him, but because the scene unfolding before him was. For the first time in years, he caught a glimpse of a life he hadn't let himself imagine—a life filled with warmth, connection, and shared purpose. The weight of that realization rooted him in place, both humbling and quietly stirring something deep within.

Caleb strode across the yard and picked up the spare shovel propped against the porch railing. Without hesitation, he joined the group, his movements smooth and practiced, as though the task was second nature. Together, they worked seamlessly, their efforts creating a steady symphony of scraping metal against compacted snow. Lively chatter drifted through the crisp air, punctuated by the occasional burst of laughter and Nathan's well-aimed snowball antics, which kept the mood light despite the winter chill.

Debbie sidled up next to Caleb at one point, her cheeks rosy from the cold, her breath fogging in the crisp evening air. "Not bad for a supervisor," she teased softly, her voice just low enough for him to hear.

"Not bad for a forewoman," Caleb shot back, his lips quirking into a grin.

Once the path was cleared, Debbie and Caleb made their way to the woodshed as Nathan and Danielle dashed toward the pole barn. Moments later, Nathan emerged, pushing a wheelbarrow, while Danielle drove the side-by-side, towing a cart behind it. Laughter rippling through the cold air as they joined their mom and Caleb near the woodshed. The foursome worked seamlessly, loading firewood into the cart and wheelbarrow with practiced ease. Each load was hauled to the cabin's back porch, where it was neatly stacked for the days ahead. Trip by trip, the four moved in steady rhythm, their teamwork transforming the work into a shared, lighthearted effort.

Caleb glanced over at Debbie, catching sight of her flushed cheeks, their rosy hue deepening against the stark white of the snow. A loose strand of hair had slipped from beneath her hat, dancing against her face in the crisp winter breeze. She bent to grab a piece of firewood, her movements precise yet carrying the quiet exhaustion of hours spent battling the cold. Caleb stepped closer, his gloved hand resting lightly yet firmly on her forearm as she straightened.

His touch stilled her, and she looked up, a question in her hazel eyes. "Why don't you and Danielle head inside for a while? Nathan and I can finish up and tackle the driveway afterward."

Debbie hesitated, scanning his face. "Caleb, I'm not about to let you and Nathan—"

"Mom," Nathan interrupted from behind her, his tone bordering on teasing but laced with warmth, "you know he's right. Go warm up for a while. Don't worry—we've got this."

Debbie looked between the two men, her son's boyish smirk and Caleb's steady, reassuring gaze. Before she could argue further, Danielle chimed in, tugging on her mother's jacket sleeve.

"Come on, Mom. I think we've earned a cup of hot cocoa and a little downtime. Let the guys handle the rest." Her voice was light, but there was a pleading note in it that made Debbie relent.

"All right," Debbie said with a small huff

"We'll hold down the fort, Nurse Ferguson," Caleb said.

"I'm sure you both will," Debbie replied as she and Danielle turned to climb the back porch steps.

·Caleb and Nathan moved the last load of firewood onto the porch, their breaths puffing into the crisp, frozen air as they worked. With a final nod of satisfaction at their neatly stacked pile, they turned and reached for their shovels.

As they rounded the side of the cabin, Caleb glanced over at Nathan, catching the glint of mischief in the teenager's eye. The look was so familiar it made Caleb pause—it reminded him of his younger self, brimming with quiet confidence and the playful edge of a challenge.

"All right," Caleb said. "Think you've got what it takes to keep up?"

Nathan's grin widened. "Keep up?" he shot back with a mock scoff. "I was about to ask if you could handle it."

Caleb let out a low chuckle. "Kid," he said with a smirk, planting the sharp edge of his shovel into the packed snow, "we'll see who's keeping up with whom."

"Keep up? I'm about to leave you in the dust... or, well, snow."

Caleb smirked, shaking his head. "We'll see about that."

The two worked side by side, their shovels plunging into the dense snow in steady rhythm, lifting and tossing what the storm had left behind. Despite the cold and labor of their work, they fell into an easy cadence, shovels scraping, boots crunching, and idle conversation filling the air.

"So," Nathan started, stealing a quick glance at Caleb, "you've been around a few days now... What do you think of my mom?"

Caleb paused mid-motion, caught off guard not by the question itself, but by the boldness of it. "I think she's a tough lady," he said simply. "The kind who doesn't back down from much. You don't meet people like her every day."

Nathan studied him, as if weighing his words for authenticity, before nodding slowly. "She is," he said with quiet pride, kicking a tuft of snow with his boot. "A bit stubborn, though."

"Yeah, I've picked up on that," Caleb replied with a chuckle, leaning back into his work.

"She's been through a lot, you know," Nathan said after a pause. "Not just with Dad... but with life. It hasn't exactly gone easy on her."

Caleb stopped and looked at the young man beside him, sensing the weight of the truth in his words. "She doesn't let it show much," Caleb said, his voice low, contemplative. "She carries herself like someone who's had to fight for everything but doesn't want to burden anyone else with it."

Nathan nodded, his Adam's apple bobbing as he swallowed hard. "She's the strongest person I know," he said firmly, his voice carrying an edge of protective pride. "Which, ironically, makes it really hard to take care of her. She's not great at letting people help her, you know?"

"I'd gathered that," Caleb replied.

"She does care about you, though," Nathan added, throwing the observation out there like a stray snowball, gauging Caleb's response.

Caleb paused in his work and turned to Nathan, his expression thoughtful yet firm. "I care about her too," he said, his voice steady and sincere. "She's an incredible woman—someone any man would be lucky to stand beside as an equal. She deserves respect, admiration, and people surrounding her that lift her up, and never diminish her. I'd never do anything to hurt her, Nathan. You don't need to doubt that."

Nathan remained quiet for a moment, his gaze steady, as if weighing Caleb's words. He extended his hand.

Without hesitation, Caleb reached out, clasping Nathan's hand in a firm, steady grip.

Without missing a beat, Nathan scooped up a shovelful of snow and flicked it deliberately in Caleb's direction, a mischievous grin spreading across his face. "On that note, don't think you're getting off easy. There's still plenty of snow to shovel."

Caleb let out a deep, rumbling laugh. "Fair enough," he replied, a faint smirk tugging at the corners of his mouth.

Chapter 20

"Frozen," Danielle declared dramatically, stamping snow from her boots onto the old rug by the back door. "Mom, I'm officially a human popsicle. Pretty sure I can't feel my toes anymore."

Debbie chuckled as she removed her scarf, hanging it on a hook near the door. "I don't want to hear it," she teased. "I've been out in colder weather than this when you were still toddling around demanding grilled cheese for every meal."

Danielle's laugh bubbled up, filling the cozy space of the cabin. "Still wouldn't say no to a grilled cheese right now." She kicked off her boots, wiggling her socked toes, then quickly walked into the living room, sticking her hands out toward the fire in the fireplace. "What's next, Mom? Is there an official guide to surviving a snowbound apocalypse? Should I start whittling a spear for hunting?"

Debbie grinned and stepped further into the warm space, rubbing her hands together to chase away the residual cold. "Step one," she said, her tone light and playful, "is adding more wood to that fire so we don't turn into human icicles. Would you mind tackling that for me?"

Danielle snapped off a mock salute. "Aye aye, Captain. Operation Firewood is officially underway."

While Danielle busied herself with stoking the fire, Debbie cast a thoughtful glance toward the kitchen.

"What's the plan for dinner? I'm starving," Danielle called over her shoulder.

Debbie's eyes swept across the kitchen as she deliberated. "I'm thinking chili and peanut butter and jelly sandwiches will work," she said as she headed into the kitchen.

Rummaging through the pantry, Debbie was relieved to find four large cans of chili. She grabbed the peanut butter and set it on the counter, adding the jelly retrieved from the fridge. A loaf of bread from a nearby shelf rounded out the lineup.

Back in the living room, Danielle gave the logs a final shove with the poker, smiling as the fire roared back to life with fresh energy. Satisfied with her handiwork, she wandered into the kitchen.

"What can I do to help?" she asked.

"Start opening these cans," she replied, motioning to the chili on the counter. "I'll be back after I get the generator running."

Debbie slipped her coat on again, pulled the back door open, and stepped out into the biting chill. She took a moment to pull her collar up higher around her neck and glanced down at the porch, noting the sprinkling of salt on the wooden planks. The sight made her stop short. It hadn't been there just a few minutes ago when she and Danielle had stepped inside together. There was only one explanation: Caleb.

She stepped down carefully, grateful for the traction. A gesture like that wasn't something loud or showy, but it spoke volumes. Caleb knew what was needed and quietly handled it.

She could faintly hear Nathan's laugh carried on the icy breeze, buoyant and free and Caleb's deep, gravelly chuckle mingling with her son's. Debbie paused mid-step, turning her head slightly, listening as the sound sparked a smile. She didn't know what they were saying, but from the rhythm of it, she could tell it was playful, relaxed.

Debbie hurried to restart the generator, the engine sputtering to life with a reassuring hum. She rushed back inside, the bitter cold trailing in behind her as she stomped the snow from her boots onto the rug by the back door and removed her coat.

"Mission accomplished?" Danielle asked, raising her brows as she emptied the last can of chili into a large microwave-safe bowl.

Debbie grinned as she stepped into the kitchen. "Generator's purring like a kitten."

"Thank goodness," Danielle replied.

Debbie nodded toward the counter. "Alright, you take sandwich duty. Bread, peanut butter, jelly... it's all yours. I'll handle the soup and setting the table."

"Are we calling the boys in soon?" Danielle asked, spreading jelly across the bread with swift, even strokes.

"As soon as this heats up," Debbie replied, punching in the time on the microwave and watching as the bowl spun slowly inside.

The warm, savory aroma of chili soon filled the kitchen. For Debbie, the simple meal carried a nostalgic charm—it transported her back to childhood winters, sitting in this very kitchen as her mom made the same hearty dish. The memory was vivid, etched with the crackle of the fire and the sound of her mother's soothing voice.

Danielle worked contentedly, a soft tune escaping her lips as she cut sandwiches into neat triangles, arranging them with care on a plate. Watching her, Debbie couldn't help but smile, the scene mirroring her own childhood. She could see herself as a young teen standing beside her mother, learning to find joy in even the simplest tasks of preparing a meal together.

Debbie turned her attention to brewing a pot of coffee, the familiar gurgle and hiss adding another layer of comfort to the cozy kitchen. As the coffee brewed, she set out bowls, spoons, and napkins, arranging them on the table with practiced ease.

"All right," Debbie said at last, wiping her hands on a towel and breaking the quiet rhythm of the room. "Let's call them in before they turn into snowmen."

Danielle bounded to the front door, her feet thudding against the hardwood floor. With a swift tug, she threw it open, the cold rushing in like an eager guest. Shivering slightly but grinning widely, she leaned out into the snowy air, cupping her hands around her mouth.

"Hey!" she called, her voice cutting through the crisp silence. "You two! Don't make me come out there—I'm too cold for that! Dinner's ready, so get moving already!"

Her playful tone carried easily across the snow-covered yard, beckoning Nathan and Caleb, who stood in the driveway, shovels paused mid-motion. They exchanged brief, knowing smiles before turning toward the house.

A few moments later, the back door opened, and Caleb and Nathan stepped into the warmth of the cabin, shaking off snowflakes and shedding their outer layers with eager haste. "Smells good in here," Caleb said, his deep voice carrying a note of appreciation.

"You're welcome, by the way," Danielle said, hands on her hips as she gestured dramatically toward the table, where the chili and sandwiches were neatly arranged. "This didn't just appear on its own."

Caleb raised an eyebrow, the corner of his mouth twitching with amusement. "I figured as much, and thank you."

"Hope you guys are hungry. We've made enough to feed an army." Danielle replied.

The twins and Caleb settled around the table as Debbie filled their bowls with generous servings of steaming chili. Once everyone was served, she took her own seat.

Nathan reached out his hand toward her. On his left, his other hand extended toward Caleb, who hesitated for a split second before taking it.

Danielle joined in with ease, clasping her mom's hand on one side and Caleb's on the other.

Nathan cleared his throat, his voice quiet but steady as he led them in prayer. "Heavenly Father," he began, his tone a little hesitant at first, "thank You for this meal, for keeping us safe through the storm, and for giving us a warm place to be together. Thank You for the help You've sent our way and for bringing Caleb to us when we needed it. Please watch over us and everyone else dealing with this weather. And...thank You for showing us that even in hard times, we've got so much to be grateful for. Amen."

"Amen," Danielle echoed softly, squeezing her mother's hand before letting go.

Caleb cleared his throat and reached for his spoon. "Well, Nathan," he began, a faint smile playing at the corner of his lips, "it seems your skills extend beyond shoveling snow and cracking jokes."

Nathan grinned, reaching for the plate of peanut butter and jelly sandwiches Debbie had set in the center of the table. "What can I say? I've got range."

Debbie leaned back in her chair and took a bite of her sandwich as her eyes drifted toward Caleb.

For a brief second, their eyes met. She smiled and returned her attention to her food.

"So, Caleb," Danielle began after a sip of water, "what's your go-to blizzard food? I mean, I imagine you've survived a few of these storms up where you live."

Caleb raised a brow, leaning back slightly in his chair as he considered her question. "Canned soups. Sandwiches... something I can throw together quick."

"Practical," Nathan chimed in, nodding approvingly.

Throughout the meal, conversation flowed naturally, effortlessly—touching on snowy weather, school stories, even a few jokes at Caleb's expense, which he took with quiet grace.

Debbie watched him in those unguarded moments, his easy laughter blending seamlessly with the chatter of her children. He seemed at home here—relaxed, present, and somehow fitting perfectly into the rhythm of her little family.

She allowed her gaze to rest on him for just a heartbeat longer, her heart swelling with gratitude. *God,* she prayed silently, *thank You—for this meal, for the laughter of my children, for the unexpected kindness of someone who feels less like a stranger and more like a blessing. Thank You for always showing up in the moments that matter most.*

Chapter 21

Debbie stepped onto the porch, her breath forming faint clouds in the crisp, wintry air. She pulled her coat tighter around herself, the chill biting at her cheeks as she crossed to the wooden railing. Above her, the stars were scattered like diamonds on black velvet, their light steady and serene against the lingering frost of the storm. The snow blanketed the world, muffling it into a peaceful silence.

She leaned against the railing, staring at the frozen expanse of snow that stretched before her, glittering faintly in the moonlight. The evening had been everything warm memories were made of—filled with laughter, the familiar comfort of her children's voices, and a meal that felt far more special than its humble simplicity. Debbie had watched as Caleb, so often reserved and hard to read, opened up in small but meaningful ways within the cozy rhythm of her family dynamic. It had been an unexpected gift these past few days, seeing him relax, witnessing the easy bond building between him and Nathan, the way Danielle's humor disarmed him.

Now, under the vast and silent sky, the warmth of that time together gave way to something quieter—something reflective, almost weighty. The absence of voices left her alone with the truth she had been trying to keep at bay. It wasn't just the storm that had left Caleb in their lives. This felt bigger, more intentional. Like the start of something.

The thought scared her, but it also warmed a corner of her heart she had nearly forgotten. A gentle shift, subtle yet undeniable, was taking place, and she couldn't pretend not to notice.

Her eyes drifted skyward, searching for constellations that never moved, even when her world had. "Beautiful," she murmured softly.

"Sure is," a deep voice answered from behind her, low and steady enough to make her start slightly.

Debbie turned quickly, her hand flying to her chest in reflex. Caleb stood there, one hand resting lightly on the door frame leading back into the house. He was already in his coat, the edges of his frame briefly illuminated by the moonlight. His expression softened when he saw her small surprise, and after a beat, his face shifted into one of apology.

"Didn't mean to startle you," he said. "I saw you sneak out and figured you shouldn't have to freeze out here alone."

Her lips quirked upward, the faintest hint of a smile appearing. "Not sneaking, exactly," she replied, though her voice carried the warmth of amusement. "I just needed a few minutes of quiet. I guess I didn't expect company."

He stepped further onto the porch. The door creaking faintly as he shut it behind him. A fresh gust of icy wind curled between them, prompting him to stuff his hands into his coat pockets as he wandered toward the railing.

Caleb stopped a few feet away from her. He leaned against the railing, his gaze following hers out over the blanket of snow that reflected the moonlight like it was sprinkled with glitter. For a moment, they stood in shared silence, the quiet of the night folding around them like a heavy quilt.

"Moments like this," he said finally, his voice quiet but rich, "remind me there's still good in the world. Even when you forget to look for it."

Debbie glanced at him, surprised by the vulnerability in his words. "I know what you mean," she said. Her gaze lifted to the stars. "Sometimes it feels like the world's too heavy to carry. But then there's a moment like this, and it's like God reminds us He's still here. We just have to notice."

Caleb turned his head toward her, his eyes holding hers for a moment. "Noticing's the hard part," he said with a quiet, self-deprecating chuckle. "I spent years trying not to notice. Felt easier that way."

Her fingers brushed the cold wood of the railing as she considered his words. "Noticing can be scary," she admitted. "Because once you notice, you can't ignore it. You can't pretend anymore."

He nodded slowly, the weight of her words settling into the lines of his face. Somewhere in the distance, a tree creaked under the snow, the sound mournful but somehow fitting.

"I think," she said softly, "sometimes the noticing is what saves us. Even when it's hard. Even when it hurts. Grace... looks a lot like noticing, I think."

His shoulders eased, as though her words had reached something inside him. "Bonnie would've liked you," he said suddenly, his voice softer now.

Debbie caught her breath, the unexpected mention of his late wife deepening the surrounding quiet. "She must've been an incredible woman," she said gently, leaving space for him to share if he wanted.

"She was," he said, a faint smile tugging at his lips. "Strong. Stubborn. Kind in a way that stayed with people." He hesitated, his voice quieter when he added, "She had this way of seeing right through me, even when I didn't want her to."

Debbie's heart ached at the grief woven into his words. "She must've seen a lot to love," she said, her voice steady and sure.

Caleb blinked, his lips parting as if to argue, but instead, he let her words hang between them like frost on the trees. "She deserved better than me," he murmured.

"You mean the man who's been looking out for my family these past few days? The one who works hard and doesn't give up?" Debbie asked gently, her brow arching. "I don't know who you were back then, Caleb, but I know who you are now. And I think she'd be proud of that man."

Her words stilled him, his shoulders stiffening slightly before he let out a quiet breath. He didn't answer right away, and Debbie didn't press, sensing the shift in his spirit—quiet but undeniable.

After a moment, he said, "Before this storm, I didn't think I had much left to notice. But you and your kids... you've made me wonder if I was wrong about that."

Debbie swallowed hard, her voice barely above a whisper. "Sometimes God shows up in the people we least expect." She stepped closer, resting her gloved hand lightly on his arm. "You're still here, Caleb. That's not an accident."

His gaze lingered on her hand before meeting her eyes again. "Maybe you're right," he said quietly.

The first flakes of fresh snow began drifting from the sky, soft and unhurried.

Caleb tilted his head slightly, a faint smile playing at his lips. "Looks like the storm's not done with us."

Debbie smiled back, her hand slipping from his arm. "Maybe that's a good thing."

This time, Caleb didn't look away, and neither did Debbie.

Chapter 22

The soft hiss of the fire greeted Caleb as he knelt in front of the hearth, gently placing another log onto the glowing embers. Firelight danced across his weathered face, the warmth battling the predawn chill that lingered in the cabin. He sat back on his heels, staring at the flickering flames as if searching for answers. Silence surrounded him, broken only by the rhythmic breathing of the twins who lay sprawled on the floor, and Debbie on the couch cocooned in a tangle of blankets. Their faces—so innocent in sleep. The realization that he would be leaving soon weighed heavily on him, and he didn't want to leave this quiet, messy, wonderful scene.

Outside, the faint rumble of snowplows reverberated through the stillness, the sound growing louder as the first streak of light broke across the horizon. Caleb shifted his gaze to the window. The snow, which had blanketed them in isolation for days, was finally being pushed aside. The roads were clearing. His way home was opening. He should've felt relieved. Instead, a hollow ache expanded in his chest.

With a grunt, he pushed himself to his feet and walked into the kitchen and grabbed the coffeepot from the counter. Power had been restored at some point in the wee hours of the morning. It felt natural, this small motion—walking across Debbie's kitchen, filling the pot with water, measuring out the grounds. It shouldn't feel natural, he reminded himself. This place wasn't his home. These people weren't his family, but it was beginning to feel like they were.

The coffee maker hummed softly, filling the cabin with its rich, familiar aroma. Caleb inhaled deeply, closing his eyes, enjoying the rich scent he enjoyed in the quiet hours of the morning. Bonnie used to brew coffee first thing in the morning, humming quietly to herself while the world was still. He banished the memory, focusing instead on grabbing two mugs from the cabinet. One, he filled nearly to the brim, black and strong. The second, he left empty, just in case Debbie emerged wanting her coffee doctored with cream and sugar. The thought brought a faint smile to his lips. For someone so steady and practical, she had a surprisingly stubborn sweet tooth.

The sound of a floorboard creaking behind him made him turn. Debbie stood in the entryway to the kitchen, her blanket draped around her shoulders like a cape. Her hair was slightly mussed, her eyes heavy-lidded with sleep. Even in the dim light, he noticed the faint crease of a pillow pressed into her cheek. She looked... real, unguarded, natural, and it tugged at something deep inside him.

"You're up early," she murmured, her voice still thick with sleep.

"And you're not far behind," Caleb replied, his tone gentle. He nodded toward the coffeemaker. "Figured you'd surface sooner or later. Thought I'd get started on some coffee."

She smiled, small but genuine, and shuffled toward the counter. "You're full of surprises," she teased, rubbing at her eyes. "I wouldn't have pegged you for the domestic type."

"I wouldn't go that far," he said, handing her the empty mug. "Let's just say I'm a man who likes his coffee. Can't survive a cold morning without it."

Debbie took the mug, her fingers brushing his as she did. The brief contact was electric, though neither pulled away too quickly. Caleb cleared his throat, turning to drink his own coffee as Debbie doctored hers with a splash of creamer and an impressive heap of sugar.

"Not a fan of bitter coffee, are ya?" he asked, quirking a brow when he saw the exaggerated amount of sugar she stirred in.

Debbie scrunched her nose at him playfully. "Not all of us have the urge to drink it black. Some of us prefer to enjoy our coffee, not suffer through it."

"You don't know what you're missing."

She lifted her mug, blowing gently at the steam while fixing him with a mock-serious look. "I think it's safe to say we have different definitions of enjoyment." Then, with a boldness rare for her, she added, "But since you're so insistent, maybe I'll try it black one day... if you promise to try my version first."

A low chuckle rumbled from Caleb's chest, and Debbie's heart gave a faint flutter at the sound. "Deal," he said, raising his mug in mock salute before taking a long sip.

Caleb glanced toward the window, where the first light of dawn illuminated the snow-covered yard. His expression grew contemplative, his jaw tightening just slightly.

"The plows are out," she said, following his gaze. "Looks like the roads will be clear soon."

He nodded, his fingers tightening around his mug. "Storm's giving us back our world."

"Yes, I guess it is," she said, her voice gentle.

Caleb walked to the living room window, his broad shoulders outlined against the faint light of the morning. The rumble of a county plow trucks broke the stillness, their amber colored lights flashing rhythmically as they worked to clear the narrow mountain road. The snow-covered world was slowly being put back in order—one pass of the plow at a time.

Debbie stepped up beside him, cradling her mug of coffee in her hands. She leaned slightly on the side of the window frame, watching him for a moment before turning her gaze to the road.

"They're making good progress," she said. "It looks like you might actually be able to head home later today."

Caleb took a long sip of his coffee. He didn't answer right away, his gaze fixed on the plow as it pushed through the icy berm along the shoulder of the road. Finally, after a long breath, he spoke.

"Yeah," he said, his voice low, gravelly. "Looks that way."

There was weight in his tone, not the relief she had expected to hear, but something heavier—something more complex.

"You don't sound too excited about it," Debbie observed, glancing up at him, her head tilted slightly in curiosity.

"I guess I'm looking forward to getting back to work," Caleb admitted, swirling his coffee absently. "I'm not used to sitting around waiting for things to fix themselves. But getting back to the way life was before the storm..." He paused, leaning a forearm against the frame, his posture stiff. "I'm not so sure I'm ready for that."

Debbie studied his expression—the faint creases of his brow, the way his jaw seemed to tighten as if holding back words that wanted to tumble out. "Meaning?" she prompted.

"Meaning..." he began, choosing his words carefully. "I've been living in the same routine for years—work, come home, get through the day. It's quiet, it's safe, it's... manageable. But it's also lonely," he admitted, the last word spoken so softly she almost thought she'd misheard it.

Debbie blinked, surprised by his honesty. Caleb wasn't one to bare his soul easily. She could see the discomfort in the way his shoulders seemed to tense, the way his hand tightened just slightly around the mug he held, like it was anchoring him.

"Lonely," she repeated gently, not as a question but as an acknowledgment. "I think I know a little about that, too."

His eyes softened as they searched hers, and for a few moments, neither of them seemed to know what to say next.

"It's just..." Caleb said, breaking the stillness as he shifted, rubbing the back of his neck with his free hand. "Being here these past few days—it felt different. I don't know how to say this without sounding... I don't know..." He trailed off, shaking his head slightly, as if struggling to corral his thoughts.

"Go ahead," Debbie encouraged, her voice steady even as her heartbeat quickened. "Say it."

He looked at her then, really looked, and whatever battle he'd been waging internally seemed to settle just enough for him to speak.

"Being here felt right," he said simply. "It felt like... I don't know... life, I guess. Real life. Not the kind you just get through because you don't know any better. The kind that feels... worth something."

Debbie's breath caught, her fingers tightening around her mug as she let his words sink in. She hadn't expected anything so raw, so honest. But she understood. Deeply.

"That's not nothing," she said after a moment, her voice soft but certain.

He turned back toward the window, his profile partly shadowed in the soft morning light. "I've spent a lot of years convincing myself that keeping everything at arm's length was how you protect yourself. How you survive after losing someone. You don't let people in, you don't let it get too complicated, and you tell yourself that's enough."

"And now?" Debbie asked carefully.

"And now..." Caleb hesitated. "Now... I'm seeing my way of life is a habit. I've lived alone for so long, it's instinct. Now I'm starting to think maybe I've been protecting myself from the wrong thing. I've let the fear of losing... or maybe a better way to put... I've let a fear of living keep me from everything."

Debbie's chest tightened. She reached out instinctively, her fingers brushing his arm lightly.

He glanced down at her hand on his arm, then back at her face. "Being here these past few days... you and the kids... it's made me see what I've done to myself... what I've missed out on."

The honesty in his words, in his eyes, was almost too much. Debbie felt a lump rise in her throat as she struggled to put her own feelings into words.

"I think we've both been doing a lot of surviving and not living," she admitted, her voice trembling.

Caleb's gaze lingered on her. Something in her chest swirled—an ache, a hope, a fear.

"Debbie," he said.

"Yes?" she answered, her voice barely audible.

"I don't know how to do this," he said, his tone resolute but tender. "But I know I don't want to walk away and pretend none of this mattered." He hesitated, measuring his next words. "Do you?"

Her breath hitched as the question hung in the air between them, fragile and full of possibility. Slowly, she shook her head, a small, vulnerable smile tugging at the corners of her lips.

"No," she said simply. "I don't want that either."

Caleb's lips curved into a genuine smile—subtle, soft, but real. They didn't say anything more, but they didn't need to. Some moments didn't need resolution. They just needed to be felt, and both of them were feeling this one deeply.

The snowplow clattered loudly outside, breaking the moment but not dissolving it. Caleb turned back toward the window, exhaling a long breath.

"I guess we'll figure out what happens next," he said.

"I guess we will," Debbie echoed, her voice steady but full of quiet hope.

Chapter 23

Debbie adjusted her scarf tighter around her neck, grabbed a snow shovel, and stepped off the porch. Her breath puffed visibly into the brisk air, but the cold didn't bother her. Mornings like this were invigorating. The world seemed blanketed in peace, untouched by the chaos of daily life. Even the air smelled fresh, crisp, and clean in the way only winter mornings could manage.

She glanced back at Caleb, who was only a few steps behind her, carrying his own shovel. His broad shoulders were encased in his thick winter work coat, the collar turned up against the chill. A knit cap sat snugly on his head. His expression carried its usual rugged charm. Debbie couldn't help but smile. He looked as if he had been born to handle winters like this—steady, capable, unbothered.

Caleb scanned the stretch of driveway leading to the freshly cleared road. The county plows had done their job, but they'd also left a massive wall of heavy, compressed snow right at the edge of Debbie's driveway.

"I'm sure glad we tackled most of this yesterday," Caleb said, his low voice laced with amusement as he studied the hefty mound of snow blocking the end of the driveway. "This might take a while."

Debbie glanced from the blockade to Caleb, pulling her scarf a little tighter against the brisk air. "Yeah, but between the two of us, we can knock this out pretty quickly." Her eyes drifted to the side yard, landing on Caleb's truck, which was practically entombed in the snow. She tilted her head slightly, a playful curiosity lighting her expression. "How are you planning to get around now that life's returning to normal? That poor truck of yours looks like it's done for."

He followed her gaze to where the vehicle rested. It's normally rugged form, now a rounded mound under the weight of the storm. With a sigh, he planted his shovel in the snow and rested his hands on the top of the handle. "Yeah, that truck's probably seen its last winter. She got me through a lot of rough patches, but I have a feeling I'll either be towing her back home to work on in the summer or sending her off to the salvage yard for good."

Debbie frowned in sympathy, but there was a hint of teasing in her tone. "That sounds like a sad end for a workhorse like that. So, what's Plan B? You can't exactly hike your way to wherever you need to go."

Caleb's lips quirked just slightly at the corners, a soft grin barely noticeable against his usual stoic expression. "Got an old jeep tucked away in the barn at home. I don't drive it much—it's more sentimental than practical—but she runs like a dream. My dad bought it for me when I was a teenager. First vehicle I ever owned. We rebuilt the engine together." His voice softened slightly, carrying the weight of a memory that clearly meant a lot to him. "She's been around forever but still knows how to handle the road, even in weather like this."

Debbie straightened, her interest piqued. "A jeep, huh? Now that's got some charm. Sounds like it's got a little history wrapped in all that horsepower."

"It does," Caleb admitted, pulling the shovel back into his grip and turning his attention to the packed snow in front of them. "One of those things I could never part with. She's reliable, though—stubborn, maybe, but reliable."

Debbie smiled as she listened. There was something endearing about the way he spoke about the jeep, his rough edges softening as he shared a piece of his past. "Stubborn and reliable, huh?" she said, with a sly glance in his direction. "Funny—sounds a bit like you."

Caleb paused mid-shovel, turning to give her an appraising look, his brow raised. "Oh, is that so?"

She shrugged innocently, but the mischievous glint in her hazel eyes gave her away. "Just an observation," she said, sticking her shovel into the snow and leaning on it. "If the jeep's anything like its owner, I'm sure it runs good, works hard, and gets the job done."

He let out a low chuckle, a sound that warmed the crisp morning air. "I'll take that as a compliment," he said, shaking his head as he resumed shoveling. "Though I'm not sure the jeep would appreciate being compared to me."

She grinned, her cheeks flushed—not just from the cold, but also from the natural ease between them.

The two fell into a steady rhythm, shoveling side by side as the conversation faded into comfortable silence. But Debbie's mind lingered on the image of a teenage Caleb working alongside his father, tinkering with an old Jeep, talking about engines and life. It was a side of him she hadn't expected to think about—a layer of warmth and sentimentality beneath his usual stoic surface. And it made her wonder just how many other layers there were.

As she worked, she stole a glance at him. Caleb was focused, his strong, gloved hands gripping the shovel as he powered through another stubborn section of snow. There was a calm efficiency in his movements, as though the physical effort gave him a sense of purpose. And despite the weight of the storm that had swept into their lives, Debbie couldn't help but feel strangely grateful. The snow had brought its share of challenges, but it had also given her this—these moments with Caleb, small but meaningful, where walls seemed to come down and something genuine took their place.

"How about you?" Caleb asked suddenly, breaking the silence as he looked over at her. His breath puffed visibly in the cold air, but his voice was steady, almost casual. "What's your vehicle story? I don't suppose you've got a secret love affair with some old classic hidden in your barn?"

Debbie laughed, shaking her head as she scooped another shovelful of snow. "Nothing quite as interesting as your jeep, I'm afraid. Just a reliable car that gets the job done. I bought it after the divorce—practical, dependable, and big enough for the kids. No sentimental value, though."

Caleb nodded thoughtfully and returned to his shoveling. "Well, practical's never a bad thing," he said after a beat.

"I've never been one for fancy cars," Debbie said. "Honestly, I just don't see the point. A car's job is simple—to get you where you need to go. It doesn't need to be flashy or sleek to do that. I guess I've always valued practicality over showmanship."

Her hands tightened slightly around the handle of her snow shovel as her gaze drifted toward Caleb's buried truck. She tucked a strand of hair back under her hat, her voice thoughtful as she continued. "Don't get me wrong, I understand why some people love the thrill of a shiny new engine and all the bells and whistles that come with it. But for me? A car's just a means to an end. It doesn't need to be anything more."

She looked back at Caleb, whose lips quirked into a faint smile as she spoke. "I think when you live a life full of all the big, messy, important things—family, work, keeping up with the day-to-day—you start to realize that what really matters isn't the car you drive, but the journey you're making. The memories you're building along the way. That's what stays with you—not whether your car had heated seats or a turbo engine."

"That perspective," Caleb said, "is why I think you're one of the most grounded people I've ever met."

"I don't know about all that," she said.

Caleb shrugged, his gaze on her steady and unwavering. "I mean it. The world we live in... it's easy to get caught up wanting more—chasing after shine and gloss. But hearing you talk about things so simply, so wisely... it reminds me that there's value in keeping your feet on the ground. I think we all need a little more of that."

Debbie paused, turning to face Caleb with a soft smile tugging at her lips.

"You know something, Caleb," she began, her voice quiet but saturated with sincerity. "You never fail to surprise me."

Caleb stopped in his tracks, hands resting on the handle of his snow shovel as he turned his attention to her. His brows lifted slightly in curiosity. "Oh yeah? How exactly do I manage to do that?"

Debbie's smile widened just a fraction, her gaze unwavering as she considered her next words. "You've got this way about you—like you're carrying the weight of the world on your shoulders, always calm, always strong... but there's so much more to you than what you let people see. Underneath all that ruggedness, you're incredibly thoughtful. Deep, even."

His expression softened, the corner of his mouth twitching upward like he was trying to suppress a smile but couldn't quite manage it. "Deep, huh?" he echoed, his tone dry but tinged with amusement. "I don't think anyone's ever accused me of that before."

Debbie gave a small, teasing laugh, but there was no mistaking the earnestness in her tone when she replied. "I mean it, Caleb. You don't just talk to fill a silence. When you say something, it matters. And when you listen... it's like you're actually hearing what someone has to say, not just waiting for your turn to speak."

He shifted his weight slightly, the faintest hint of color rising in his cheeks. "I've just always figured there's no point in saying much unless it's worth saying," he said.

"Exactly. Most people don't take the time to think about their words the way you do, or to pay attention to the little things that really matter."

Caleb's gaze flickered to the snow-covered ground for a moment before returning to her.

"You give me too much credit," he said gruffly, though his smile finally broke free, softening his features in a way that made her heart stutter.

"Not a chance," she countered, her voice gentle but firm. She took a cautious step closer, the snow crunching lightly beneath her boots. "I've noticed how you are with Nathan and Danielle. You've got this way of making them feel seen—like you're really on their side, without saying much at all. And the way you've opened up these past few days with me... that's no small thing, Caleb. It tells me that there's so much more to you than anyone realizes—including you."

"You make it sound like I'm some kind of puzzle waiting to be figured out."

Debbie tilted her head. "Maybe you are," she said. "But you're a good one. You're worth the effort."

Caleb let out a short, disbelieving laugh, shaking his head slightly. "Worth the effort?"

"You are," Debbie said simply, the firmness in her voice leaving no room for doubt.

"What do you mean by that?" he asked, his deep voice carrying a softness that hinted at both curiosity and self-protection.

She bit her lip briefly before stepping closer, the crisp air swirling around them like an invisible curtain blocking out the rest of the world. "I mean... there's something about you, Caleb. Something I don't think you even realize."

The sincerity in her tone made his chest tighten, and he tipped his head slightly, his eyes narrowing just enough to show she had his full attention. "And what's that?" he asked.

Debbie let her shovel fall gently into the snow, the dull thud muffled by the thick powder. She closed the space between them and lifted her hands, resting them lightly on his shoulders. He stood still, watching her face as her hazel eyes gazed up at him, earnest and steady.

"I think," Debbie began, her voice gentle but deliberate, "that all the time you've spent alone has given you something rare. A gift, really—one that more people would do well to learn."

Caleb blinked, his brow furrowing slightly. "I'm not sure I follow," he murmured. There was no trace of skepticism in his tone, just the genuine confusion of a man unaccustomed to being seen so clearly.

"You know how to think, Caleb," she said, her voice quiet but steady, as though declaring a powerful truth. "You know how to discern what matters in life. You've had the space, the silence, and the time to really understand it."

Debbie took a deep breath, her fingers curling slightly into the fabric of his coat for emphasis. "We live in a world full of noise," she continued, her words picking up a quiet intensity. "Constant chatter, endless distractions, people running themselves ragged trying to chase after things that don't really matter—trying to keep up, to fit in, to fill the emptiness with the wrong things."

Her hands shifted slightly on his shoulders, grounding her thoughts, as if the words themselves needed something solid to anchor them. "But you... you stepped away from all that. You pulled back and let the noise fade. And somehow, in doing that, Caleb, you've learned something most people never figure out: what's truly important."

"Debbie," he began, his voice softer now, hesitant. "I don't know if that's something to admire. Cutting myself off... it wasn't exactly a noble choice. It was survival. A way to keep the pain at arm's length."

Debbie shook her head gently, her smile softening as her hands remained where they were. "I'm not saying it's how anyone should live forever. And I'm not saying it didn't cost you something. But I am saying this: stepping away gave you clarity. It gave you perspective that's so rare these days. You don't care about keeping up with the Joneses or impressing anyone, Caleb. You know what it means to focus on what truly matters—on people, on meaning, on connection."

Her hands slipped down slightly, resting just above his elbows in a gesture that felt both grounding and intimate. "That's not something just anyone can do," she said earnestly. "Most people are too busy chasing after everything they think they need to even realize what they already have. But you... you've lived in the quiet. You've sat with your thoughts, your fears, your regrets, and your hopes. And because of that, Caleb, you see things differently. You see, what most of us miss until it's too late."

Caleb's throat tightened, and for a moment, he didn't trust himself to respond. He stared at her, his gaze flickering from her eyes to the faint crease of concern that shadowed her brow, as though she half-feared she'd said too much.

Finally, he spoke, his voice low and raw with sincerity. "I never thought of it that way," he admitted. "I've always looked at the years I spent alone as—" He paused, searching for the right word. "—as lost time. As a sign of weakness or failure."

Debbie shook her head, her grip on him firming slightly, as though physically countering his words. "It wasn't lost time, Caleb," she said softly. "And it wasn't weakness. It was healing. Finding yourself again."

The faintest hint of a smile tugged at the corner of Caleb's mouth, and he looked away briefly, shaking his head as if to clear the weight of her words. "You see too much, you know that?" he said, his tone lightly teasing but laced with an undercurrent of amazement.

Debbie grinned, the tension breaking just enough for a touch of playfulness to return. "Part of my charm," she quipped lightly before her expression softened again. "But seriously, Caleb. I'm not saying solitude is the answer to everything, and I'm definitely not saying you should stay there. But I think... I really think that time alone gave you a kind of wisdom—an understanding of what matters—that most people spend their whole lives searching for."

Caleb let out a soft laugh, the sound rough around the edges but genuine. "And here I was thinking I'd turned into a hermit who forgot how to talk to people."

Debbie's smile widened, and she chuckled. "If this is forgetting, I'd like to see what happens when you remember."

Chapter 24

Debbie's playful side sparkled to the surface as she and Caleb worked side by side to clear the driveway. She paused, her breath curling in the cold air, and cast a sly glance in his direction. Crouching quickly, she scooped up a handful of powdery snow. The chill seeping through her gloves. The glint in her eyes gave away her mischievous intent as she shaped the snow into a compact ball, her hands moving deftly.

Straightening, she turned her attention back to Caleb. He was focused on the stubborn snowbank ahead of him, completely oblivious to the ambush about to take place. The faint crease between his brows made her smile; he tackled every task with quiet determination, even something as ordinary as shoveling snow.

It had been far too long since she'd allowed herself to relax like this, to embrace a moment of lighthearted fun. "Why not?" she murmured under her breath, the words barely audible.

With a quick flick of her wrist, she launched the snowball. It arced through the crisp winter air, landing squarely on its target. The snow burst harmlessly against Caleb's broad shoulder, leaving a soft white mark in its wake.

He froze mid-shovel, his posture straightening as the realization hit. Slowly, he turned, one brow arched high, his rugged face a mix of amused disbelief.

"Tell me that wasn't on purpose," he said, his deep voice edged with playful challenge.

Debbie pressed her lips together to stifle her laughter, but it was no use. A giggle escaped, and then another, until she was laughing freely. "What if it was?" she teased, unable to keep the humor out of her voice. "What are you gonna do about it?"

The corner of Caleb's mouth twitched, a smile threatening to break his otherwise stoic expression. He set his shovel down, brushing his gloves together as though preparing for battle. "Oh, you're gonna wish you didn't start this..."

Debbie barely had time to react before Caleb bent down, scooping a handful of snow and packing it into a firm ball. She gasped, her heartbeat quickening as she realized his intent. "No, Caleb, wait—"

Her plea dissolved into a squeal as he launched the snowball directly at her. She ducked, but she wasn't quick enough—half of it caught her on the arm, scattering in a soft spray.

Debbie stumbled back, laughing as she grabbed another handful of snow, her hands fumbling in her haste. "You asked for it now!" she declared, tossing another snowball his way.

And just like that, the driveway became their battlefield. Snowballs flew fast and furious between them, laughter echoing through the crisp morning air. Caleb quickly proved to be a formidable opponent—his aim was annoyingly accurate, and his competitive streak was evident in the wide grin across his face.

"You're supposed to miss occasionally, you know!" Debbie called out, dodging behind the corner of the porch for cover.

"Where's the fun in that?" Caleb retorted, his deep laugh rumbling as he hurled another snowball her way.

Debbie peered out cautiously, her breath puffing in visible clouds. She spotted him kneeling to gather more snow, his movements swift but unhurried. Her heart gave an unexpected flutter as she watched him—his boyish energy, his warm smile, the way the snow clung to his dark coat and knit cap.

Before he could catch her staring, she darted from her hiding spot, tossing another snowball in his direction. It hit him square on the back, and she couldn't help but cheer. "Ha! Gotcha!"

"Oh, is that how we're playing now?" Caleb's voice held a mock warning tone as he straightened and began closing the distance between them.

Debbie yelped and took off toward the yard, the snow crunching beneath her boots as she ran. She could feel him chasing her, could hear the steady thud of his boots behind her. Her laughter bubbled uncontrollably, a mix of exhilaration and pure, unfiltered joy.

She zigzagged through the yard, her cheeks flushed and her heart racing. But in her rush to escape, her foot caught a slick patch of icy snow. Time seemed to slow as she felt herself falling, her arms flailing uselessly. She landed with a soft whoomp on her back, the cold snow pressing against her coat. For a split second, she was too surprised to do anything but blink up at the pale blue sky.

The sound of Caleb's footsteps grew louder—and then, suddenly, he was falling too. He must have hit the same icy patch because he lost his footing and toppled forward. The moment felt almost comical, and Debbie braced herself as he landed with a soft thud right beside her.

"Ugh," Caleb groaned, his breath forming visible wisps in the frosty air. For a moment, neither of them moved, both too stunned to process what had just happened.

And then Debbie started to laugh and Caleb let out a low chuckle that turned into a deep belly laugh.

"Well, this is definitely not how I planned my morning workout," Debbie said between gasps of laughter.

Caleb shook his head, a faint grin tugging at his lips. "I think I might've pulled something," he teased. "Getting old is no joke, huh?"

"Oh, we're definitely gonna feel this tomorrow," Debbie agreed, her laughter subsiding into a smile. She looked over at him, her hazel eyes meeting his dark ones.

Caleb's face was closer than she'd realized, his breath warm despite the chill in the air.

"Debbie..." His tone was low, with a slight hesitation.

Her heart quickened in response. She didn't need words to understand what this moment was. She didn't need to hear the rest of whatever Caleb was trying to say—because she already knew.

Debbie shifted onto her knees, her breath steady and measured as she moved closer to Caleb with quiet determination. Her hands reached out and found the thick fabric of his coat, gripping it firmly at the shoulders. With gentle but deliberate strength, she guided him into a seated position, her movements carrying an unspoken certainty.

Her hands slid up to cradle his face, her touch tender yet grounding. And then, without hesitation, she leaned forward, closing the distance between them.

The first touch of her lips against his was soft yet resolute, a blend of vulnerability and quiet strength. It wasn't rushed or uncertain—it simply was like the natural culmination of something long building beneath the surface. For a moment, she worried he might retreat, but instead, Caleb stilled, as though caught off guard by the sheer clarity of the moment.

Then, like snow melting under the touch of sunlight, his initial tension dissolved. She felt the change in him—the way his hesitation gave way to something deeper, something unspoken that neither of them could deny. Slowly, cautiously, Caleb leaned in, meeting her kiss with a tenderness that was quiet and restrained.

The kiss deepened slightly, not in haste, but in a kind of unhurried discovery. Every heartbeat seemed to bring them closer, the world around them fading into irrelevance.

When they finally parted, it was slow and natural, their breaths mingling in the cold air. For a heartbeat, neither of them spoke. Debbie's hands lingered on his face, her hazel eyes searching his as if trying to memorize the tender vulnerability she saw there.

"I—" he started, but Debbie pressed a gloved finger gently to his lips, the glimmer of a smile tugging at the corners of her mouth.

"Don't," she said. "Sometimes, Caleb, words get in the way."

Chapter 25

The back door creaked as Caleb stepped inside, arms laden with firewood. His boots thudded softly against the wooden floor as he moved through the kitchen toward the hearth in the living room. Debbie glanced over her shoulder as she stood at the sink, rinsing off the last lunch dish.

He crouched by the fireplace, stacking the thick logs in the firewood rack.

Debbie dried her hands on a dishtowel as she turned and leaned back against the kitchen counter. "Caleb," she said.

"Yeah?" He said as he turned to her.

"What do you think about going for a ride to check on the road and your place?" Debbie asked.

Caleb raised an eyebrow, his forehead creasing slightly in confusion. "A ride?"

"On the side-by-side," Debbie clarified, a small smile playing at the corners of her mouth.

His expression shifted to mild skepticism. "Not to rain on your idea, but don't you think it might get a little cold out there?"

Debbie shook her head, her smile widening with a touch of mischief. "It won't be so bad," she said lightly. "It has a heater in the cab. As long as we don't drive like we're filming an action movie, we'll be perfectly fine."

Caleb studied her for a moment, his gaze lingering as if trying to gauge her sincerity. The truth was, barely anyone had ever stepped foot on his property, just a select few in all these years. Finally, a soft chuckle escaped him, breaking the silence. "All right," he said, his voice low yet carrying the faintest touch of amusement.

Debbie moved to the base of the stairs and called up toward the second floor. "Nathan! Danielle! Caleb and I are taking the side-by-side to check on his place. We'll be gone for a couple of hours, so behave yourselves!"

Nathan shouted, "Okay! Be careful!"

"Have fun, mom," Danielle called back.

They bundled up in their coats, gloves, scarves, and boots, bracing against the cold as they made their way to the pole barn. Inside, Caleb checked the oil, and topped off the gas in the side by side. His large, capable hands moved confidently as he inspected the vehicle. Once satisfied, Caleb slid into the driver's seat, his broad shoulders and strong build making the side-by-side's compact cabin feel snugger than it was. Debbie followed, settling into the seat beside him.

The engine roared to life with a deep, reliable hum, breaking the quiet stillness of the barn. Caleb put it into gear and they exited the barn. The vehicle bouncing lightly over the uneven snow as Caleb guided it across the yard, up the driveway, and onto the narrow mountain road, climbing steadily upward into the waiting expanse of white that waited beyond.

For the first couple of miles, the conversation meandered, touching on everything from the best hiking trails in the area to Caleb's occasional run-ins with wildlife on his property. Their words came easily, punctuated by the occasional tease or quip.

The road narrowed about a mile from Caleb's driveway, flanked on either side by towering trees dusted with fresh snow. Up ahead, two state trucks diligently worked to clear the road, their amber lights pulsing in steady rhythms against the quiet wilderness.

Caleb leaned back in his seat. "Well, looks like we're not getting through this way."

"So, what now?" Debbie asked.

He looked over at her, one brow raised. "Shortcut."

Caleb skillfully maneuvered the side-by-side off the main road, guiding it steadily up the snow-dusted mountainside. He steered the vehicle through the towering trees, its tires crunching over the packed snow. The engine's low hum reverberated in the stillness of the forest, the occasional bump jolting them slightly. Debbie gripped the frame tightly, a laugh bubbling up, unbidden, and full of exhilaration, as they climbed a gentle rise. Caleb, ever steady, navigated with an almost effortless confidence. His strong hands guided the vehicle with practiced ease, his steady gaze fixed on the snow-draped trail ahead, which unfurled like a pale ribbon disappearing into the quiet embrace of the wilderness.

"Do you hike out here often?" she asked as they followed the snow-covered trail.

"This trail stretches pretty far—it's popular for ATV riders exploring the mountains," Caleb explained, his tone easy but edged with a familiarity born from years of wandering these woods. "If we keep following it for about another mile, it'll start getting a lot rougher.

When I hike, though, I steer clear of these trails. I prefer to just wander through the woods on my own land, far off the beaten paths."

"I haven't explored this ATV trail before," Debbie admitted, casting a curious glance toward Caleb. "I usually stick to the ones closer to home. They're not too challenging—just nice, easy rides through the mountains."

As they rounded one last bend, Caleb cut off the trail and once again meandered through the woods, steering through the trees expertly. When they broke through the treeline several minutes later, Caleb stopped the side by side. His property sprawled before them. The cabin itself was a masterpiece of practicality and care, its sturdy design accented by thoughtful touches—the wraparound porch, the neatly stacked firewood under the woodshed, the sloped roof dusted with snow. The barn stood proudly nearby, its red facade a warm contrast against the white landscape.

"Caleb..." she said. "This is...incredible."

He shifted in his seat, his expression unreadable. "It's just a cabin and a barn."

"No," she said, her voice full of quiet conviction. "It's not 'just' anything. You built all this?"

His gaze dropped briefly to the steering wheel. "Yeah, the cabin I did myself. Dad and my brothers actually came up and helped me build the barn."

"It's beautiful," she said softly, her voice tinged with awe. "So peaceful." As her gaze traveled past the rustic cabin and barn to the left, she caught sight of something that made her breath hitch. The land spilled away into an endless panorama of snow-dusted peaks and valleys, the kind of untouched beauty that might appear in a picture-perfect postcard. The sky, a blend of pale blue and soft white wispy clouds, framed the rugged peaks in the distance like a painting.

She shook her head in disbelief. "Caleb," she murmured, her words slow and deliberate, as though afraid to disturb the stillness of the moment. "This view... sitting out on your front porch, it must feel like the whole world is laid out in front of you."

Caleb didn't need to look—he already knew the view by heart.

"It's pretty special," he admitted, his tone modest.

Debbie shook her head again, as if she couldn't fully comprehend its beauty. "This is literally heaven on earth, Caleb," she said.

He smiled as he released the brake on the side by side and rolled closer to his cabin. When he parked and turned the engine off, the only sounds were the soft hush of the wind moving through the trees.

"Come on," Caleb said, as he stepped out of the side-by-side. "Let me show you around."

Debbie hopped out of the vehicle, her boots crunching softly against the undisturbed snow. Her eyes roamed across the serene expanse of Caleb's property, taking in the simple yet exquisite charm of his surroundings.

"How far away from the main road are we?" she asked, pulling her scarf tighter around her neck. The stillness of the place felt striking to her, nearly otherworldly. There wasn't a single hum of a plow or the faintest sound of distant traffic—just the crisp rustle of the breeze moving through nearby trees.

Caleb chuckled, the sound low and grounded. "Two miles, give or take," he replied. "That's why you don't hear the plows. Once you get this far in, it's just you, the forest, and maybe a bear or two."

Debbie gave him a wide-eyed look. "A bear or two? That definitely makes me feel better."

The corner of his mouth quirked. "Don't worry. They're more scared of you than you are of them. They're hibernating right now anyhow," He paused, his tone taking on a note of quiet pride as he glanced at the surrounding property. "But yeah, it's pretty isolated. I like it this way."

"I can see why. But with weather like this, how do you manage to keep your driveway clear when it snows?" she asked.

Caleb shrugged, his answer as unassuming as the man himself. "I've got an old plow in the barn. It used to belong to the mill. Dad upgraded to a newer one after I finished this place, so he gave me the older model." He chuckled, his breath visible in the cold mountain air. "She's seen better days, but she gets the job done."

"Well," Debbie said after a moment, her voice lighter as she gestured toward the cabin. "You did promise me a tour. Lead the way, Mr. Warren."

That elusive smile twitched on Caleb's lips again, and he motioned for her to follow. "Prepare yourself," he said with mock gravity. "It's no five-star mountain resort and definitely not as nice as your place."

Debbie laughed as she trailed behind him.

Caleb opened the front door to his modest cabin, revealing an interior that was simple and welcoming. The living room was the definition of practical comfort: a sturdy couch with worn, plaid upholstery, a well-loved recliner angled toward the fireplace, bookcases lined with various novels, and little odds and ends that hinted at years spent carving out a life here.

"Caleb, this is... perfect. Perfectly you," she said.

"Thanks," he said gruffly, rubbing the back of his neck. "It does the job. Keeps me warm, the roof doesn't leak. What else does a person need?"

Debbie's eyes scanned the room, catching sight of a small framed photo resting on the mantel above the fireplace. She stepped closer, tilting her head slightly to take a better look. It was an image of a younger Caleb, standing arm in arm with a petite woman with bright eyes and a beaming smile: Bonnie.

"You both looked happy," Debbie said softly, her voice tinged with gentle reverence as her eyes lingered on the photo in front of her.

"We were," he said.

"She was beautiful."

A faint flicker of a smile crossed Caleb's lips, though it didn't quite reach his eyes. "Yeah," he said. "She really was."

"Come on," he said, his tone steady. "There's more to see."

The kitchen was small but functional, with gleaming wood countertops that Caleb had clearly taken the time to maintain. The cabinetry was amazing, all handcrafted from oak and detailed. The appliances were simple and well taken care of. A small pantry was built into one corner of the room. A simple table and chairs nearby, a gorgeous set of handcrafted woodworking.

The bedroom was understated, yet it carried a quiet charm. A neatly folded quilt rested at the foot of the bed, offering a hint of homely warmth against the otherwise rugged simplicity. The bed frame, crafted with care, showcased the natural beauty of oak through its intricate yet subtle woodworking details. Across the room stood a matching dresser, its clean lines and delicate craftsmanship a testament to the talent and thoughtfulness that had shaped it.

"Who made this quilt?" Debbie asked, her fingers grazing the edge of the intricate patchwork.

"My mom," Caleb said, his gaze growing distant. "She loved quilting and was always working on one. I can still picture her stitching away while my brothers and I watched TV. She passed away when I was twelve."

Debbie's hand found its way to his arm, a gentle and comforting gesture. "I'm so sorry, Caleb. Losing your mom at such a young age... I can't imagine how hard that was."

A faint smile ghosted across his face, though his eyes held a lingering sadness. "It was tough. Life was never quite the same without her. Dad tried his best with us boys, but we all felt the void she left behind. My mom... she was one of a kind."

Debbie gave his arm a light squeeze, her voice tender. "She sounds like an amazing woman. I bet she'd be so proud of who you've become, Caleb."

He tilted his head slightly, his expression unreadable for a moment before he simply nodded.

Debbie wandered back into the living room, her steps slowing as her gaze landed on the built-in bookcases that framed one of the walls. Her fingertips traced the smooth wood, the craftsmanship evident in the details. She marveled at how perfectly the shelves fit the room, a testament to both skill and care.

Her hazel eyes swept over the spines of the books, taking in the variety of titles—everything from classic literature to thrillers, and even a few dog-eared faith-based volumes nestled among them. Tilting her head, curiosity piqued, she glanced over her shoulder at Caleb, who had trailed behind her.

"You built these too, didn't you?" she asked.

He nodded, a sheepish smile softening his rugged features. "Yeah. Took a few weekends, but it was worth it," he said, leaning against the door frame. "Most of those books belonged to my mom. She loved reading. I guess I picked it up from her."

Debbie turned back to the shelves, her expression thoughtful as her fingers brushed one particularly well-worn spine. "These aren't just random books on a bookshelf, Caleb. It's... it's a piece of her, isn't it? A way for you to keep her close."

"It is," he admitted. "She used to say books are like old friends—you can always return to them when you need to."

"Wise words," Debbie murmured softly, her fingers pausing on an old, weathered Bible. She gently pulled it from the shelf and turned it over in her hands, smiling as she opened the front cover to see an inscription in delicate handwriting: For Caleb, Love Always, Mom. Her hand stilled as she read it, her smile deepening.

"Your cabin, the work you've put into it, your life... it's all about creating something lasting. Something meaningful," she said.

Caleb's mouth curved into a small, appreciative smile as he pushed away from the door frame and stepped closer. "I don't know about all that," he replied modestly, though his eyes betrayed a glimmer of pride.

Debbie slipped the Bible back onto the shelf, turning to face him fully. "You're selling yourself short, Caleb," she said gently. "You didn't just build a house here. You've built a home. And a life that matters.

He blinked, momentarily caught off guard by the depth of her words. Then he nodded, a quiet acknowledgment of the truth she'd revealed.

"Caleb," Debbie began, her voice tinged with both gratitude and admiration, "thank you for sharing all of this with me—your home, your world. It's so much more than I expected." She turned to face him fully, her hazel eyes warm and glistening. "Standing here, I see something extraordinary. This isn't just a house or a piece of land—it's a reflection of who you are."

Caleb's eyes flicked to hers, his expression softening. He didn't speak, but the way he held her gaze said more than words ever could. Encouraged by his quiet attention, Debbie continued.

"Your mother's books, the view from your porch, the craftsmanship in every detail of this cabin—they all tell a story. You didn't just walk away from the world. You've taken your pain and shaped it into something meaningful. What you've built here isn't about isolation. It's about love, memory, and purpose." She paused, her voice dropping to a gentler tone. "Most people spend their lives chasing distractions, but you've created something real—something that's both strong and gentle, grounded and free. That's rare, Caleb. And it's remarkable."

Caleb shifted his weight, his hands settling on his hips as his dark eyes grew thoughtful. After a moment, he exhaled, the breath visible in the cool cabin air. "Yeah," he said. "Most people don't get that."

Debbie stepped closer, positioning herself in front of him. She leaned in gently, pressing her head against his chest as her voice carried steady conviction. "Everything about this," she said, gesturing subtly with her words, "adds up to you—a man who cares deeply without needing to announce it. You've created a home that feels safe, warm, and honest. If that's not a meaningful life, Caleb, I don't know what is."

A faint smile curved Caleb's lips as he wrapped his arms around her, holding her against him. His tone held a trace of wry amusement. "You get me, Debbie Ferguson," he said softly. "Didn't see that coming when we first met."

"Oh?" she replied, her voice alighting with playful curiosity. "And what did you expect when you first met me?"

He smirked, his dark eyes gleaming with mischief. "A sharp-tongued nurse who would probably drag me out of these mountains kicking and screaming if she thought I needed help."

Debbie laughed lightly, shaking her head. "Well, sharp-tongued, I'll admit. But I'm not one for dragging anyone unless there's an extreme medical emergency."

"Good to know," he said.

Chapter 26

Debbie sank into the couch, tugging the woolen throw across her lap. She cradled her phone in her hands, the remnants of the conversation with her boss lingering in her mind. Tomorrow, her days of snowed-in reprieve would end, and everything would go back to its usual rhythm. Her heart twinged at the thought.

Caleb sat at the other end of the couch, leaning forward with his elbows on his knees, staring into the fire. The edges of him, the rugged lines of his figure, looked softer in the firelight. Debbie noticed the way he rubbed his hands together, a motion that seemed more of a habit than necessity.

"Well," she began, snapping out of her thoughts. "That was my boss. Looks like I'll be back on the road tomorrow." Her tone was light, but there was an undercurrent of reluctance.

Caleb's gaze shifted, his dark eyes meeting hers briefly before they returned to the fire. "Guess the world's gotta keep turning," he said.

She chuckled, though it didn't quite reach her eyes. "Trust me, my patients don't stop needing care just because I want another snow day."

"These last few days have been nice, though," Caleb admitted.

Debbie smiled, tucking a stray strand of hair behind her ear. "It really has been," she said softly, pausing before continuing, "I guess you'll probably want to go home tomorrow?"

"Yeah," Caleb replied thoughtfully, his deep voice steady. "It's probably time. I need to clear my driveway. I called my dad while you were on the phone. He's already lined up a crew to start clearing the snow at the mill first thing tomorrow. We'll be back in business soon enough."

Debbie bit her lip for a second. "Do you want an extra set of hands to help with your driveway? Nathan's always itching for a project, and I bet he'd love to help you."

"I wouldn't mind it a bit if he wants to come up and help me."

She leaned forward, calling toward the stairwell. "Nathan! Can you come down for a minute?"

"Coming!" came the muffled reply.

A minute later, he appeared. "What's up?" he asked, a curious look flashing between his mom and Caleb.

Debbie gestured toward Caleb. "Caleb's planning to clear his driveway tomorrow with his tractor, and I thought you might want to tag along. Take the side-by-side, help him with whatever he needs?"

Nathan's face lit up, though he masked it with a nonchalant shrug. "Sure. I mean, sounds like a decent way to kill some time."

Caleb smirked, resting his hands on his knees. "Appreciate it."

"Yeah, no problem. Who's driving the tractor? You trust me behind the wheel?"

"I'm sure you can handle it," Caleb said with a grin.

"What's going on? I could hear you guys while I was upstairs trying to read," Danielle said as she bounded down the stairs.

Nathan rolled his eyes. "You can hear everything. Mom's just volunteering my services to help Caleb clear his driveway tomorrow."

Danielle's eyes flitted to Caleb, then back to Nathan, before she crossed her arms dramatically. "What about me? I've been stuck here too, y'know."

Before Debbie could reply, Danielle's demeanor shifted. "Actually," she said, a spark of excitement lighting her hazel eyes. "Can we do something tonight? Just... get out of the house for a little while? Please?"

Debbie tilted her head. "What do you have in mind?"

"I don't know," Danielle said, throwing her hands up in exaggerated exasperation. "Go out to eat or something. Martha's Diner is probably open by now, right? I'm sick of staring at the walls in this house."

Nathan snorted. "You're being dramatic."

"Am I?" she retorted. "Or am I channeling the voice of everyone here? Come on, Mom. You've got to admit—dinner out does sound good."

Debbie turned to Caleb. "What do you think, Caleb? Feel like joining us?"

For a moment, Caleb's face was unreadable, as though the invitation caught him completely off guard. But then, something flickered—hesitation at first, followed by quiet acceptance.

"Sure," he said. "Might as well."

Debbie laughed, shaking her head as she stood. "Alright. Guess we're doing this. Go get yourselves ready."

***

As they pulled into the gravel parking lot of Martha's Diner, the building seemed to radiate the warmth of the community. Light poured through the windows, where tiny snowflake decals clung to the glass, catching the soft glow from inside. The chalkboard sign propped near the door cheerfully announced, "Welcome Back from the Blizzard, Laurel Ridge! Specials Tonight—Pot Roast and Apple Pie!"

Debbie couldn't help but smile as they stepped inside, the familiar jingle of the bell overhead welcoming them like an old friend. The comforting aroma of fresh coffee and warm bread wrapped around them immediately. Behind the counter, Martha bustled about, her salt-and-pepper hair pulled into a neat bun. At the sound of the bell, she turned, her face lighting up with recognition and joy.

"Well, now," Martha exclaimed, brushing her hands on the front of her apron as she approached, her smile as warm and welcoming as fresh-baked bread. "If it isn't the Ferguson's... and Caleb Warren! Mercy me, Caleb, it's been what? Ten years, at least since you've stepped foot in my diner?"

"Martha," Debbie greeted, stepping forward and enveloping the older woman in a heartfelt hug. "I've missed you."

"And I've missed you, too, honey," Martha replied, pulling back just enough to take Debbie in with a fond, motherly gaze before setting her sights back on Caleb. Her expression shifted instantly to one of wily delight, her sharp eyes twinkling. "Caleb. My word," she said, her voice picking up steam like a kettle about to whistle.

Before Caleb could muster so much as a polite response, Martha lunged forward and wrapped him in a bear hug so enthusiastic it sent him stepping awkwardly back to steady himself. The sheer force of it left even Nathan and Danielle standing behind him, stifling amused grins.

"Well, now, that's what I call a welcome," Caleb said. He straightened as Martha released him, brushing his calloused hands against his coat. "Figured it was about time for a change."

"Well, whatever finally dragged you down from your mountain, I approve," Martha teased. "Y'all take a seat anywhere you like. I'll send Sarah over with menus."

They chose a booth near the window, and the twins quickly dove into an argument about which pie was more superior—cherry or apple—with Danielle breaking into laughter when Nathan's enthusiasm became too dramatic to take seriously.

As they settled into the cozy booth by the window, Caleb found himself at ease. The warmth of the diner, the rhythmic hum of distant chatter and laughter—all of it felt like a portal to a simpler time in his life—a time he now realized he missed. It wasn't just the smell of fresh coffee or the murmur of voices layered over the faint crackle of the old jukebox in the corner; it was the sense of being part of something.

"Well, now," Martha began, her voice brimming with that signature blend of sass and affection that had made her diner the heart of Laurel Ridge for decades. She placed a tall glass of water in front of Caleb, followed by Debbie. "Here I was thinking the blizzard might've scared people off for good. But look at y'all, braving the snowbanks like true mountain folk." Her blue eyes twinkled as she shifted to Nathan and Danielle, placing their glasses down last. "Though I'd wager you two are hoping we still have pie."

Nathan smirked, leaning back in the booth. "You know us too well, Martha. Is your cherry pie still king around here?"

"You'd better believe it," she shot back. "But my apple pie might just dethrone it tonight. Fresh out of the oven. Practically smells like heaven back in that kitchen."

Danielle crossed her arms, glancing at Nathan. "Told you apple wins every time."

"Oh, you wish, Dani," Nathan said with a mock scoff, shaking his head. "Cherry is superior, and deep down in your soul, you know it."

Martha's chuckle spilled out as she poured coffee into a plain white mug and set it in front of Caleb. "The twins are at it again—arguing like those pie slices don't both belong on the same dessert menu."

Debbie laughed, her hazel eyes gleaming. "This is how about half of our family dinner conversations go. Food debates are a very real thing in our house."

Caleb leaned forward slightly, a small grin tugging at the corners of his mouth. "Good to know pie diplomacy is a priority. I guess I'll need to weigh in once I get a taste."

Debbie tilted her head, giving Caleb a teasing look. "Are you serious? You've lived in this town your whole life, and you've never tried any of Martha's pies?"

Caleb shrugged, his shoulders broad under the flannel shirt he wore. "Guess I've always been more of a coffee kind of guy. I remember my mom's apple pie was the best, though."

Danielle's jaw dropped theatrically. "Fix this situation immediately, Mom. No one leaves tonight until we've converted him into a Martha's apple-pie enthusiast."

Nathan raised his hand as if in protest. "Whoa now, easy there. Let's not sway the man before he's had a chance to properly taste-test. Let him experience the superior cherry pie first. You'll thank me later, Caleb."

"Hogwash. The poor man deserves a shot at both. Life's too short to pick sides," Martha said.

Caleb chuckled, enjoying the back-and-forth. "Alright," he said, holding up two fingers. "Let's be fair. One slice of each after dinner, and I'll give my official verdict tonight."

Nathan and Danielle groaned in mock frustration at Caleb's diplomatic decision.

"Looks like we've got a level-headed judge in our midst," Debbie teased, leaning slightly toward him. "You might regret this, though. They'll be talking about your decision for months."

"Months? Try years," Nathan quipped. "This is legacy stuff, Mom. I'll tell my future kids about tonight."

Martha laughed. "You folks decide what you want to eat yet, or are we skipping straight to dessert tonight?"

Debbie flipped her menu closed, glancing at Caleb. "I'm thinking the pot roast dinner—with apple pie for dessert."

Caleb leaned back as he folded his menu. "Pot roast for me as well," he said, his deep voice steady. He then glanced at Martha. "And if you wouldn't mind, keep the coffee coming. Sounds like I'll need it to survive the dessert debate."

"Smart man," Martha said approvingly, jotting down the order. "And what about you two?" She eyeballed Nathan and Danielle. "I'm guessing grilled cheese and fries for Danielle, plus apple pie, and a bacon cheeseburger with fries for Mr. Cherry pie?"

"It's like you're inside my head, Martha," Danielle said.

Nathan gave a sheepish shrug. "What can I say? You've got us figured out."

Martha tapped the pen against her notepad before tucking it expertly into her apron. "That's what happens when you practically grow up in my diner. Now, y'all sit tight, and I'll be back with your food in a jiffy."

As she walked away, Debbie turned to Caleb, her smile softening. "So, what is your favorite dessert?"

Caleb leaned back against the booth, his dark eyes meeting hers as he considered the question.

"Favorite dessert," he repeated slowly, his voice carrying that familiar low timbre. "Never been one to think much about dessert. But if I had to choose... I'd say peach cobbler."

Debbie's eyebrows lifted in pleasant surprise. "Peach cobbler? Really?"

He gave a small shrug. "My mom used to make it on Sundays when I was a kid."

Debbie nodded. She could picture it—young Caleb, dirt on his jeans and sunburn on his nose, sitting at his mother's kitchen table, the smell of peaches and cinnamon filling the air. It was a simple image, but one that seemed to match him perfectly.

Martha reappeared from the kitchen with a tray balanced effortlessly on one hand, the smell of rich gravy and roasted vegetables preceding her. "Alright, folks," she announced with a triumphant gleam in her eye, "your delicious dinners have arrived."

She set the plates down with practiced ease, the steaming portions of meat and sides drawing appreciative murmurs from Debbie and Caleb. Nathan was quick to grab his cheeseburger, while Danielle inspected her grilled cheese with critical precision before nodding her approval.

As they dug in, the conversation ebbed and flowed without effort. Debbie caught herself stealing glances at Caleb as he interacted with her kids. The way his reserved demeanor softened around their haphazard energy. It felt... natural, as if he had always been sharing a table with them.

***

Martha arrived with the desserts, her trademark charm in full swing as she set the plates down with care. Debbie, Nathan, and Danielle each received their chosen slices, the sweet aroma filling the air as forks were eagerly poised to dig in. But when she placed the two plates in front of Caleb—one cherry and one apple—she couldn't help but add a little flair.

Leaning in conspiratorially toward Debbie, she gave a sly wink. "You're the referee, honey," Martha teased, her grin broad and mischievous. "Just in case this turns into a full-blown pie war."

Debbie laughed, picking up her fork with playful trepidation. "I'm not sure if that's a job anyone can handle."

As they all took their first bites, the table fell into silence, save for the occasional groan of delight or exaggerated gasp. Caleb chewed slowly, his expression a picture of deliberation.

"Well?" Nathan prompted, his voice almost cracking with impatience. "What's the verdict, Caleb? Your reputation depends on this moment."

Caleb smirked, setting his fork down purposefully. "They're both good," he said simply. "But... I think I'm going to have to give the edge to apple."

Danielle threw her fists into the air, triumphant. "Yes! I knew it!"

Nathan slumped dramatically against the booth. "Traitor."

Debbie laughed so hard she nearly dropped her fork, and Caleb's deep chuckle joined hers—a sound she realized she enjoyed hearing.

"Enjoy those desserts, everyone," Martha said with a warm smile, her sharp blue eyes lingering on Caleb. "And Caleb, don't be such a stranger, alright? It's been too long since we've seen you around here. And tell that daddy of yours I said hello. Bet he didn't mention that we were in the same high school graduating class, did he?" Her grin widened as she leaned ever so slightly closer, a teasing twinkle in her eye. "Course, I'm not saying who had the better report card, though I'm sure it wasn't him."

Caleb chuckled, his deep voice rumbling like distant thunder. "Dad always said he learned more in the woods than he ever did in a classroom. I'll pass your message on to him."

Martha smirked as she turned her full attention to Debbie. She rested one hand on her hip, and the other gave Caleb's broad shoulder a playful pat. "Well, Miss Debbie, I'm not sure what magic or mountain spell you cast to drag this man off his ridge and into civilization, but I'm dying to hear the story. It must be somethin' worth telling, don't you think?"

Debbie laughed, her cheeks warming lightly under Martha's teasing gaze. "I didn't drag him anywhere, Martha. Turns out, the snow played a part in it."

Martha raised an eyebrow, her curiosity laced with amusement as she leaned forward. "Oh? Now this I've got to hear. Come on, spill it."

"Well," Debbie began, "the night the storm hit, Caleb found himself in my driveway in a rather... unplanned fashion."

Martha's eyes widened with intrigue, her gaze darting between the two of them like she was savoring the opening chapters of a juicy small-town story.

"Yeah," Caleb said with a slight grin. "Tried to head home after my shift at the mill and hit an icy patch on the road. Next thing I know,

I'm off the road, headed down the embankment and landing smack in her front yard."

Martha's eyes widened, but the corners of her mouth lifted knowingly as she set her coffee pot down. "Well now, mercy me," she drawled, folding her arms as her gaze flicked between Caleb and Debbie. "Sounds like that snowstorm was rather interesting for y'all."

"It was interesting for sure," Debbie said with a laugh. "He practically gave me a heart attack, showing up the way he did. But, uh, I think it ended up working out alright."

"Sounds like it," Martha said, her sharp-eyed intuition blurring the line between observation and playful meddling. Her grin widened. "The Lord sure does work in mysterious ways, doesn't He?"

"Yeah, mysterious is a good word for it," she murmured.

Caleb shifted slightly in his seat, his rugged hands wrapping around the coffee mug in front of him. "Sometimes life just surprises you," he said, his voice steady but thoughtful.

Martha arched an eyebrow as she refilled Caleb's coffee mug. "Well, surprises or not, sounds to me like you found yourself right where you needed to be, Caleb."

"Kids," a voice interrupted their conversation, disarmingly casual yet charged with an undercurrent that froze Debbie in place. "Well, this is a surprise. Didn't think I'd bump into you all tonight."

The fork slipped from Debbie's fingers, landing on her plate with a sharp clink that echoed louder than it should have. Time seemed to slow as the voice sent a chill coursing through her. James Ferguson, her ex-husband, stood just a few feet away.

Chapter 27

Nathan, who had been mid-bite, froze with his fork halfway to his mouth. He glanced at his sister before muttering, "Hey, Dad."

Danielle, sitting up straighter, managed a tight, polite, "Hi," though her hazel eyes betrayed her disquiet.

Debbie worked to regain her composure, instinctively straightening in the booth while trying not to appear ruffled. Her eyes quickly darted to Caleb, who frowned almost imperceptibly, a watchful look in his deep brown eyes. He leaned back slightly, his arms resting on the side of the booth, embodying a quiet but steady presence.

James, of course, seemed oblivious—or downright indifferent—to the tension his arrival brought. His face bore the same self-assured grin that had once charmed Debbie, but now only grated. His dark hair was gelled a little too perfect, his shirt untucked in a way that seemed intentionally careless, and his arm rested a little too comfortably around the shoulders of the young woman standing next to him.

James gestured toward her as though presenting a prized trophy. "This is Piper," he announced, his voice carrying easily over the subtle hum of the diner. "Piper, these are my kids—Nathan and Danielle—and their mom, Debbie." His delivery was breezy, as if their family dynamic wasn't steeped in years of fractured trust, resentment, and complicated histories.

Piper gave a small wave, her hand barely leaving the pocket of her trendy jacket. "Hi, nice to meet you," she said, her voice light and sweet, though her lack of eye contact hinted she had no real interest in anyone at the table.

For a moment, no one spoke. The air hung heavy, like a stillness right before a summer storm. Nathan was the one to break the silence, pushing his plate slightly aside. "Nice to meet you," he said, his expression unreadable—a mask Debbie recognized all too well as his way of deflecting discomfort. Danielle, on the other hand, simply nodded, narrowing her eyes slightly as she studied Piper.

"Well," James continued, rubbing the back of his neck. "I guess it's good to see you all out and about. Figured you'd be holed up at the cabin, Deb." He laughed awkwardly, the sound forced, as though he was trying too hard.

"It's good to get out," she said, folding her hands in her lap to keep them steady. She wasn't about to let James rattle her, not with Nathan and Danielle sitting right there. "The kids needed a break, and so did I."

Her eyes flicked toward Caleb, who remained silent but watchful. Realizing he deserved an introduction, Debbie cleared her throat. "James, this is Caleb Warren."

Caleb stood, extending a hand as his deep voice broke the tension. "Nice to meet you."

James gave Caleb a once-over, his grin tightening. Whether it was the easy confidence in Caleb's tone or the sheer height and strength of the man in front of him, something about Caleb clearly unsettled him. Still, James clasped Caleb's hand for a quick shake, though his posture stiffened noticeably. "Yeah, good to meet you," he said, his tone polite but clipped.

If Caleb noticed the shift, he didn't show it. "Snow's been rough up on the mountain," Caleb added casually, his hand dropping back to the table. "I'm sure your kids could tell you all about it. They've been a big help."

James's gaze flickered between Caleb and Debbie for a moment. Then, regaining his overly relaxed posture, he chuckled. "Yeah, well, they're good kids." His words felt hollow, more like an empty platitude than genuine affection.

Piper shifted on her feet, tugging at the sleeve of her jacket. "James," she murmured, just loud enough to catch his attention, "I'm going to go grab a table."

"Right," James said quickly, seeming almost relieved by the excuse to move on. He glanced back at Nathan and Danielle with a half-smile. "I'll check in with you guys later, okay?"

"Sure," Danielle said, her voice tight. Nathan just nodded.

James and Piper left, weaving their way toward a small table on the far side of the diner. Debbie exhaled, not realizing she had been holding her breath. The kids exchanged a glance but said nothing, each retreating into their own thoughts.

Caleb broke the silence, his voice calm but firm. "You alright?" The question was directed at Debbie, though his gaze shifted briefly to Nathan and Danielle.

"Yeah," she said, offering Caleb a small, grateful smile.

Danielle shrugged, though her expression betrayed her frustration. "I just don't get it. How can someone act like everything's fine when it's not?"

Nathan leaned back in his seat, playing idly with the fork on his plate. "It's easier to pretend," he muttered, his tone carrying an edge of bitterness.

Danielle glanced at her mom, her expression softening slightly. "It just... feels weird seeing him with someone else... especially so young. It's like he's moved on, but we're still stuck."

Debbie's chest tightened at her daughter's words. "I know how that feels," she admitted softly. "We're not stuck, Danielle. We've carved out a new life for ourselves. Your dad may just need more time to figure out where he fits into this new picture."

Nathan and Danielle exchanged looks, their expressions shifting ever so slightly, though they remained silent.

"I know it's not easy," Debbie said softly, "but let's just try to have a little faith. Add your dad to your prayers. I'm sure that God will listen."

Danielle nodded, her shoulders relaxing as she picked up her fork again, though her brow furrowed as she processed her mom's words. Nathan pushed his cherry pie around on his plate.

Across the diner, James and Piper seemed oblivious to the storm they had stirred. James leaned back in his chair, laughing at something Piper had said, his voice carrying across the room. Debbie turned her gaze away.

Danielle set her fork down with a sigh, drawing everyone's attention back to her. "I guess you're right," she admitted grudgingly, her eyes flicking between her mom and Caleb. "It just still feels...ugh. Like, how does he not even think about how this all makes us feel?"

"Danielle," Debbie said gently, reaching out to place a hand on her daughter's, "your dad is going through his own stuff. Sometimes people deal with guilt or sadness in ways that make little sense to others. It doesn't excuse it, but it does explain a little."

Nathan, who had finally started eating his pie again, piped up. "Or maybe he's just terrible at dealing with guilt," he muttered, though there was no venom in his voice—just a quiet frustration.

Danielle looked at her brother and nodded wordlessly, her expression softening.

Martha reappeared at the table, sweeping in with her usual mix of warmth and energy. "Everything tasting alright over here?" she asked brightly, her gaze flicking from one face to another.

"Fantastic, as always," Debbie replied, her tone lighter now as she smiled up at the older woman. A glance at the table confirmed that everyone's plates were either empty or close to it.

"Good, good," Martha said with a satisfied nod. Then she leaned in conspiratorially, lowering her voice. "You know, it's been a long time since I've seen a table like this one—a whole lotta love going on right here. And might I add, Caleb Warren, you fit in with this crew like you've been sittin' with them for years."

Caleb chuckled softly, his expression unreadable but warm. "Just happy to be here tonight, Martha."

"Well, don't make it a onetime thing," she said with a wink before bustling off to another table.

Chapter 28

Caleb sat nursing a cup of coffee at the kitchen table. His broad shoulders were relaxed, but his expression attentive as his dark eyes followed Debbie's movements around the kitchen as she prepared her lunch for work tomorrow.

"Harold and Mildred will be my first visit tomorrow," Debbie said over her shoulder, pulling a ziplock bag from the drawer. She placed the sandwich she'd made inside, sealing it with a satisfying snap. "They're such a sweet couple. Married for over sixty years, can you imagine? Sixty." She said. "That sort of commitment feels like a miracle these days."

Caleb tilted his head, his voice low and thoughtful. "Sixty years is something special. Sounds like they could teach the rest of us a thing or two."

"They definitely could," Debbie said with a soft laugh, turning around to face him. "Even with all the challenges they've faced—health issues, losing two sons—they're still so deeply rooted in their faith. It's like, regardless of what happens, they're unshakable."

She leaned back against the counter, her arms crossed loosely, fingers brushing her sweater sleeves as if grounding herself. "That kind of resilience amazes me."

Caleb nodded. "Reminds me of my grandmother," he said after a moment. "When my grandpa passed, she could've let the grief swallow her whole. But she didn't. Every morning after he passed, she'd sit by the window with her Bible, just reading and praying. That was her anchor." He paused, eyes distant as he recalled the memory. "She used to tell us, 'Hope doesn't depend on what you can see. It depends on who you trust.'"

"That's beautiful," she said.

He gave a small nod, meeting her eyes. "I think you've got a bit of that in you," he said. "Harold and Mildred might be unshakable, but you're not far behind."

Debbie's cheeks warmed, and she turned back toward the counter under the guise of grabbing the bag of carrots she'd prepped earlier. Her heart thudded heavier in her chest, a mix of emotions she didn't dare unpack just yet.

"Thank you," she murmured. "But most days, it just feels like surviving."

"Even surviving takes strength," Caleb countered, his tone low but sure.

Before Debbie could respond, the sound of footsteps interrupted the moment. Danielle appeared in the kitchen doorway, her phone in her hand and an uncertain crease in her brow. "Mom?" Her voice carried a hesitant edge, the kind Debbie knew well—it was the voice of someone unsure how the next few minutes might unfold.

Debbie straightened immediately, bracing herself. "What's up, sweetie?"

Danielle held up her phone slightly. "Dad just texted. He... wants to talk to me and Nathan. He asked if we'd come over."

Debbie swallowed, maintaining a calm expression even as her thoughts began to swirl. James's unpredictable nature always left her on edge. His rare attempts to reach out had a pattern of raising expectations, only to let them crash. She didn't want this to be one of those times—but history had taught her to be cautious.

"What do you want to do?" Debbie asked, her voice gentle but careful to hand her daughter the reins.

Danielle frowned, chewing her lip. "I don't know."

"Maybe he really does want to talk," Debbie said. "Only one way to find out."

Danielle fidgeted with the phone in her hand.

"It's up to you and Nathan. You're both old enough to decide." Debbie continued.

Danielle's hazel eyes searched her mother's for a moment, her expression shifting between doubt and hope. "But what if he—"

Debbie cut in softly, recognizing her daughter's unspoken concern. "I can't promise he won't disappoint or upset you. But I can promise you this—you're stronger than that."

Danielle nodded, her shoulders dropping slightly as some of the tension eased.

A sound from the stairs signaled Nathan's arrival. He padded into the room, his hair slightly tousled, his phone gripped loosely in his hand. "I guess we better go," he said.

Danielle glanced at her brother, then back at her mom. Debbie nodded solemnly. "The keys are hanging by the front door," she said, forcing her voice to stay steady even as her chest tightened.

As the twins retrieved their coats, Debbie moved toward them, wrapping them both in a quick, tight hug. "I'm proud of you both," she said. "No matter how this goes, I want you to remember that."

Nathan nodded wordlessly, his jaw tight. Danielle lingered in her mom's embrace for half a second longer before whispering, "Thanks, Mom."

They stepped out into the cold, their boots crunching on the snow-covered porch. Debbie watched from the doorway, her arms folded across her chest as she fought the tug of worry and pride warring within her. She prayed silently as the car's headlights cut through the darkened driveway and turned on the road leading to town.

When the taillights disappeared out of her sight, Debbie closed the door, her eyes flicking toward Caleb. He'd moved to lean against the kitchen counter, watching her with an expression both empathetic and steadying.

"You okay?" he asked, his voice low.

Debbie smiled, shaking her head. "It's strange... being proud, mad, and terrified all at once." She walked into the kitchen and leaned against the counter beside Caleb. "I get that this is their choice to make. I do. But watching them walk out that door... it's hard not to think about all the times James has let them down before."

"You can't control what he does, Deb. You've given the twins the tools to deal with life. You've taught them how to face tough things and come out stronger. That's what matters."

Her eyes lifted to meet his, gratitude mingling with something deeper—something unspoken but palpable. "You make it sound like I actually know what I'm doing," she said, her lips curving into a faint, self-deprecating smile.

"You should give yourself more credit," Caleb replied, his tone sincere. "Being a parent doesn't mean having all the answers. It means showing up. And you do that every single day."

She nodded in response, lost in her thoughts.

"I think I'll step out for some fresh air," he said, his voice quieter now. He grabbed his coat from the back of the chair and slipped it on.

Debbie watched him go.

The door clicked softly behind him, and Debbie exhaled. Alone in the quiet cabin, she placed her hands flat on the counter and let her head bow slightly. "Lord," she whispered, "help me trust You with this—not just for Nathan and Danielle, but for all of it."

Chapter 29

Debbie sat curled on one end of the couch, her Bible open on her lap, and a coffee cup resting on the end table beside her.

She breathed deeply, her fingers idly tracing the margins of the Bible's thin pages. Her eyes moved over a passage in Psalms: He heals the brokenhearted and binds up their wounds. The words felt heavier tonight, their personal significance not lost on her. She didn't need a blizzard to remind her how life's storms—be they swirling snow or soul-deep struggles—could push faith to its limits. And yet, here she sat, drawn to a man she never expected to meet in such circumstances, wrestling with emotions she hadn't dared to explore for years. Her children, meanwhile, were navigating their own battles at their father's house, each facing the uncertainties of love, trust, and forgiveness in their own way.

The back door clicked open. She glanced up as Caleb stepped inside, his tall frame silhouetted against the dim light spilling in from the porch. Snow clung stubbornly to his coat and boots, and his cheeks carried the telltale redness of the bitter cold outside.

He shrugged off his coat and boots. When his eyes met hers, they softened just enough to send a flicker of warmth through her chest.

"Cold out there?" she asked, her voice quiet but tinged with gentle humor.

"Freezing," he replied, his lips twitching into a faint smile.

He moved into the kitchen and poured himself a cup of coffee, his movements unhurried and deliberate. Debbie watched him carefully. There was something both reassuring and disarming in the way he had settled into her home, carving out his space without ever overstepping.

When he walked into the living room, he hesitated for just a moment before choosing the spot beside her on the couch. The cushions dipped under his weight.

"You're in the thick of it, huh?" Caleb nodded toward the Bible in her lap, taking a sip of his coffee.

"Psalm 147," she said, tapping the page lightly. "I was reminding myself about healing."

Caleb's gaze lingered on her for a moment before he looked down at his coffee. He cradled the mug in his hands, as though willing its heat to seep into more than just his fingers. "I used to think healing was something that just... happened, so long as you kept your head down and powered through." His eyes lifted to meet hers again, the weight of his words like a stone sinking in a river. "Turns out, it's not quite that simple."

"No, it's not." Debbie closed the Bible slowly, her hands resting gently over its cover. "You can't outrun pain any more than you can outrun a storm. Believe me, I've tried."

Caleb's gaze lingered on the fire, the glow of the flames flickering across his rugged features. His deep voice carried a thoughtful intensity as he broke the comfortable silence that filled the room. "Tell me about your divorce," he began, his tone hesitant, the words edged with curiosity and care. "What happened between you and your ex?"

Debbie stilled for a moment. The logs crackled softly in the background, the sound filling the brief pause as she processed his question. Caleb had rarely asked personal questions—especially ones like this. She glanced at him, noticing the way he stared at the fire, like he wasn't entirely sure he had the right to ask, but couldn't ignore the question pressing on his mind.

"That's not exactly light conversation," she said.

"No, I don't suppose it is," he admitted.

"Well," she began, her voice steady but thoughtful, "James and I met in high school. We had been casual friends. After we graduated, we started dating. He enrolled in college, and I had no clue exactly what I wanted to do with my life. He went off to college, and I stayed here and worked at the grocery store. We were young, full of plans, and we thought we had everything figured out. I think, at the time, we both wanted the same things—a family, a home, a good life together. And for a while, we had that. But life... life happened." Her gaze flickered toward the firelight, her eyes reflecting memories both bittersweet and painful. "The stress kept piling on. Jobs, bills, raising twins... We stopped working with each other and started working against each other without even realizing it." She paused, her brows knitting together as she chose her next words carefully. "In the end, it wasn't just the stress. It was the betrayal."

Caleb's eyes shifted to her, a flicker of understanding darkening his expression.

Debbie hesitated, her thumb tracing idle patterns along the armrest of the couch. Her voice, when it came, was soft but imbued with a quiet strength she'd earned the hard way. "James was unfaithful," she began. "I wish I could say that it was a onetime mistake. But it wasn't. It became a pattern." She paused, as though steadying herself with an invisible thread of resolve. "The first time, I forgave him. I wanted to believe we could make it work, but forgiveness doesn't mean much if the other person isn't willing to change. And the second time?" Debbie drew in a slow breath, her lips pressing together. "It was like the first betrayal had left cracks I didn't see before, and with the second, everything started shattering."

She leaned forward, placing the Bible carefully on the coffee table. As she rested her forearms on her knees, her gaze turned distant, drawn into the swirl of a memory she would never forget. "The third time? That was the end. No room for excuses, no room for doubt." Her voice softened, each word coming slower, heavier, laced with the weight of old wounds. "It happened on Main Street. Just me, Nathan, and Danielle—walking side by side like we often did. They were fourteen back then, old enough to catch things and understand.

"We'd just left the bookstore. It was supposed to be a normal day. Then Nathan stopped so abruptly, it startled me. He pointed, his voice hesitant but curious. 'Mom,' he said, 'who's Dad with?' I'll never forget that moment." She paused, her fingers tightening briefly against her knees as though bracing herself. "I followed his finger, and there James was... walking down the street hand in hand with another woman. Bold as daylight."

Her breath hitched ever so slightly before she drew herself back into the present, and her next words carried a quiet grief laced with resilience. "That was the moment everything broke. Not just for me—but for Nathan, for Danielle as well."

She sat back with a deep exhale, her eyes briefly closing, as if releasing the weight of those words all over again. "We ducked into one of the shops nearby. We stayed there for a while, and I tried my best to distract them—bought them their favorite candies, talked about anything except what they had just seen. Later, when we went home, I had already made up my mind. That moment—the look in their eyes, the trust he'd shattered not just with me but with them—that was it. There was nothing left to repair. I knew it was over."

Debbie turned her gaze toward the fire, its light reflecting in her eyes. "I don't regret leaving him. I don't regret filing for divorce," she said. "What I regret is that my kids had to witness so much. That their faith in love and loyalty took such a hit so young. I'll always wish they hadn't been caught in the middle of it."

Caleb reached over and gently took her hand, the warmth of his touch grounding her amidst the steady hum of the crackling fire. "That couldn't have been easy—for any of you," he said, his voice quiet, but rich with understanding.

"It was," Debbie admitted. "But staying in a marriage where the foundation had crumbled wasn't an option anymore. The kids needed stability, and I... I needed to show them what self-respect looked like, even if it meant making the hardest decision of my life." She glanced at him, a small, bittersweet smile softening her expression. "I don't regret the divorce. I regret not doing it sooner. I've made peace with it. I know I did what was right, even if it wasn't easy."

Caleb nodded, his gaze steady. "A lot of people stay in situations like that because they're scared. Scared to start over, scared of what the world might think." His voice softened almost reverently. "But you? You chose what was right over what was easy. That says a lot about you, Debbie."

"Thank you," she said. "It wasn't pretty, and it wasn't graceful, but we've made it through. And trust me, I made plenty of mistakes. Nathan and Danielle—they're my world."

"They're good kids," he said. "Smart, respectful, and tough—in the best way. You've done something special raising them."

He hesitated for a moment before continuing, his voice steady, reflective. "I'll admit, I'm not the most social guy. Outside of my brothers, my dad, and the folks at the mill, I don't spend much time talking to people. But there's one thing I've never been able to wrap my mind around—how someone could break the bond of marriage so easily. It's supposed to mean something. A promise before God, a commitment to stand by someone, even when it's hard. I just... I can't understand how someone could look at the person they vowed to stay faithful to and betray that promise."

Debbie nodded, her expression thoughtful. "I think some people let fear and selfishness take over," she said softly. "And there are others who chase the thrill of sneaking around, convincing themselves they'll never face the consequences."

Caleb nodded.

Debbie let out a soft sigh, her gaze drifting to the flickering flames. "Even through all the ugliness and pain of a divorce, I still believe in love," she said, her voice steady, yet laced with quiet conviction. "I believe I went through everything I did for a reason. Just like you, everything you've gone through, there's a reason for it all."

Chapter 30

Debbie sat propped against a stack of pillows on her quilt-covered bed. A book lay open on her lap, though she had read the same paragraph three times without fully grasping it. Her thoughts kept drifting, her heart half-focused on the quiet prayer she'd been murmuring since Nathan and Danielle drove away earlier that evening.

The bedside lamp cast a soft light over the room, warm and inviting, as if coaxing her to trust the stillness. Yet, no matter how calm the exterior—the soft hum of the heater, the occasional whisper of wind outside—Her mother's heart held a whisper of unease, a blend of worry layered like fine threads. She wasn't just concerned about the snow-laden roads they'd have to navigate on their way home—though the thought of icy bends brought its own kind of tension. No, it was more than that. It was the uncertainty of what might weigh on their hearts after time spent with their father. That quiet tension, the possibility of disappointment or hurt resurfacing, settled inside her like a knot she couldn't untangle.

When she finally heard the creak of the front door opening and the low murmur of Nathan and Danielle's voices downstairs, Debbie released a quiet breath. She glanced at the digital clock on the nightstand—10:47 p.m. Most nights when they would be out with their friends or at a church or school activity, the twins would have breezed past her door with a quick goodnight, but Debbie had left her door wide open, hoping the small gesture would be enough to let them know she was waiting.

Nathan appeared first, his broad shoulders nearly filling the doorway. Danielle trailed a step behind, their unspoken twin bond evident as they moved together. Nathan stepped inside and perched himself on the end of her bed, his long legs stretched toward the floor, hands clasped loosely in his lap. Danielle wordlessly slipped under the covers beside Debbie, like she had done as a little girl after a bad dream. They were no longer small children, but this closeness—the way they gravitated toward her in moments of uncertainty—reminded Debbie just how universal some aspects of mothering would always be.

"You guys okay?" Debbie asked, keeping her voice calm and steady, offering an open door but not a push.

For a moment, the only sound in the room was the faint ticking of the clock on the wall. Finally, Danielle sighed. "It was... weird," she said, her tone soft but tinged with a mixture of frustration and thoughtfulness.

Nathan nodded, his brow furrowed, as if he were still sorting through his own emotions. "He... I don't know. He tried, I guess. But it's like..." He trailed off, searching for the right words. "It's like the doesn't know how to just be a dad."

Debbie's chest tightened. She kept her expression neutral, careful not to project her own emotions.

Danielle shifted slightly, her words slower now, as though she were parsing through the experience as she spoke. "He said he wants to be more involved. That he wants to... try. But it felt kind of... forced, you know? Like he was saying what he thought we wanted to hear, but it didn't feel real." She frowned, her fingers fidgeting with the edge of the quilt. "It's confusing because part of me wants to believe him. I mean, he's our dad, right? Shouldn't we want to give him another chance?"

Nathan leaned forward, resting his elbows on his knees. "But how many chances does that make now?" he asked quietly, his voice steady but tinged with an edge. "It's like trying to rebuild something out of matchsticks. You know it's gonna fall, so what's the point?"

Debbie's heart ached at his words—not because he was mistaken, but because she knew how draining it could feel to hold on to anger and disappointment, even at their age.

"I don't think there's a right or wrong way to feel about it," she said finally, her words slow and intentional. "It's okay to want to protect yourself from more hurt. And it's okay to hope for change, too. They're both honest emotions."

Danielle lifted her head slightly, turning to look at her mom. "Is that what it was like for you?" she asked. "When you—when everything fell apart?"

Debbie hesitated, not because the answer wasn't there, but because she wanted to choose her words carefully. "I think... I think it was a lot like that," she admitted. "I wanted to believe, wanted to hope. But at some point, you realize that love isn't just about words or promises—it's about action. And when someone isn't willing to fight for your trust or your love, it becomes very hard to keep extending it."

Nathan glanced at her then, his jaw tight but his eyes softer now. "What if the trust's already on crutches?" he asked.

Debbie smiled faintly, her eyes meeting his with a quiet steadiness. "Then you tread carefully. You don't have to give him everything at once—all the hope, all the trust. If you feel led, you can give him small pieces and see what he does with them. God doesn't ask us to lower our guard completely; He asks us to be wise and discerning. And forgiving someone doesn't mean you have to let them deeply into your life if they haven't earned it."

"It's just... hard to know where to draw the line, you know? I don't want to stop hoping, but... I don't want to get hurt again, either," Danielle said.

"You're stronger than you think," Debbie said. "And you're wise. You'll figure it out in time, and when you do, I'll be here—no matter what."

Her gaze shifted to Nathan, who was staring at the quilt pattern as if it might hold some hidden answer. "Both of you will," Debbie added firmly. "You've come through so much already, and you've done it with grace, with faith, and with strength I can't even put into words. I'm so proud of both of you. And I know this is hard right now, but he is your dad, and he always will be. There is not one single person on this planet who has never made a mistake."

Nathan glanced up at her, the weight in his expression lifting slightly. "You always think we're stronger than we feel, Mom," he said, his tone laced with affection.

Nathan and Danielle exchanged a look, that unspoken twin conversation passing between them in a way Debbie had grown accustomed to over the years. She could see a flicker of hesitation in Danielle's hazel eyes, mirrored by the slight tilt of Nathan's head. Then, with a quiet nod from her brother, Danielle spoke, her voice tentative but steady.

"Mom," she began, tucking her legs under her as she shifted on the bed, "since we're being honest tonight, we've got a question."

Debbie set her book down on the nightstand, folding the corner of the page to mark her place. Her warm hazel eyes met her daughter's with an openness that invited trust. "Alright," she said gently, her posture relaxing as she leaned back against the headboard. "Lay it on me. You know I'll always give you the truth."

Danielle looked at Nathan for a moment, as if waiting for him to jump in, but when he didn't, she took a slow breath and pressed forward.

"So..." Danielle hesitated, then let the words tumble out. "Do you think you'll ever... I don't know, date again? Like, really date someone?" Her cheeks flushed, and she gave a nervous laugh, brushing a stray strand of hair behind her ear. "I mean, not that we're trying to put you on the spot or anything. But dad has obviously moved on... well, he moved on a long time ago. But when will you?"

Debbie blinked, caught off guard by the question, but her lips curved into a soft, understanding smile. She glanced between her children, her heart swelling with a mix of love and bittersweet amusement.

"Well," she began, her tone thoughtful, "that's a fair question. And I think the honest answer is... yes. Yes, I will date again. For a long time, my focus has been on you two—making sure you're okay, that we're okay, and building a life we can all feel safe and proud of. Dating just hasn't been at the top of my list."

She paused, glancing toward Nathan, whose brow furrowed slightly as he stared at the floor, seemingly deep in thought. Danielle, on the other hand, was studying her mom closely, her gaze searching for something unspoken.

Danielle tilted her head, her expression curious. "So... what kind of person would you want to date? Like, if you could choose."

Debbie laughed softly, reaching out to ruffle her daughter's hair, which earned a playful groan of protest. "You two have more questions than the Sunday school kids at Vacation Bible School," she teased, then turned thoughtful. "Let's see... someone kind. Honest. Reliable. A man of faith who knows how to laugh and doesn't mind the chaos of family life." Her smile deepened. "And someone who sees the blessing in being part of us, the three of us."

Nathan lifted his head, his gaze serious as he met his mother's eyes. "But what if they're not... you know, like Dad was before he got all crazy acting? Like he was when we were younger?"

Debbie's expression softened immediately as she leaned forward, resting a hand on her son's knee. "Sweetheart," she said gently, "I don't expect anyone to be like your dad used to be. But I will expect the person that I choose to bring into this family to treat us with honesty, with respect, and with love. That's the standard, and that's what I'd hold anyone to if they came into our lives."

"Even Caleb?" Nathan added, his voice quieter now, as if testing the waters.

"Caleb is a good man," she said simply. "I think he's still figuring some things out for himself, just like we all are. But what I can say for sure is that I trust him. And trust is a pretty big deal in this house, don't you think?"

Danielle's lips curved into a small smile, and Nathan gave a tiny nod, though neither said anything.

Debbie took the opportunity to reach out, one arm pulling Danielle close and the other nudging Nathan to snuggle up to her. "I know it's been a lot—this life, the changes we've all had to weather—but you both make everything worth it. Even the hard days. I know it's hard on you both to see your dad with someone else, I get that, but there is no need to worry about me." Her voice softened, carrying an edge of emotion that made Danielle hug her a little tighter. "And you know what? I'm so proud of both. The way you handled yourselves tonight, the grace and strength you showed with your dad... it makes me so proud to be your mom."

Nathan ducked his head, a faint smile tugging at the corners of his mouth, while Danielle pressed her face into Debbie's shoulder with a muffled, "Thanks, Mom."

"No, thank you," Debbie said, holding them both a little longer, grounding herself in the presence of her two greatest blessings. She pulled back slightly, her hands resting on each of their shoulders as she added with a playful raise of her eyebrows, "Now, go get some sleep. We've all got a new day to tackle tomorrow."

Danielle groaned lightly but climbed off the bed, yawning as she stretched. Nathan followed, lingering at the doorway just a moment longer to glance back at his mom. "Night, Mom," he said, his voice softer than usual, but laced with sincerity.

"Goodnight, sweet boy," Debbie replied, her smile warm and steady.

Chapter 31

"It's always a pleasure to see you, Debbie," Mildred said warmly, waving her in with one hand while holding a broom with the other. Her silver hair was neatly pinned back, though a few playful wisps had escaped the tidy bun, softening her already welcoming demeanor. "Now, before anything else, let me say this: we owe you and Caleb more thanks than I can put into words for what you did during that storm. If it weren't for the two of you, Lord only knows how we'd have managed."

Debbie stepped through the doorway, enveloped almost instantly by the comforting scent of sugar cookies and wood smoke. She shrugged off her coat, a modest smile gracing her lips. "You don't need to thank me, Mildred. Helping you and Harold was the least we could do. Honestly, the two of you are like family to me."

Mildred clucked her tongue and arched a brow. "Family or not, don't you dare downplay what you both did for us. Caleb practically hauled this entire mountain on his back to make sure Harold and I had firewood, and you, young lady, well, you acted like a modern day Florence Nightingale."

Debbie laughed softly, holding up her hands in surrender. "Alright, I'll take the compliment—but only if it comes with one of those cookies I smell baking."

Mildred broke into a conspiratorial grin as she hung Debbie's coat on the peg by the door. "Oh, I've got more than cookies coming your way. But first, you sit yourself down and let me put some coffee on. We've got plenty to catch up on."

Harold's gruff but cheerful voice carried from the next room. "Is that Debbie I hear rescuing us again?" He appeared in the doorway, leaning his weight on a sturdy wooden cane but looking far better than he had during the storm. His smile stretched wide. "About time someone showed up and brought some good company to balance all this bossy business, Mildred's been throwing my way."

"Bossy?" Mildred sniffed dramatically, though her eyes sparkled as she grabbed coffee cups from the hutch. "You'd still be trying to crawl across the back porch if it weren't for my bossiness."

Debbie laughed, dropping her medical bag onto the table as Mildred set a bouquet of mismatched cookie tins in front of her. But Harold wasn't done. He shuffled toward the table, pointed a gnarled finger at Debbie, and said with mock solemnity, "You tell her, Debbie, that I'm a perfectly capable man—"

"Capable of making a mess, maybe," Mildred interjected with a smirk, sitting down across from Debbie.

Harold huffed, but his grin remained intact.

Mildred, her expression softening, reached across the table to place a hand gently over Debbie's. "Let's get back to the other subject. Just knowing there are people like you and Caleb in this world—steady, reliable folks who show up when it matters most. You've made my heart so happy. You helped us when you didn't have to."

"It's not a one-way street, Mildred. You and Harold have done your share of taking care of others, too. Your kindness spreads farther than you probably even realize," Debbie said.

Mildred gave Debbie the kind of look that only decades of living—and meddling—could perfect. Her sharp blue eyes sparkled with mischief as she stirred a spoonful of sugar into her coffee, refusing to let the subject drop. "Speaking of Caleb," she began, her tone casual, though her pointed expression revealed her true intent, "how's that man of yours doing?"

Debbie felt the heat rise to her cheeks, her composure faltering under the combined weight of Mildred's relentless curiosity and Harold's raised eyebrow from the nearby chair. "He's... fine," she said carefully, shifting her weight as she fiddled with the blood pressure cuff she was strapping around Harold's arm. "He's been keeping busy—spending today clearing out his driveway after the storm. Nathan volunteered to go help him out." Her voice quickened, as if speed could steer her away from the real target of Mildred's question. "And, for the record, he's not 'my man.' We're friends—good friends."

"Friends," Mildred repeated. "Well, isn't that something special? Forgive me, dear, for assuming otherwise. Still, the good Lord does have a knack for weaving people's paths together in ways none of us can predict, doesn't He?"

Debbie barely had time to open her mouth before Mildred pressed on, her words flowing like warm honey. "Though, if I'm being honest, it does sound like one of those stories that makes you stop and wonder. A man like Caleb landing in your yard in the middle of a blizzard?" She gave an exaggerated shrug, like the answer was plain as day. "If that isn't a sign, I don't know what is."

"Mildred," Debbie interjected, fighting the urge to roll her eyes. "You know better than anyone that storms don't just move people—they reroute everything in their path. Caleb ending up at my place? That could've been a coincidence… or maybe it wasn't. I don't have it all figured out yet."

"But you will." Mildred lifted her coffee mug in quiet acknowledgment, her grin playful but layered with purpose. "Mark my words. God doesn't put people on the same path accidentally."

Debbie sighed in mock exasperation, the corner of her mouth twitching toward a smile despite herself. Mildred had a way of sewing faith and humor into her words so seamlessly that resistance was nearly impossible. "I'll be sure to let you know when the heavens send me a memo about Caleb's divine purpose in my life."

Mildred stifled a chuckle, tilting her head with a motherly amusement that disarmed Debbie completely. "Oh, I have a feeling you'll figure it out soon enough. You may not see it clearly yet, sweetheart, but remember this—storms don't last forever. And sometimes, when the snow clears, you find something standing in its place that's stronger, warmer, and more beautiful than what came before."

In the defiant flicker of silence that followed, Debbie focused on Harold's reading, the steady rhythm of the cuff's release grounding her. But even she had to admit—through Mildred's teasing, there was truth. A gentle, disarming truth that nestled quietly in the space between what had been, and what might someday come to be.

Harold chuckled as the cuff deflated with a faint hiss. "Don't get too flustered, Debbie. Mildred's just nosy by nature—it's the only exercise she gets some days."

"I heard that," Mildred retorted.

With a chuckle of her own, Debbie shook her head. "Your blood pressure's good," she informed him with a reassuring smile. "Right where we want it." She leaned in closer, speaking in a conspiratorial tone. "I think the real question is whether being married to Mildred all these years has kept your heart healthy—or if it's given you a little extra endurance."

Harold broke into a laugh, slapping his knee. "Now there's a question worth pondering."

Mildred set her coffee down with a mock offense that was, of course, betrayed by her beaming smile. She wagged a finger at Debbie. "You watch it, young lady. Keep it up, and I won't share my lemon pound cake with you next time."

"Oh, not that!" Debbie gasped, pretending to look horrified. "Anything but the pound cake."

Their shared laughter filled the room, but Mildred wasn't about to let the moment distract her for long. Her expression softened as she leaned forward slightly, her fingers tracing the rim of her cup as she turned back to Debbie. "Joking aside," she said, her tone now warm and earnest, "I always thought that Caleb was a good boy growing up. He and his brothers—why, they used to come by with their daddy, delivering truckloads of lumber scraps to anyone who needed them during the colder months. They were strong kids—had to be working at that mill. But out of all of them, Caleb always seemed the most... intense. Like he carried more than the others did. He had this quiet nature about him. He studied people. And then Bonnie..." she trailed off, her smile faltering as the memory shifted.

"Yes," Debbie said softly, nodding. "He's definitely carried his share of heartache. Losing his wife the way he did—I can't even imagine what that was like for him."

"And the drinking," Mildred said softly. "Everyone in this town knows how far Caleb fell into the bottle when he was in his teens. After Bonnie passed, though..." She paused, her blue eyes brimming with a mix of awe and respect. "He quit drinking, just like that. Faster than I've ever seen anyone do it. We were all really worried about him living up on that mountain all alone. I think a lot of us wondered if he'd ever find his way back."

Harold shifted in his chair, resting his arms on the table as his typically playful tone gave way to something deliberate and reflective. "But let me tell you something," he added, a faint spark of conviction lighting his expression as he tapped the table softly for emphasis. "I have no doubt that God was working on him during those years—shaping him. Sometimes, it's the hardest chapters that set you up for the kind of reckoning that leads to something better. I believe the Lord put him on a new path—not just to pull him out of what was breaking him, but to prepare him for something good."

Debbie glanced between the two as they spoke, her hands busy with her work as she applied fresh, clean bandages to Harold's leg. She stayed silent, letting their reflections fill the warm kitchen air. When Harold winced slightly, she paused and looked up at him, offering a gentle smile. "Sorry about that, Harold. Almost done." She smoothed the bandage with care, her touch practiced and steady.

"No worries, young lady," Harold replied, his tone lightening as he flashed her a wink. "You can poke at me all you want if it keeps these old bones ticking a little longer."

"You know," Mildred said, leaning back in her chair and folding her hands in her lap, "I think Caleb's carrying more strength now than he ever did before. It's not the loud, boastful kind—it's the quiet kind. The kind that sneaks up on you and takes root when you've fought through seasons of heartbreak and come out the other side."

Debbie carefully secured the final piece of bandage tape, smoothing it lightly with her fingers. Her voice, when she spoke, held a quiet thoughtfulness, as though she were sifting through her own reflections. "He's shared pieces of all that he went through with me," she said, glancing between Mildred and Harold. "He didn't sugarcoat anything—not the drinking, not the grief, not how losing Bonnie felt like losing himself. He was honest about what it took to crawl back from rock bottom, and it says a lot about the kind of person he is now. There's a resilience in him, a strength beneath the surface, that's hard to miss."

She paused, her gaze dropping briefly, as if replaying moments from her conversations with Caleb. "What stands out the most, though, is the peace he's found in solitude. It's not loneliness he's escaped to; it's a deliberate choice to live more quietly and intentionally. And I have to admit, I see the clarity it's brought him."

Debbie's voice softened further, an edge of curiosity threading through her words. "But I do wonder sometimes... is solitude still serving him, or is it just a habit he's grown comfortable with over the years? Habits—good or bad—are hard to break, especially ones that feel safe. Yet... maybe that safety, that quiet, is part of what's given him the calm and thoughtfulness he has now. It makes you question—when you've rebuilt a life that brings you peace, is there even a need to disrupt it?"

"Rebuilt is exactly the right word," Harold said, his mouth quirked in a thoughtful half-smile. "It's like he was standing on shaky ground for years, but instead of letting it all crumble, he got out his tools and started hammering in a new foundation. Sturdy and solid."

Debbie paused mid-motion, her hands momentarily still as she packed away her supplies. "You two are determined to send me home with a lot to think about, aren't you?" she teased, her gaze shifting between their knowing expressions.

"It's what we do best," Harold quipped, crossing his arms over his chest with mock pride. "Now, take a break from always lookin' after everyone else and let the words of two old folks who've seen some things settle in for a change."

Debbie smiled warmly at them both, her heart full of the quiet intimacy of their shared moment. "I promise to think about what you've said," she said. "As long as you promise me you'll focus on keeping your bandages clean and dry, Harold. You're healing beautifully. You keep doing what you're doing and don't overdo it, okay?"

Harold raised his hand as though making a solemn vow. "I'll be good, cross my heart."

Mildred reached across to pat Debbie's arm affectionately. "You're a good person, you know that? You brighten every room you step into. And if you ever get the feeling that maybe you're good for Caleb, too… well, I reckon you won't hear us arguing about it."

Debbie smiled as she stood up, slung her bag over her shoulder, and slipped her coat back on. Harold and Mildred walked her to the door, their combined presence as warm as the firelight glowing in the hearth behind them.

"Take care of each other," Debbie said with a playful smile as she stepped onto the snow-dusted porch.

"We always do," Mildred replied with a wave. "And you take care of yourself, too, young lady. You deserve it."

Chapter 32

The steady hum of Caleb's space heater blended with the occasional metallic clink of tools against the car engine. The barn was alive with the kind of quiet productivity that had always centered Caleb—a space that made sense when the rest of the world didn't. The scent of old motor oil mingled with the faint tang of sawdust, and the two men inside the barn worked side by side like it was the most natural thing in the world.

Nathan, his jacket shed and sleeves rolled to his elbows, leaned over the hood of Caleb's car, eyes wide with interest as he examined the intricate workings of the engine. Streaks of oil smudged his hands—a badge of honor he was quick to admire with a grin every time Caleb handed him a new tool.

"What year did you say this baby was?" Nathan asked, brushing a hand lightly against the cool metal of the car's exterior.

"1972 Plymouth Road Runner," Caleb replied from the other side of the engine, his voice steady, tinged with pride. "I've had her since

I was eighteen years old. Found her rusting away in a salvage yard upstate."

Nathan let out a low whistle, eyes sweeping over the sleek curves of the aging muscle car. Even in its unfinished state, there was something beautiful about it—the raw potential, the quiet promise of what it could become under Caleb's care. "It's awesome," Nathan said earnestly. "You really know what you're doing, huh?"

Caleb chuckled, reaching for a wrench and handing it to Nathan without missing a beat. "Takes time and patience more than anything else," he said. "Working with cars isn't about chasing perfection right off the bat—it's about understanding how each part works with the others. You rush through, you miss something important. Take your time, and you start to see how even the small stuff makes a big difference."

Nathan glanced at the wrench in his hand like it had just become a knight's sword, his expression a mix of eagerness and caution. "Alright, so what should I start on without completely wrecking this thing?"

Caleb tilted his head, assessing both the car and the young man across from him. Nathan had a sharpness in him—an alert curiosity that reminded Caleb of himself at his age, eager to learn, even if a little unsure at first. "Here," he said, coming around to Nathan's side, "see that bolt right there? Adjust it, but go slow. We're working on timing right now—start cranking it one turn to the right and let's see if we make any progress."

Nathan's brow furrowed in concentration as he crouched closer, angling the wrench carefully, but his enthusiasm bubbled up in a string of fast-paced questions as he worked. "So, timing—that's like making sure all the moving pieces are... synchronized, right? Or am I totally making that up?"

"Close enough," Caleb said, his mouth quirking with a faint smile. He crouched down beside him, careful not to hover but close enough to guide. "Timing on an engine is about precision. If the spark plugs don't fire in sync with the engine's pistons, you're gonna have a whole mess of problems. A car's heart is its rhythm. Get it steady, and you're golden."

Nathan nodded, biting his bottom lip in concentration as he carefully tightened the bolt. "So you're kind of like a doctor for cars, huh?"

The comment made Caleb pause. He didn't laugh—it wasn't patronizing, just unexpected. His eyes crinkled slightly as he considered it. "I guess you could say that," he said finally. "Though I'd argue, your mom's got me beat in the lifesaving department. Her job's the real deal."

Nathan straightened, resting his forearms on the edge of the car as he glanced sidelong at Caleb. "She's definitely good at patching stuff up. Always in fix-it mode, I guess."

Caleb leaned back on his heels, his eyes catching Nathan's carefully neutral tone. "Fixing people up, or life in general?"

"Both, I guess," Nathan admitted, shrugging slightly before picking up one of Caleb's screwdrivers and twisting it between his fingers absentmindedly. "She's always been that way—making life better for people. Even if it's just little things, like baking cookies for church or stitching ripped jeans. She doesn't like sitting still. It's like she's got this sense of duty about every little thing."

Caleb nodded, leaning against the car. "Not a bad quality to have."

"Yeah," Nathan agreed slowly, his gaze shifting toward the barn window, where the snowy woods stretched endless and still. "It just makes you wonder if she's ever gonna relax, you know? Actually, let herself be happy, not just busy."

Caleb thought about that for a long moment, long enough that Nathan turned back toward him with slightly narrowed eyes.

"You got to spend a lot of time with her lately," Nathan said, keeping his voice breezy, but Caleb caught the undercurrent of something else—a sense of responsibility, maybe even caution. "You ever see her relax? I mean, how's she really doing in your opinion?"

Caleb let out a slow breath, weighing his words carefully. "Your mom," he said finally, keeping his voice steady as he chose honesty over diplomacy, "is one of the strongest people I know. She doesn't just get through life—she makes life better for everyone around her. And I guess... no, I haven't seen your mom relax much."

Nathan watched him closely, his expression unreadable. Then, leaning forward slightly, he said, "You're not just friends, are you?"

Caleb straightened to his full height, scratching the back of his neck as he considered how to answer.

"She's important to me," Caleb admitted, his voice quiet but firm. "And as long as the door is open to more... yeah, I'd want to be more than just friends. I'd like the chance to get to know her better."

Nathan processed that for a moment, the tiniest glimmer of approval breaking through his steady gaze. "You care about her."

"I do," Caleb said plainly. No hesitation.

"What about us?" Nathan asked. "Me and Danielle?"

"Nathan," he said, meeting the boy's eyes squarely, "you and Danielle come with your mom. Loving her would mean loving you two as well. And if we continue down this road that's opened up to us all? I wouldn't take it lightly. I'd want her whole world—as messy, beautiful, and complex as it is."

Nathan studied him for a lingering moment before nodding slowly. "Alright," he said at last, his tone softening. "As long as you... always keep a smile on her face."

"I'll do my best, Nathan. That, I can promise," Caleb replied sincerely. He paused for a moment, considering his next words. "Can I ask you something? What brought all this up about your mom?"

Nathan hesitated, the question hanging in the air as he tried to untangle the knot of emotions inside him.

"You know, Danielle and I went to my dad's house last night," he began, his tone low and guarded. "And... well, it was confusing. Upsetting, really. It left me thinking about a lot of things—about him, about Mom, about all of us."

Nathan paused, glancing at Caleb to gauge his reaction. Caleb stayed quiet, his expression open and attentive, which gave Nathan the courage to keep going.

"It's just... with him, things always feel so surface-level," Nathan admitted, his voice slightly unsteady now. "Like, he tries to say the right things, tries to act like he cares, but it doesn't feel real. It's almost like we're strangers, you know? Like I'm just some guy he used to know instead of his son. And I can't tell if it's because he doesn't know how to connect with us, or if he just doesn't care enough to try."

Caleb tilted his head slightly, his brow furrowing in thought. "That must be hard to deal with," he said gently. "Feeling that distance from someone who's supposed to be so close to you."

Nathan nodded slowly, his jaw tightening as he clenched his hands into fists and then released them. "Yeah, it is. But last night, it hit me all over again how much mom's had to carry on her own because of him, and it made me so angry. She deserves more—better—than what he ever gave her."

Nathan's voice sharpened slightly, anger flickering to the surface like a sudden spark. "And then I started thinking about everything else. About how hard she's worked to keep things steady for Danielle and me, and how she always puts us first, even when I can see she's exhausted or stressed. She's... she's amazing, you know? And maybe that's why I feel so protective. I don't ever want to see her hurt again—not by Dad, not by anyone. I won't allow it."

"That's a lot to carry, Nathan," Caleb said, his tone gentle but firm. "Worrying about your mom, wanting to shield her from more pain—it says a lot about the kind of man you're becoming. But can I share something with you?"

Nathan glanced at him, hesitant but curious. "Yeah... sure."

"Your mom's been through her share of hard things, no doubt about that. But each time, she's come through stronger, a better person. And while I know it's your instinct to protect her—because you care, and because you've got a good heart—you don't always have to."

Nathan frowned slightly, his brows knitting together. "What do you mean? I can't just stop caring about her."

"I'm not saying that," Caleb said quickly, shaking his head. "Caring about her is a good thing—an important thing. But sometimes, the best way to love someone is to trust them to take care of themselves, too. Your mom's been through more than most people ever will, and she's still standing. That tells me she's got a strength that runs deep—deep enough to handle whatever life throws at her."

Nathan didn't respond immediately, but Caleb could see the wheels turning in the younger man's mind.

"Alright," Nathan said finally, his voice carrying a note of cautious acceptance. "Just... don't mess this up, okay... I kinda like having you around."

Caleb chuckled softly, the sound warm and reassuring. "I wouldn't dream of it."

Chapter 33

Debbie pushed open her front door, the familiar creak of the hinges echoing into her unnaturally quiet home. The early evening light filtered through the living room curtains, casting warm streaks of light across the hardwood floors. She slowed her steps, immediately noticing the stillness. No sound of Danielle's music playing softly upstairs, no muffled laughter from Nathan. Not even the faint buzzing of activity that typically came with the twins doing their own thing. It was too quiet.

"I'm home," she called, hanging her coat on the hook near the entryway. The silence remained unbroken, save for the faint ticking of the clock above the mantle. "Danielle? Nathan?"

After tugging her boots and coat off, Debbie ventured toward the staircase. She'd barely reached the banister when she heard the soft thud of Danielle's footsteps descending, her long hair pulled into a loose braid and her phone in one hand.

"Hey, Mom," Danielle greeted with a small smile.

"Hi, sweetheart." Debbie scanned her expression, looking for any signs of alarm. "Where's Nathan? It's awfully quiet around here."

"He's still with Caleb," Danielle said casually, tucking a stray strand of hair behind her ear. "He texted me earlier—said he was going to hang out with Caleb for a while longer."

Debbie's brow knitted slightly. She glanced at the clock hanging above the entryway—nearly five o'clock. Caleb's long driveway might have been a challenge after the recent snowstorm, but surely, they were finished by now?

"He's not home yet... huh?" Debbie said.

Danielle shook her head. "Nope. He seemed pretty excited about whatever Caleb was showing him in the barn, though. Haven't really heard from him since."

Debbie chewed the inside of her cheek for a moment, mulling it over. "I think I'd better check on him," she said. "I haven't actually driven up to Caleb's house using the main road before. When we checked on his place the other day, we had to cut through the woods instead. But I'm pretty sure I can figure it out."

"I'll come with you." Danielle said.

"Are you sure? I don't mind going alone."

"Oh, I'm sure," Danielle said, grabbing her coat. "Besides, this could be fun. You and Caleb always act so..." she trailed off with a sly grin, wiggling her eyebrows.

Debbie arched an eyebrow. "So what?"

"You know, like you're trying really hard not to like each other," Danielle teased, her tone lightly sing-song.

Debbie let out an exasperated laugh as they both bundled up, slipping into their coats and boots. She grabbed her keys. "Come on, Danielle," she said, her voice laced with affectionate amusement.

The mountain road twisted and climbed, each turn revealing a vista more breathtaking than the last. The setting sun spilled across the snow-draped landscape in soft strokes of lavender, blush, and gold, painting the world in twilight's gentle embrace. Debbie gripped the wheel with steady hands, guiding her car carefully along the serpentine curves. Her thoughts, however, wandered far from the road ahead. She found herself wondering what Nathan and Caleb had spent their day doing besides clearing his driveway, their easy companionship drifting into her mind like the warmth of a remembered melody. But beneath her curiosity, another realization had taken root—a growing awareness of how much Caleb had come to mean to her. With each passing day, the feeling grew stronger, no longer something she could easily set aside.

Danielle, sitting in the passenger seat, tapped her fingers against her phone screen. "You're worried about him, aren't you?"

"I'd said curious more than anything," Debbie tightened her grip on the steering wheel as the incline steepened. "I know Nathan's old enough to take care of himself, but... I promised myself I'd never be the kind of parent who just assumes everything's fine. That's what being a mom is about—making sure your kids know you're there, even when they don't realize they need you."

Danielle smiled at that, her expression soft. "You've always been good at that."

Debbie glanced at her daughter, her heart swelling. "Thanks, sweetie."

By the time they reached a mailbox that bore "Warren" painted in neat black letters, Debbie felt a flutter settle in her chest. She turned onto the newly cleared driveway, the tires crunching over the frozen ground as the trees arched gracefully overhead, their branches heavy with snow.

"Wow," Danielle breathed, her voice tinged with awe as the car emerged from the tree-lined driveway moments later into a clearing. Caleb's home sat nestled against the backdrop of the snowy mountains. "This is... incredible. Who would've guessed Caleb lived somewhere like this?"

"It's beautiful, isn't it?" Debbie replied, slowing the car as she took in the scene. "Feels like it fits him perfectly. Quiet, strong, and a little rough around the edges, but... solid." She glanced at her daughter, who was already eyeing the barn with fascination.

Danielle smirked, raising a sly eyebrow. "Careful, Mom. You're starting to sound like someone who's more than just friends."

Debbie shot her a quick look, half-exasperated, half-amused. She put the car in park near the barn, her heart fluttering slightly.

Danielle climbed out of the car, her boots crunching against the packed snow. Debbie followed, inhaling deeply as the crisp mountain air filled her lungs. There was something utterly serene about this place, as if the world paused here.

As they approached the barn, the hum of activity, music, and soft laughter reached their ears. Danielle glanced over at her mom, grinning. "Sounds like someone's having a good time."

Debbie smiled. "Let's see what they're up to."

When she opened the barn door, the scene inside stopped her in her tracks. Overhead light illuminated the space, casting long shadows across the tools and workbenches, creating a warm cocoon against the winter's chill. Music played from overhead speakers. A large wood stove was going, heating the space. Nathan stood beside Caleb, his face alight with excitement as he pointed to something under the hood of a car. Caleb, sleeves rolled up, leaned casually beside him, nodding in approval as Nathan explained whatever discovery he'd made.

"Looks like Nathan's found a buddy," Danielle quipped, stepping inside.

Nathan's head whipped around, his face splitting into a broad grin. "Danielle! Mom! What are you doing here?"

Debbie folded her arms and raised an eyebrow. "What are you still doing here? You've been gone all day."

"Sorry," Nathan said, sheepishly rubbing the back of his neck. "We were working on the car, and I guess I lost track of time. Caleb's kinda of awesome at showing me this stuff."

Caleb glanced up from the car, his expression warm as he stood to his full height. "Hey. I'm glad you came up." His gaze lingered on Debbie, a flicker of something unspoken passing between them.

Debbie's heart softened at the sight—Nathan, so animated and alive, surrounded by the kind of positive energy she'd always wanted for him. And Caleb, standing steady like a strong anchor.

"Hey yourself," Debbie remarked with a soft laugh, her tone light but edged with playful teasing. "Looks like you two are enjoying yourselves. Just promise me, Caleb, you won't let him completely dismantle your car."

Nathan groaned, dramatically rolling his eyes. "Mom, Caleb's got it under control." He nudged Caleb with his elbow, silently pleading for backup.

Caleb chuckled, his trademark lopsided grin as easygoing as ever. He raised his hands in mock surrender, his tone playful. "Don't worry, no permanent damage—I promise. Believe it or not, I've actually got a system."

Debbie arched an eyebrow, adjusting her scarf with deliberate precision before shifting her gaze to Nathan. "You," she said pointedly, though her words were softened by the faint curve of a smile, "could've at least texted to let me know you'd be gone this long."

"Sorry, Mom," Nathan mumbled, his voice tinged with sheepishness as his shoulders slumped slightly. "I should've, but... I lost track of time. Got a little caught up, I guess."

Debbie sighed with exaggerated exasperation, shaking her head. "Alright, apology accepted—this time," she said with a wry smile. "But next time, at least check in every few hours, okay? You know how I worry."

Nathan gave her an easy grin. His confidence restored now that the storm had passed. "Deal."

Danielle, who had been snooping around the barn, paused in front of the car. "This thing is amazing," she said, her voice somewhere between awe and curiosity. "What is it?"

"1972 Plymouth Road Runner," Caleb answered. "She's not quite ready to roll yet, but we're getting closer."

Danielle whistled low. "I didn't think cars like this still existed. You must really love it."

Caleb smiled, his hand resting lightly on the hood. "It's less about the car itself and more about the process," he said. "Taking something broken and putting it back together—making it even stronger than it was before. It's... satisfying." His words were straightforward, but there was a depth to them that struck Debbie, like they meant more than just the car.

Danielle's gaze shifted between Caleb and her mom, her smile widening. "Yeah," she said softly. "I bet it is."

The next hour passed in a blur of shared stories and lighthearted banter. Danielle eventually jumped into the action, daring Nathan to guide her through one of the simpler tasks Caleb pointed out under the hood. Her laughter filled the barn when she struggled to figure out which way to turn the wrench, and Nathan offered a teasing commentary that only a twin brother could get away with.

Debbie hung back, watching it all unfold with quiet wonder. Caleb caught her gaze, his expression soft but unreadable, as if he was as caught up in the moment as much as she was.

He walked toward her and leaned against the workbench beside her, crossing his arms. "They're good kids," he said, nodding toward the twins. "That's no small credit to you."

Debbie felt her chest tighten, emotion pressing against her usual composure. "They're my world," she said, her voice softer now.

Caleb nodded, his gaze steady. "It shows."

Nathan was gesturing animatedly toward the old car, pointing out its various parts to Danielle, who occasionally chimed in with playful teasing. Their easy banter filled the barn, weaving through the air like a melody that spoke of comfort and love.

Caleb cleared his throat gently, drawing Debbie's attention. "You know," he began, his tone low and thoughtful, "Nathan and I had a good talk this afternoon."

Debbie turned to him, curiosity flickering across her face. "Oh?"

Caleb nodded, his fingers brushing against the edge of the workbench. "Yeah. Don't mention this to him—last thing I want is to break his trust—but he shared some things with me. He worries about you. A lot."

Debbie's brow furrowed, her smile fading into something softer, more introspective. "Worries about me?" she repeated, her voice barely above a whisper. She glanced back toward her kids, who were now arguing lightheartedly over whether Nathan's explanation of the carburetor made any sense.

"He does," Caleb said gently, his eyes steady on hers. "He sees how much weight you carry—how you pour yourself into taking care of everyone, making sure everything's steady and secure. But he also sees the cost. The way you don't allow yourself much time to stop, to just breathe, to... be."

Debbie's lips parted slightly, but no words came.

"And before you say anything," Caleb said, a soft yet knowing smile flickering across his lips as his fingers brushed hers, steady and unhurried, "he didn't bring it up to find fault, Debbie. It wasn't that at all. It's love—pure, fierce love."

"I know he loves me," she murmured. "And I love them both more than anything. The visit with their dad last night brought out a lot of emotions for them. But..." Her voice trailed off, and she glanced back at her children, her warm hazel eyes misting over. "Kids really do see more than we give them credit for, don't they?"

"Yeah, they do," Caleb said, his voice steady and reflective.

Debbie sighed softly, her gaze lingering on Nathan and Danielle, who were now laughing over some inside joke only they seemed to understand. "They've grown up so quickly," she murmured, her tone carrying a bittersweet weight. "It feels like just yesterday, they were running through the house in mismatched pajamas, leaving a trail of markers and glitter behind them. And now... now they're nearly ready to step out into the world."

Caleb followed her gaze, his expression thoughtful as he watched the twins. "Well, I'm not fortunate enough to be a parent but, that's the paradox of parenting, isn't it?" he said after a moment.

Debbie smiled faintly, a mixture of pride and longing flickering across her face. "Yes. I want to see them thrive, to chase their dreams and build lives that make them happy. But it's hard to imagine the house without them in it—without their laughter, their arguments, even their chaos. It's been us three, you know? This little team trio. It's hard to think about not having that anymore."

Caleb shifted slightly and reached for her hand, which she accepted without hesitation. "Debbie, they might move out someday, but they'll never truly leave you. The foundation you've laid for them—it's there in the way they carry themselves, in the way they speak about you. That kind of love? It's the unshakable kind."

Her eyes softened as she glanced his way.

He met her gaze, unwavering. "I think they'll carry pieces of it with them wherever they go. You've done more than raise them—you've poured yourself into their lives in a way that most parents can only hope to. That kind of love is a constant."

Debbie tilted her head toward Caleb, studying him with quiet appreciation. "You know, I really like how deeply you think."

He chuckled softly, looking down for a moment before returning his eyes to hers.

The sounds of Nathan and Danielle's chatter mingling with the faint crackle of the wood stove. The barn felt warm, not just from the heat of the fire but from the grounding presence of everyone in it—a moment suspended between the past, present, and all the unknowns of what lay ahead.

"I'm scared sometimes," Debbie admitted quietly. "That I'll let go too soon. Or not soon enough. That I'll mess it up somehow."

Caleb's brow furrowed, the faintest hint of sadness touching his features before he responded. "You know what I've learned about fear, Debbie? It's just another way of showing how much you care. You fear because you love. And that love? That's what's going to guide you."

Debbie looked at him, her chest tightening. She offered a small, tired smile, one that didn't shy away from the honesty of it all. "You really do have a way with words, Caleb Warren."

He grinned, his voice tinged with warmth. "One of the perks of spending too much time with my own thoughts, I suppose."

She laughed at that, the sound light but genuine, as Nathan and Danielle seemed to catch on to their quiet exchange and approached.

"All good over here, Mom," Nathan announced with a grin, holding up his grease-smeared hands. "Think I might've fixed something on the car... or maybe I broke it. Not totally sure yet."

Debbie let out an exaggerated groan, giving him a pointed look. "Nathan Isaiah Ferguson, if you've made Caleb's car worse, I'm grounding you until graduation."

Caleb waved a hand dismissively, chuckling. "Don't worry, Debbie—he hasn't broken anything beyond repair. Yet."

Danielle snickered, bumping her brother with her shoulder. "Looks like you've officially been adopted as Caleb's apprentice. Congrats. Don't forget the grease-resistant party hats."

Debbie stepped closer, brushing a strand of hair out of Danielle's face and smoothing a stray smudge of oil on Nathan's cheek. "Don't tease your brother too much. It's good to see him so excited about something. It gives me hope he'll finally clean his room." She grinned, earning matching eye rolls from both twins.

"You ready to head out, Mom?" Danielle asked, slipping her arm around Debbie's shoulders. "I'm kind of starving."

"Yeah, same here," Nathan said, his voice warm and easy as he wiped his hands on a nearby rag.

Debbie gave him a small smile, her gaze lingering for a moment on her son, before she turned back to Caleb. The barn felt warmer somehow—not just from the heat of the wood stove, but from the laughter and connection shared between all of them.

"Alright," she said, her tone signaling it was time to move. "Let's head home and figure out dinner. Nathan, you drive the side-by-side home. Danielle, are you riding with Nathan or coming with me?"

Danielle shot a teasing look at her twin. "I'll ride with Nathan. Who else is going to keep him from wrecking the thing?"

Nathan groaned dramatically, rolling his eyes. "Gee, thanks for the vote of confidence."

Debbie laughed. "Alright, just be safe."

As the kids headed toward the barn doors, Debbie lingered for a moment, turning to face Caleb. "Thank you," she said with sincerity, her hazel eyes soft. "For putting up with Nathan all afternoon—and honestly, for showing him a little piece of your life. It means a lot that he has someone like you to look up to."

Caleb shrugged, though there was a warmth in his expression that contradicted his casual tone. "He's sharp, picks things up fast—and he's got that spark. Your son's a good kid, Debbie. Both of them are."

Debbie nodded, her smile genuine. "Well, you're welcome to join us for dinner, if you're up for more chaos. I can't promise it'll be peaceful, but we always have plenty of food."

"I think I'll stay up here tonight. Get a bit settled after the storm and finish up a few things around the place. Rain check, though?" Caleb asked.

Debbie tucked a loose strand of hair behind her ear, a soft smile playing on her lips. "Rain check it is," she said, her voice warm but lighthearted.

Caleb leaned in, pressing a gentle kiss to her lips, and for a moment, the world grew quiet around them. It wasn't just the stillness of the night; it was the unspoken understanding that passed between them, grounding and comforting in ways words couldn't express.

As she turned to leave, Caleb's voice followed her, steady and sincere. "Drive safe."

There was nothing extraordinary in the words themselves, but the way he said them—low and full of meaning—made her pause mid-step. She glanced back over her shoulder, catching the quiet intensity of his gaze. It was a look that held more than simple concern, a look that promised something steady, something real.

"I will," she replied before stepping out into the chilly evening air. Danielle and Nathan were already pulling away in the side-by-side, their laughter trailing behind them as they disappeared down the snow-lined driveway.

She glanced back at Caleb, catching his steady gaze fixed on her with an intensity that was neither invasive nor demanding. She raised her hand in a small, hesitant wave.

Caleb's response was just as understated, yet profound. He lifted his hand in return, a simple gesture that somehow conveyed volumes—steadfastness, understanding, and the quiet assurance of his presence.

Chapter 34

The sharp scent of fresh-cut pine mingled with the faint tang of motor oil as Caleb Warren stood by the loading dock, clipboard in hand. The rhythmic hum of machinery and the occasional grind of saws filled the air, a steady backdrop to the organized chaos of the mill. Caleb's eyes skimmed the delivery sheet again, meticulously cross-checking for any errors, though his focus wavered. His hands were busy; his mind, decidedly less so.

It had been over a week since the snowstorm had disrupted daily life, and the town had gradually settled back into its usual rhythms. For Caleb, that meant returning to the unrelenting grind of the Warren Family Lumber Mill. He'd thrown himself into tasks with his characteristic determination—hours of backbreaking work soothed something restless in him, a familiar balm for a heart that often strayed toward solitude. But no matter how much sawdust clung to his boots or how weary his muscles felt by the end of the day, one thing remained constant. His thoughts always drifted back to Debbie.

After work, Caleb would be sharing a meal with Debbie and her kids again. It wasn't just the thought of a warm, home-cooked dinner that he was looking forward to. It was the laughter and love that always seemed to echo around her kitchen table, filling the space with a kind of life he wanted. It was the effortless way Nathan and Danielle bantered back and forth, their sharp wit softened by the unmistakable thread of sibling loyalty. It was the way Debbie made everything feel steady and normal, even amidst the chaos of their busy lives, and how her hazel eyes held a gentle spark whenever she glanced his way.

Caleb leaned against the frame of the dock door and looked out at the mountains surrounding the mill and let his mind wander. Debbie and her kids had come into his life unexpectedly, but they seemed to have carved out their own space in it almost instantly. He hadn't been looking for them—it wasn't like he'd planned to get tangled up in someone else's life—but now he couldn't imagine his days without them. They were tethering him in a way that felt nothing like restraint and everything like belonging.

At 44, the weight of the past still settled on his shoulders like an old coat, frayed here and there but familiar, nonetheless. Life with Bonnie had shaped him in ways he couldn't deny, carving out pieces of him, both good and bad. Years of solitude had done their part too, sanding down his edges until he thought he might be better off keeping others at arm's length forever. Yet here he was, standing at the edge of something new, something he hadn't dared to think he'd ever want again. And it wasn't just a want. It was a need, a quiet certainty he couldn't ignore. Building a life with Debbie wasn't just an abstract idea—it was solid, tangible, something he felt in the marrow of his being.

The weight of it wasn't unwelcome, though. If anything, it felt grounding, like he was finally planting roots in soil that wouldn't crumble beneath him. For a man who had spent the better part of a decade convinced that isolation was safer, the ease with which Debbie and the kids had slipped into his life—and his heart—should have been unnerving. But it wasn't. It just felt...right.

Caleb!" a voice rang out, pulling him from his thoughts. He turned to see his brother David approaching, wiping the sawdust from his hands as he closed the gap between them.

"What's up?" Caleb asked, his brow furrowing slightly at the seriousness in David's tone.

"There's someone here asking for you. Guy's name is James Ferguson. Says it's about a lumber order," David said, his expression laced with curiosity.

The name hit Caleb like a lead weight, settling uneasily in his chest. He straightened his stance, rolling his shoulders as if shaking off the unwanted tension. "James Ferguson," he repeated slowly, his voice measured, almost wary.

"Yeah," David added, folding his arms as he watched Caleb carefully. "He's waiting in the front office. Something wrong?"

Caleb took a deep breath, slipping off one of his work gloves and adjusting the other. "Not sure," he replied. His tone was calm, but there was an edge to it that didn't escape David's notice.

"You want me to stick around?" David offered, his tone casual, though his eyes sharpened slightly, scanning Caleb's expression for any sign of what this was about.

Caleb shook his head. "No, I've got it," he replied, though the sinking feeling in his gut told him otherwise. He nodded at his brother, who gave him a lingering look before heading back toward the mill floor.

Adjusting the cuff of his jacket, Caleb made his way toward the front office. The scrape of his boots against the concrete floor echoed faintly in the otherwise quiet corridor, the sound underscoring the unease that settled heavier with each step.

Pushing open the door, Caleb stepped into the space with deliberate calm. His eyes immediately landed on James, whose presence radiated the kind of confidence Caleb instinctively distrusted. James was dressed well—too well for someone stopping by a lumber mill—with a tailored coat bearing the sleek logo of his construction company embroidered over the breast. He exuded a practiced charm that Caleb recognized instantly, though the undercurrent of smugness in James's smile didn't sit well with him.

James glanced up, his face splitting into an easy, self-assured grin, as though he hadn't just walked into another man's territory uninvited. "Caleb," he said, stepping forward with a hand extended. "Appreciate you taking the time."

Caleb hesitated for the briefest moment before clasping James's hand for a firm, professional shake. "You're here about a lumber order?" His tone remained neutral, his stance grounded.

James's handshake lingered just a heartbeat too long before retreating. "That's right. Thought I'd deal with someone high up—get the details straight from the source. Big project coming up. Figured your mill might be a good fit."

Caleb gave a curt nod, his expression unreadable. "We're always happy to work with local companies. What kind of project are you planning?"

"Oh, you know, just one of those big developments," James said vaguely, waving a hand as if the specifics were hardly worth mentioning. "New builds, revitalization... stuff to put Laurel Ridge on the map. You know how it goes."

Caleb's eyes narrowed slightly, watching James with quiet scrutiny. There was an easy confidence in the man's tone—a rehearsed, polished way of speaking. It put Caleb on edge, though he forced himself to maintain an air of professionalism. "I'll make sure our sales team gets the details so they can set you up with the right materials."

James smiled, the kind of smile that didn't quite reach his eyes. "Appreciate that. But if I'm honest, Caleb, I didn't come here just to talk about a supply order. I came to talk about Debbie."

Caleb's chest tightened without warning, though he didn't let it show. His jaw ticked once before he calmly replied, "Don't see what Debbie has to do with placing an order."

James tilted his head, his grin widening ever so slightly as he shoved his hands into his pockets. "Relax, man. Just making conversation. I mean, you and I both spend time with her—we've got that in common, don't we?"

Caleb's gaze went cold, his arms crossing loosely over his chest as a subtle barrier. "If you've got something to say, just say it," he replied flatly.

James chuckled, the sound low and almost condescending. "Alright, fair enough. Look, Debbie and I... we've got history. Long history. She can be a little... complicated, you know? But hey, that's part of what makes her so unforgettable."

Caleb's fingers curled slightly against his biceps, though his expression remained calm and steady. "Seems like wherever you're going with this is your business, not mine."

"You think so?" James said smoothly, his tone taking on a sharper edge. "See, the thing about Debbie is... she's been through a lot. And yeah, maybe I deserve a little blame for that. But some things between us? They don't just go away."

Caleb's lips pressed into a firm line, his silence sharpening the tension in the air. James stepped forward slightly, clearly emboldened by Caleb's restraint.

"I guess what I'm saying," James continued, his tone almost too casual now, "is that it's easy to step into someone else's story and think you can rewrite the ending. But Debbie? She's not like other women—not as easy to figure out as she seems. I'm just saying... be careful getting comfortable. Might not work out how you think."

Caleb didn't bite. Instead, his voice came out cold and even, his eyes locked on James's face. "You done?"

James blinked, clearly not expecting the composed response. But he quickly recovered, flashing another grin as he pulled his hand out of his pocket and gestured to the room. "Yeah, I guess I am. Thanks for chatting, Caleb. I'm sure I'll be seeing you around."

He turned toward the door but paused just before exiting, throwing a parting shot over his shoulder. "Oh, and hey—take good care of her, alright? For as long as she lets you."

The door swung shut behind him, leaving Caleb standing in the silent foyer.

For a moment, he didn't move. The tension in his shoulders, the clench of his jaw—everything screamed at him to shake off James's words like the manipulative noise they were. But deep down, the seeds of doubt were already taking root. What if James was right? What if stepping further into Debbie's life—into her family—was a mistake?

Caleb sighed heavily, rubbing the back of his neck before turning and heading back to the mill floor, his thoughts swirling in a way that no amount of physical labor could untangle.

Chapter 35

Debbie glanced at the large wooden clock hanging on the wall. Caleb would be arriving any minute, and though she told herself it was nothing out of the ordinary, she couldn't quiet the flutter in her chest. What was it about him—his steady presence, his quiet strength—that had her feeling like a teenager waiting on a first date?

It was just dinner.

Nothing extraordinary—roast chicken, green beans, and potatoes.

And yet, Debbie caught herself smoothing the edges of the tablecloth for the second time, ensuring the ceramic salt and pepper shakers were evenly spaced on the oak table. She glanced around the room. Everything was tidy, cozy, welcoming... perhaps too welcoming? Had she lit too many candles? Was the flickering glow too intimate?

"Mom, are you okay? You've been staring at the table for like five minutes," Danielle teased from the doorway, leaning against the frame with a sly smile. Her leggings and oversized sweatshirt somehow made her 17-year-old form both laid-back and graceful at the same time.

"I have not," Debbie protested lightly, brushing a loose strand of hair behind her ear.

Danielle walked over to the table, exaggeratedly craning her neck to inspect the settings. "What's with the napkins? You never fold them this fancy unless it's Christmas."

"They're not fancy. It's just... a little nice. We're having company, that's all," Debbie muttered, feeling the heat rise to her cheeks.

"Company?" Danielle repeated, raising an eyebrow. "You mean Caleb."

Debbie tilted her head, giving her daughter a pointed look. "Caleb is our guest tonight. Danielle and I just felt like making this dinner special."

Danielle smirked, leaning closer, her hazel eyes—so much like Debbie's—sparkling with mischief. "You never get this flustered. But Caleb comes over, and suddenly, it's napkins folded and candles everywhere?"

"Excuse you," Debbie retorted, biting back a smile as she lightly swatted at her daughter's arm. "And we always have folded napkins and candles when we have guests."

Danielle took a step back, clearly enjoying how easily she could ruffle her mother's feathers. "Sure, Mom. Whatever you say. By the way, Caleb's Jeep just pulled into the driveway."

Debbie's stomach flipped, and she tried to play it off with a nod, busying herself at the counter to give the appearance of being nonchalant.

"Well, go let him in, Danielle," Debbie said with a grin.

Debbie exhaled quickly, her cheeks still warm as she heard Caleb's boots crunching outside on the porch.

When Caleb stepped inside, brushing the snow off his shoulders, he was met with the warm smell of home-cooked food and the kind of coziness that immediately made him feel simultaneously welcome and nervous. His flannel shirt hung open over a gray Henley, and the hint of a shy smile tugged at his lips as he stepped into the entryway.

"Wow," he said, shrugging off his jacket as his eyes swept over the living room and into the adjoining kitchen and dining area.

"Nothing fancy," Debbie said quickly, as she stepped into the living room, though her cheeks betrayed her with the faintest pink tinge.

"Thanks for having me," he said, his deep brown eyes meeting hers, that soft sincerity of his making her heartbeat unsteady.

"Hey there," Nathan greeted from the couch, flashing a quick smile at Caleb.

Danielle leaned casually against the wall in the living room. "Mom won't admit it, but she just spent the last hour panicking over napkin folds—for you, of course." Danielle teased.

"Out," Debbie said with a laugh, ushering her daughter toward the kitchen.

Danielle, laughing, disappeared with a cheerful wave, leaving Caleb smiling and Debbie shaking her head.

"Sorry about that," Debbie said, rubbing at the towel slung over her shoulder. "She has a gift."

Caleb's brow lifted just slightly. "For teasing?"

"For making me question every life decision I've ever made," Debbie replied dryly, though the humor in her voice softened the words.

Dinner was anything but quiet, a lively chorus of voices and laughter filling the kitchen as sure as the scent of roasted chicken and freshly baked rolls filled the air.

Danielle was seated across from Caleb, gesturing animatedly with her fork as she recounted the latest drama from school. "—and then, Amelia tripped over her backpack and accidentally spilled her iced coffee all over Ethan. And instead of getting mad, Ethan just laughed, which, of course, made Amelia blush like a tomato. I swear, her crush on him is getting ridiculous!" She paused, eyes wide with indignation. "And Ethan? Clueless. Totally clueless."

Nathan smirked. "Maybe because, unlike you girls, some of us aren't constantly launching into secret operas about feelings. Maybe the guy's just trying to survive chemistry, not land himself in some teenage girl rom-com."

Danielle rolled her eyes, stuffing a bite of mashed potatoes into her mouth to hold back what was bound to be a pointed retort. Caleb, sitting beside Nathan, chuckled softly at their sibling banter.

"Sounds like poor Ethan's going through a lot," he offered dryly, his tone so deadpan that it sent Nathan into a fit of laughter.

"See? Caleb gets it," Nathan said through a grin, gesturing toward him with his fork before popping another piece of chicken into his mouth.

Debbie couldn't suppress her smile. She cut into her chicken, the clinking of her knife and fork adding a rhythmic hum to the conversation. "I think Amelia's crush is sweet," she said, her voice calm but teasing. "And Ethan sounds like a kind boy. Maybe we could all learn a little something from his patience."

Danielle brightened immediately. "Exactly, Mom! See? Ethan's a good guy. It's not his fault Nathan doesn't believe in romance."

Nathan feigned offense. "Whoa, whoa, who said I don't believe in romance? I've just got better things to do than obsess over someone dumping coffee on me."

Danielle gasped dramatically. "Better things? Please..."

***

Debbie sat curled into the corner of the couch, tucking her legs beneath her, nursing a cup of coffee. She glanced toward Caleb, sitting across from her in the recliner nearest the fire. He was leaned back, one leg resting casually over the other, but there was a tension in the way he tapped his thumb against the armrest. A quiet rhythm she almost didn't notice until her focus settled on it.

"Thanks for coming tonight," Debbie said. The corners of her mouth curved into a relaxed smile, her hazel eyes reflecting the firelight. "I know this place can feel like chaos with the kids, so I appreciate you surviving it."

Caleb chuckled, the sound low and warm as it broke through his contemplative expression. "Chaos?" he repeated, with a slight tilt of his head. "Your version of chaos is peaceful compared to the mill."

Debbie's eyebrows quirked at his words, and she let out a soft laugh. "Peaceful chaos. Now there's a phrase I don't hear often."

Caleb chuckled.

"You've been kind of quiet tonight. Everything alright?"

Caleb glanced toward the fireplace, the warm flicker of the flames casting shadows across the room in a way that felt both soothing and introspective.

"Yeah," he replied after a beat, his tone steady though not entirely convincing. "Just a long day at the mill."

Debbie tilted her head slightly, studying him from where she sat curled up on the couch. She'd always been good at reading between the lines—better than most, really.

"Sounds like more than just a long day," she said, her hazel eyes fixed on him. "Want to talk about it?"

Caleb hesitated, his hand reaching up to rub the back of his neck—a habit Debbie had noticed he slipped into whenever he was weighing his words carefully.

He let out a slow breath. "You know... I wasn't going to bring this up, but you'll probably hear about it eventually from someone. I had an unexpected visitor today," he admitted, his voice low but firm.

"Oh?" Debbie sat up a little straighter, her curiosity now fully piqued. "Someone from town?"

Caleb's jaw tightened, and he looked down at the callused fingers intertwined in his lap. The memory of James's smug grin was still fresh, but he wasn't sure how much Debbie needed—or wanted—to hear about it. He wasn't the type to stir up trouble, but ignoring it completely felt wrong.

"Your ex-husband," Caleb said finally, his deep voice cutting through the quiet. His gaze lifted, meeting hers. "He showed up at the mill today."

Debbie blinked, her expression faltering ever so slightly before she caught herself. Crossing one leg over the other, she leaned back into the couch cushions, her arms folding in front of her. "James came to see you?" she repeated, her tone carefully controlled.

Caleb nodded, his expression unreadable. "Yeah. Said it was about placing an order for a project, but... that wasn't really why he came."

Debbie's brows furrowed, the faintest trace of a frown tugging at her lips. "What did he want, then?"

Caleb shifted in his seat, his movements slow and measured. "A little bit of posturing, mostly," he said, his voice calm but edged with irritation. "Wanted to remind me of his history with you, how deep it runs. Tried to... I don't know. Paint this picture of you as someone weighed down by everything that came before."

Debbie's frown deepened, her arms tightening across her chest. "That sounds like James, alright," she said, her voice brittle. "Always knows just which strings to pull."

Caleb's eyes softened as he took in her expression—the sharp flicker of hurt she was trying so hard to mask. "Debbie." He rose from the recliner and moved to join her on the couch, settling in beside her. "I need you to know something, and I need you to hear me out."

"Go on," she said, her voice quieter now.

"I don't care about James," Caleb said firmly, his tone leaving no room for doubt. "I don't care about what he has to say or whatever version of the past he thinks he gets to control. That's his baggage. It's not yours—not anymore. And it sure doesn't define who you are now."

Debbie's arms unfurled, her hands resting in her lap as she processed his words.

"You've been through a lot," Caleb continued, his rough voice softening. "I see it. Anyone who takes the time to look will see it. But everything you've been through doesn't make you less—it makes you more. Stronger. Wiser. More determined to find the good in everything, even when it's hard. And that? That's not something any-one—not even James—gets to take away from you."

Debbie's throat tightened, and she pressed her lips together for a moment, unsure of what to say. She hadn't expected him to speak with such conviction or to understand her so well.

"Caleb..." she began, her voice wavering slightly. "Thank you for saying that. Truly. But James... he has a way of making things compli-cated, even when they don't need to be. And I'd hate for his issues to spill over onto you. Onto us."

Caleb leaned back, his broad shoulders relaxing slightly. "Let him try," he said simply, his expression steady. "It won't change anything for me."

"You're... something else, Caleb Warren," she said softly, a faint smile playing at her lips.

He smirked, the corner of his mouth quirking up as he shrugged. "Guess I'm just too stubborn to scare off," he teased lightly, though the sincerity beneath his words was unmistakable. Caleb reached over and took Debbie's hand. Debbie glanced down at their joined hands, the roughness of his calloused fingers contrasting with her softer grip, and yet the connection felt natural, steady—almost as if it had been there all along, just waiting to happen.

"You might be the most stubborn person I've ever met," she said with a small laugh, her voice light but tinged with admiration, "and I've spent what feels like a lifetime raising two teenagers."

Caleb chuckled, his thumb brushing lightly over the back of her hand, an almost subconscious gesture of reassurance. "Sounds like I've got some competition, then," he replied, his deep voice warm.

Debbie tilted her head, her hazel eyes searching his face. "I don't know how I got so lucky to have you crash into my life, Caleb," she said, her voice almost lost beneath the crackle of the fire. "But I'm glad you did."

Her words hung in the air, her honesty raw and vulnerable in a way she rarely allowed herself to be. Caleb's gaze didn't waver, didn't falter. Instead, he leaned slightly closer, his deep brown eyes holding hers with the kind of sincerity that left no room for doubt.

"I'm glad I did too," Caleb said. "More than you know."

"I think," Debbie said, her voice steady though her chest felt tight with emotion, "that my little world got a whole lot better the day you crashed into it."

"I'd call that divine intervention," he said with a smile.

Chapter 36

Debbie kicked off her shoes with a groan, leaning back against the door just long enough to take a deep breath. The quiet of the house wrapped around her as her tired muscles screamed for rest. After a long shift and a few too many emergencies in one day, all she wanted to do was microwave leftovers, collapse onto the couch, and catch up with her kids about whatever antics they'd gotten into that afternoon. She'd call Caleb to catch up on his day and see if their plans for dinner tomorrow were still on as well.

Straightening, she called out, "Danielle? Nathan?" There was no reply. Her eyes landed on a folded piece of paper perched neatly on the entryway table. Debbie picked it up, her lips twitching into a smile as soon as she read the note.

Mom

We got bored, so we decided to take the side-by-side up to Caleb's to see what he's up to. Don't worry—we called first to make sure it was okay.

P.S. You should come join us!
Love, your absolutely perfect children.

Rolling her eyes, Debbie shook her head and set the note down.

"Perfect, huh?" she murmured, grabbing her phone and typing out a quick text. "Be there soon. I hope you haven't caused Caleb too much trouble today!"

She hit send.

The kids adored Caleb. He had slipped into their lives so unexpectably and fit in perfectly, filling all the gaps in her life and making her feel whole again. She didn't have to worry. In fact, she trusted him—more than she ever thought possible when it came to her kids.

She heaved a happy sigh and slipped her boots back on, stifling the voice in her head that begged her to stay home and rest.

***

The drive up the mountain road never failed to take her breath away. Evening shadows stretched across the endless winter landscape, but the dusting of snow covering the trees made everything gleam under the faint blush of the setting sun. Debbie switched on her headlights as the narrow road curved and wound its way upward, her smile softening at how peaceful it all felt.

Debbie steered her car carefully up the snow-packed driveway, her headlights cutting through the twilight as the trees gave way to Caleb's clearing. The sight of him standing on the cabin's porch came into view, still and steady, hands tucked into the pockets of his coat. Warm light spilled from the windows behind him, casting a soft ambiance that framed his rugged silhouette, the edges of it catching on the snow-dusted scene like a picture brought to life.

Debbie stepped out of the car, her boots crunching against the packed snow. She waved, glancing around. "Where are the kids?" she called as she approached.

"They're inside," Caleb replied, moving down the porch steps toward her. His slow, steady stride made the corners of her mouth lift into a full smile.

"Hopefully, they haven't caused you too much trouble today."

He stopped before her, his deep brown eyes meeting hers with a quiet confidence that unraveled her composure in the best way. Caleb slipped one hand from the warmth of his coat pocket and gently took hers, the roughness of his calloused fingers familiar. With a small tilt of his head, he gestured toward the side of his cabin, his voice soft but steady. "Come, take a walk with me. Just for a few minutes," he said.

Debbie hesitated, narrowing her eyes in playful suspicion. "Alright, are we just taking a stroll around the snowy yard, or are you about to lead me on a full-blown hike through the mountains at dusk?"

Caleb chuckled. "Just trust me."

She shrugged and nudged him with her gloved hand. "Alright. But if I fall in the snow, you're pulling me back up."

The path they followed around the cabin was meticulously shoveled, its edges marked with delicate rows of twinkling Christmas lights. Debbie's curiosity deepened with each step, her gaze flicking to Caleb's strong, steady form beside her as they moved along the glowing trail.

"What did you do here?" she asked, her breath forming soft clouds in the cool air. Her eyes traced the string of lights twinkling in the snow. "These look like my holiday lights."

Caleb just smiled, tipping his head down the path. "You'll see."

The lights guided them through the yard, the snow on either side of the path piling higher with each drift they passed. And then she spotted it—a soft, amber glow radiating in the distance, casting a warm brilliance over the snow. Debbie squinted, slowing her steps.

"Is that... what in the world is that?" she asked, looking toward Caleb. "It looks like an igloo."

"Well, not exactly," Caleb admitted, his grin tilting boyishly. "It's a dining igloo dome. Your kids found the idea online and decided it was non-negotiable."

Debbie blinked. She wasn't sure what she'd expected, but as they stepped closer, the dome came fully into view, and her breath caught. Inside the clear structure sat Caleb's dining table, dressed in winter whites with tiny flickering faux candles and two steaming mugs arranged alongside plates and silverware. A portable heater hummed in one corner, lines of fairy lights draped carefully along the interior ceiling of the dome like stars caught in glass.

Caleb stepped ahead, slipping into host mode as he opened the igloo's small door with a flourish. "After you."

Debbie ducked inside, and it was like stepping into a snow globe. She spun slowly in place, taking in every detail—the warmth, the sparkle, the laughter echoing in her mind as she thought about her kids sneaking around to help orchestrate this.

"This is..." She paused, her throat tight, forcing the words through the sudden rise of emotion. "Caleb, this is beautiful. I don't have—there aren't words."

"You don't need words," he replied, stepping in behind her and scratching the back of his neck. "I just wanted you to feel appreciated. You deserve something like this. Something special."

Her chest swelled, warmth spilling over where there had been exhaustion mere moments before. She turned to thank him but paused at the sound of voices growing louder outside.

"Surprise!" Danielle's voice carried as she and Nathan appeared, each balancing a tray piled high with covered bowls and serving spoons.

"Save the gratitude for later, mom. It's time for you to enjoy your evening," Nathan announced, maneuvering his way through the igloo door.

Debbie laughed as Caleb held the door open, the rich scent of roast beef wafting in as the kids set the trays down on the table. Danielle looked like she might burst with pride, gesturing to the setup.

"You're welcome," she said cheekily. "Caleb made us his sous chefs today. He's... well, let's just say cooking's not his spiritual gift."

Nathan smirked. "Yeah. But he tries. Gold star for effort."

Caleb rolled his eyes, his laugh low and warm as the twins retreated.

"Enjoy, Mom," Danielle called over her shoulder, a grin lighting up her face as she slipped out through the igloo dome's door.

"Have fun, Caleb," Nathan added with a wink, his tone teasing as he carefully secured the Velcro on the door behind them to keep the warmth inside.

Debbie blinked, still taking in the cozy beauty of her surroundings. She reached for one of the bowls on the table, fingers brushing against the lid before Caleb stopped her. His calloused hands were gentle as they closed over hers, halting her movement.

"Sit," he said, his voice soft but firm. "Let me take care of this. You relax for once."

For a moment, she hesitated, caught off guard by his insistence. But the quiet confidence in his eyes made her relent. She sank back into one of his dining chairs, the tension of the day beginning to melt away as Caleb moved with easy purpose.

He filled her plate with care, arranging the food as if he wanted it to be just right. Then he set it down in front of her, his eyes meeting hers with a look that was steady and kind. Once her plate was full, he took the seat across from her and filled his own.

He reached across the table, his large, calloused hands extending toward hers. Debbie hesitated for only a moment before sliding her hands into his, her fingers curling around the rough warmth of his grasp. When Caleb bowed his head, she instinctively followed, surprised by the quiet reverence of the moment.

"Lord," Caleb's deep voice rumbled, the timbre low and quiet but heavy with meaning. "Thank you for this meal, for the hands that prepared it, and for the moments we get to share here tonight. Thank you for the second chances you give, for the grace that holds us together, and for the unexpected blessings we don't always see coming." He paused, the silence stretching just long enough for the words to feel unhurried. "Help us to stay grateful, to trust Your plan, even when the road's steep. And teach us, Lord, how to love the way You love us. Amen."

As he lifted his head, Debbie opened her eyes, feeling an unmistakable lump in her throat. Caleb's sincerity had caught her by surprise—not just by the act of praying, but by the weight of his words. It wasn't just a blessing over the food; it was a reflection of the life they were piecing together, one small moment at a time.

"Caleb," she said softly, her hazel eyes searching his as their hands remained joined across the table. "That was... beautiful."

He squeezed her hands gently, his gaze steady and grounding as the corners of his lips lifted in his subtle smile. "It's hard not to feel grateful when I look at you."

"You and the kids," Caleb continued, his deep voice steady with emotion, "you're the prayer I didn't even know I had the courage to ask for."

Debbie blinked, her throat tightening as his words sank in, raw and genuine.

"And this," she said softly, her voice trembling but full of warmth, "is the first time you've ever initiated a blessing over one of our meals." Her hazel eyes shimmered. "You amaze me every single day."

Leaning back, Caleb let his lips curve into a small, boyish smile. "Well," he drawled, his dark brown eyes flickering with something unspoken, "you amaze me right back."

With a gentle laugh, Debbie reached for her fork, the soft clink of utensils filling the air as she began cutting into the slice of roast Caleb had plated for her.

"So," Caleb said, his deep voice breaking through the quiet, "how was work? Did anything interesting happen today?"

"Exciting might be a bit of a stretch. It was mostly the usual—overworked, understaffed, and trying to squeeze in visiting too many patients in one day and still take time to visit with each of them. But there was this one patient who..." she trailed off, searching for the words.

Caleb raised an eyebrow, his brow furrowing slightly as he studied her. "Go on," he prompted gently.

She exhaled, her eyes drifting to her plate for a moment before meeting his gaze again. "I had a patient today who reminded me why I chose this work," she began, her voice softening. "She's this sweet older woman—a recent widow—recovering from surgery on her arm after a bad fall. She was so weighed down by worry and still grieving the loss of her husband and feeling all alone." Debbie paused, a gentle warmth threading through her tone. "It made my whole day to just sit with her for a while, talk with her, and help her see she's not as alone as she feels. Sometimes, all someone needs is a little comfort to remind them that they're still part of the bigger picture."

Caleb's expression softened, his deep brown eyes holding hers with quiet reverence. "Sounds like you really made a difference in her day," he said.

Debbie felt the blush creep into her cheeks, but didn't look away. "It's just... part of the job."

"No," Caleb said simply, shaking his head. "It's more than that. It's who you are."

His words were so earnest, so unvarnished, they left her momentarily speechless. She looked down at her plate, deflecting with a soft laugh. "Well, remind me of that next time I'm pulled in twenty directions and forget to eat for twelve hours."

"Deal," Caleb said, his lips quirking into a smile.

Debbie chuckled, relaxing further into her seat. The warmth of the igloo, the comfort of the food, and the quiet intimacy settling between them all felt like an oasis in her otherwise busy life.

"I have to admit," she said after a moment, studying the twinkling lights above them, "this wasn't what I was expecting when I came up here tonight. But... it's perfect. Thank you, Caleb."

He tilted his head slightly, his gaze soft as it lingered on her. "You deserve perfect, Debbie. A lot more than I could fit into one evening. But I hope this is a start."

Her chest tightened at his words, and she reached for her glass of water, taking a sip to calm the sudden rush of emotion.

Dinner stretched into one of the most lighthearted, joy-filled evenings Debbie could remember in years.

It was only when the kids returned with homemade cupcakes, their grins unusually wide, that Debbie realized something was really up.

"Alright, you two," Debbie said, her eyes narrowing with playful suspicion as she watched Danielle and Nathan clear the table with a quick efficiency that was highly unusual for them. All the bowls, serving utensils, and empty plates were swept away, leaving only two perfectly frosted cupcakes—one placed neatly in front of her, the other in front of Caleb. She folded her arms and raised an eyebrow. "What exactly are you two up to?"

Instead of responding, Danielle nudged Caleb with her elbow, still seated at the table. Nathan crossed his arms, a smug grin on his face.

"Actually," Caleb said, clearing his throat and glancing at Danielle and Nathan, who were barely containing their grins. "We three are up to something. Nathan and Danielle need to be here for the most important part of your special evening, if that's okay with you."

Debbie frowned, confused. "Most important part of this wonderful evening? How could it get any better... but okay, of course they can stay?"

Caleb nodded, pushing his chair back with quiet intention. Rising to his full height, he moved toward her, his steps slow and deliberate. When he reached Debbie's side of the table, he extended a hand, his touch warm and steady as he gently entwined her fingers with his. With a small, encouraging squeeze, he guided her to her feet, his deep brown eyes never leaving hers. Her heart skipped in the quiet, the growing warmth in his gaze setting off a flutter of nerves.

"You've really done enough for one night," she said with a nervous laugh.

The atmosphere seemed to change, growing still and heavy with meaning as time slowed to a near standstill. Danielle and Nathan shared a quick, knowing glance before stepping closer, positioning themselves on either side of Caleb. His deep, steady gaze never wavered, locking onto Debbie's as though her response was the only thing that truly mattered in the world.

"Debbie. Being around you and the kids—it's given my life something I never thought I'd feel again. Hope, peace… love," he began, his voice low but steady. "You've shown me that brokenness doesn't have to be the end, that grace is big enough to carry the hard days and turn them into something beautiful."

Tears welled in Debbie's eyes, spilling over before she could stop them, her breath hitching at the sincerity in his every word.

"The thing is," Caleb continued, glancing at the kids for a moment before locking eyes with her again, "I don't want just pieces of this life you've built. I want all of it—all of you. The laughter, the chaos, the faith—the tough days, too. I've wasted too many years of my life alone, and I don't want to spend the rest of my time here on earth without you and the kids in it."

Her hand flew to her mouth as he slipped to one knee, pulling a small velvet box from his coat pocket.

"Debbie Ferguson," he said, his deep eyes filled with steady love, "will you marry me?"

"Yes," she whispered shakily. "Yes. Of course, yes."

Caleb stood, sliding the ring onto Debbie's trembling hand as a chorus of cheers erupted from the kids. Without hesitation, he drew her into his arms, his embrace strong and sure.

Faint music began to play—soft, melodic, and impossibly perfect. Danielle and Nathan exchanged wide-eyed grins before slipping out of the dome, giving them space. Debbie barely registered their departure, her focus entirely on Caleb, whose deep brown eyes danced with a light she hadn't seen before.

In an uncharacteristically smooth gesture, Caleb took her hand and spun her gently, her laugh spilling out like a melody of its own. "Dance with me," he murmured, his voice low and warm.

She hesitated only for a heartbeat. Dancing was something she hadn't done in years. But with his calloused hand steady in hers and his quiet strength pulling her close, she caved. They swayed together, a rugged, quiet mountain man and the woman who had unknowingly pieced him back together.

As he twirled her again, the dome lights shimmered like stars caught in glass, and Debbie realized something profound: this wasn't just a magical moment—it was her moment. The one she never saw coming, the one that made every heartbreak, every hard decision, and every lonely night worth enduring. Caleb had stepped into her life and taught her that sometimes, love shows up quietly, like snow falling unnoticed—until suddenly, it blankets everything, softening even the hardest edges.

They moved together as though the rest of the world didn't exist, her head resting against his chest as he held her, steady and sure. And as they danced beneath the heavenly sky, Debbie finally let herself believe in not just the beauty of the moment—but the beauty of a future where each of them was no longer alone.

For the first time in years, she felt completely and utterly at peace. And she knew, deep down, that this was just the beginning.

Leave A Review

If you enjoyed this book, please consider leaving an honest review on Amazon or Goodreads.

Visit Our Website:

www.tarabaisden.com

Visit Our Amazon Author Page HERE

Find Us On Social Media:

Facebook

Instagram

TikTok

Pinterest

GoodReads